GIRL IN
THE CREEK

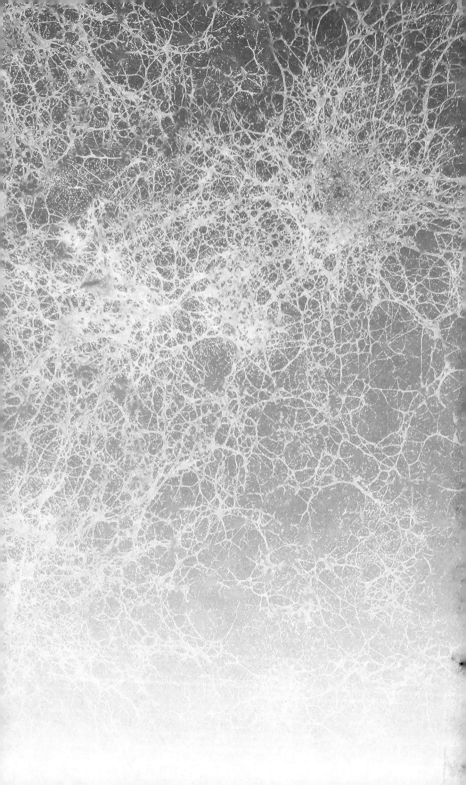

GIRL IN THE CREEK

Wendy N. Wagner

NIGHTFIRE
TOR PUBLISHING GROUP
NEW YORK

GIRL IN THE CREEK

Copyright © 2025 by Wendy N. Wagner

A Nightfire Book
Published by Tom Doherty Associates / Tor Publishing Group
120 Broadway
New York, NY 10271

www.torpublishinggroup.com

Nightfire™ is a trademark of Macmillan Publishing Group, LLC.

EU Representative: Macmillan Publishers Ireland Ltd, 1st Floor, The Liffey Trust Centre, 117–126 Sheriff Street Upper, Dublin 1, DO1 YC43

The Library of Congress Cataloging-in-Publication Data is available upon request.

ISBN 978-1-250-90864-3 (hardcover)
ISBN 978-1-250-90865-0 (ebook)

Our books may be purchased in bulk for specialty retail/wholesale, literacy, corporate/premium, educational, and subscription box use. Please contact MacmillanSpecialMarkets@macmillan.com.

First Edition: 2025

Printed in the United States of America

10 9 8 7 6 5 4 3 2 1

*Dedicated to Rebecca Stefoff
for all the encouragement and
nature talk along the way*

GIRL IN
THE CREEK

CHAPTER ONE

THE BODY LAY AT THE VERY LIMIT OF DAYLIGHT, THE last clear place on the stones before the wood framing in the ancient adit began to peel away from the walls and pile up in moldy heaps.

The coyote studied the cold, pale thing even though the air here was very bad, the rusty water in the bottom of the tunnel giving off sour vapors that burned her nose and would have irritated her lungs if her lungs were still a normal coyote's. The coyote had not been normal in a very long time, though. She stood in ankle-deep water and took in the details of the trouble someone had brought into the Strangeness's territory.

The body's head—it was a human head, the coyote knew—rested sideways in the iron-sick water, the chin pointing beyond the limit of its shoulder as the figure lay on its belly. Eyelids still curved over the full spheres of eyes. Whoever this was, they had not been lying here long. Even deep within the earth, eyeballs quickly caught the attention of anything hungry.

Compelled by the threads of the Strangeness twitching beneath her skin, the coyote trotted closer to the body. Risked a sniff at the backside, the traces of blood here and down the legs. More blood at the head, as well, hidden within the long dark hair. The human's fingers brushed against the plume of the coyote's tail like the points of some kind of mushroom springing up from the forest floor. Something secured the hands behind the corpse's back, a strong artificial scent on the stuff. The coyote had smelled it on many human things in the woods, a bitter substance both flat and flexible. Once, long ago, the coyote had curiously bitten into some and found its gray surface tough but its underside tacky. The stickiness had clung to the coyote's lips for most of a day, no matter how she had licked at it.

Now she sniffed at the body's mouth, which still smelled faintly of food and, yes, breath. Barely a breath. The body would give up soon. The coyote felt sure of it, and her own mouth moistened at the thought.

The Strangeness sent a surge of discouragement, a mother snapping at her pup's nose when it nuzzled for milk at an unwanted time. The coyote felt her limbs tighten, the corners of her mouth pull backward. Colors flitted behind her eyes, colors she knew without seeing, shades skewing outside the canine blue-yellow scale and into a sunset spectrum. A ribbon of saliva dripped from the coyote's lips.

Outside, the Strangeness urged, goading the coyote with a sense of light and clean air. A burst of energy in her limbs. The coyote took hold of the body's filthy ankle and pulled hard. Her jaws were strong, but the Strangeness lent her more strength, toughening her neck, bracing her legs. This had happened a few times in the past, and she knew she would sleep for many hours after this, afterward awakening very hungry and sore in every muscle.

Rocks shifted and splashed beneath the body and the coyote's paws. The bad smell of the water grew stronger, but the coyote kept pulling. The Strangeness tickled inside her mouth, keeping her grip on the leg even as the flesh shredded beneath her teeth. She could already smell the Strangeness entering the human body through the abrasions in the ankle. The smell comforted her. Better Strange than human, after all.

Outside the adit, the land plunged into a narrow creek funneling water down the steep flanks of the mountain. A recent, unusually warm rain had raised the water level, and dampness continued to settle out of the trees and bushes. Any minute the rain would begin again, harder this time.

Another mind tugged at the Strangeness's awareness, directing it away from the coyote, and for a moment the coyote was very nearly herself again, almost ordinary. Almost. She was still changed enough that her goal remained in the forefront of her mind even when the breath stopped coming from the dying human's body. The coyote whined to herself, knowing the Strangeness could not bond with a dead animal.

But further thoughts on the matter lay far beyond the coyote's understanding of the world. Her mind circled back to the prompt the Strangeness had given her and fixed on that duty.

The coyote gave one last fierce tug and the now-dead body slid over a hummock of sword ferns, gravity urging it toward the creek. It hung up for a second on a thorny salmonberry, and the coyote had to nudge it along.

When the body splashed into the creek, the coyote broke into a steady run, eager to leave the bad smells of the adit and find a place to shelter out of the rain. But even a mile away and resting inside a hollow log, part of her watched the body in the creek, slowly floating higher and higher in the rising water. Any unease she retained melted at the sense of the Strange emanating from the dead thing.

The coyote put her tail over her nose and let the Strangeness comfort her with its gentle thrum beneath her skin. Deep within the log, the ancient rotting wood hummed along, a sound that carried through the soil and into the trees, one soft hum stretching for miles in every direction. The coyote listened to her fellow

Strange throughout the forest, frogs and trees and all kinds of beings, even the male who had fathered the pups growing in her belly. His mind ran in soft blue circuits much like her own, flickering at the edge of their territory.

Suddenly, a sharp pain ripped through his blue humming. An image of two humans floated across the network of plants and creatures, the humans barking with laughter as the biggest of the pair picked up the coyote by his neck. Something sharp pierced the male's side again and again as he shrieked in pain.

Within her log, the female coyote whimpered, and the pain spread from her to the fern growing nearby. To the pair of vine maples sheltering her den. Onward and outward, the unpleasant sensation rippled throughout the Strangeness, and then the male coyote's voice went quiet completely.

The human body began to float away from the creek's bank and drift downstream.

CHAPTER TWO

THERE WERE CERTAIN SPRING DAYS IN OREGON, Erin thought, endless damp days when green saturated the air: the lights and darks of every color slanting to emerald, everything alive wavering with an intensity of viridian the human eye was not meant to see. Especially here, on the edge of the forest, where the trees sang a chorus of green as if their lives depended on it.

She wondered if she closed her eyes whether she could hear it, the true sound of the color green.

The rain stalled Erin's hand on the wiper switch, her whole body pleasantly toasted by the blasting heater. She needed to pee, but the steadily sifting rain promised to suck the heat from her bones if she left the car. She kept staring out at the woods. Spring was such a sodden, sluggish time in her home state. From February to May, the rain seemed like it might fill her throat and lungs when she breathed, drowning her in gray and green. Her heart craved color as much as her skin craved a break from the dampness.

Her brother Bryan had loved spring. The rain never bothered him, but instead gave him more energy for hiking and fishing and all his other outdoor adventures. He would have adored this view, the Clackamas River swirling aquamarine and white around the moss-covered rocks, cedars and alders and maples springing up from the water all the way to the sky. "We gotta get out in it," he would have said, and for a second, Erin could almost see him, a pale figure on the far side of the water beckoning to her, urging her into the green. She leaned forward, unsure if she was seeing just trees and lichens or if she was actually looking at a man.

The knock on the passenger window made her shriek and reflexively slap the wipers into overdrive. The older man outside shouted "Sorry!" and waved insistently.

For a second she wasn't sure what to do first—smile at the stranger? hit the wipers?—but the maniacal thudding and squeaking of the latter demanded her attention, and she finally fumbled them off, smiling apologetically at him the whole time. She found the switch for the passenger window and lowered it.

"Can I help you?" She still worked retail sometimes, so the fake smile was automatic.

"Good morning!" His face lit up with genuine cheer as he leaned in the window. The smell of moss and damp rolled off him like the forest itself was saying hello. "Saw your bumper sticker, thought I'd take a chance you were a foodie."

"The 'hug a farmer' one?"

"Yep." He hoisted a cardboard flat onto the window frame. She could just make out brown-and-black lumps in the folds of the canvas inside. "Any chance you like morels? I was on my way down to Sandy to sell them to the IGA, but I saw the fish jumping in the river and had to stop. Be happy to sell you a few first, though."

"Oh, that's so thoughtful. I'm not actually—"

He raised a hand. "Just think on it a second or two. No rush. I'll be setting up on the riverbank if you decide you want some."

He hauled the box back out of the window and headed toward the battered little pickup that had pulled up behind her.

She watched him in the rearview mirror, making mental notes about his beard and the fishing pole he took from behind the pickup's seat. She had no doubts she'd find plenty of local color for her article, but old habits and all that.

Erin's bladder reminded her again why she had stopped at the picnic area in the first place. She grabbed her toiletries bag off the passenger seat and got out of the car. Portland was only an hour behind her, but it felt a world away. The air smelled bracingly of forest—decomposing pine needles, wet moss, and the verdant briskness of freshly budding leaves. The river, higher than usual after a warm, wet March, grumbled in its banks. Other than that, though: silence.

When the sun arrived in a few weeks the area would be overrun by tourists, but for now, she and the mushroom seller had this picnic site to themselves. She could see him perched on a rock, casting into an inlet at the edge of the river. Back when her dad used to take her and Bryan fishing, he would have pointed them toward a spot like that, away from the main current with plenty of little nooks and crannies where the fish could relax. It was hard not to picture Bryan standing beside the old man, rod and reel in hand. He would have picked the same spot.

With a grimace, Erin turned away from the river and followed the path toward the site's vault toilet. She ground to a halt beside the Forest Service bulletin board, her eye caught by the photograph pinned up beside reminders to leave no trace. MISSING: ELENA LOPEZ. Without meaning to, Erin brushed pollen from the girl's black-and-white cheek. From the terse paragraph below her pretty, smiling face, it sounded like nineteen-year-old Elena Lopez had gotten off work at Cazadero Brewing a little more than a week ago and then fallen off the face of the earth.

In the photo, she looked younger than her age, her eyes bright as a child's.

Erin wiped her hand on the back of her jeans. That poor girl. Anything could have happened to her. A covetous customer. A pushy boyfriend. A hit-and-run. She was pretty, so that gave the first two a little extra weight. She had probably dealt with assholes hitting on her every shift, learning the necessary balance of subservient flirting and calculated avoidance. Erin knew the routine. Every woman who worked in customer service did. It didn't matter the job—Erin had worked in a feminist bookstore, a copy place, a bougie coffee joint, a diner—all the same.

"So sorry, Elena," she said, and went into the vault toilet.

Like all vault toilets, it encouraged hasty use. She hurried back outside and stood in the drizzle as she used hand sanitizer. The mushroom man cast into the water, and she thought again of Bryan.

The memory hurt. Thinking about him always did; her last therapist said she needed closure, that the families of missing people struggled their whole lives with it. But there was no closure when someone just vanished into the woods, even though the cops had closed Bryan's case after finding his journal full of talk about suicide. After the ruling, Erin's parents refused to talk about Bryan—hell, her mother refused to *talk*, unless it was to order another vodka tonic.

It was Bryan that brought her here. She looked at the flyer about Elena Lopez and felt her lips compress. After five years, Erin had finally joined a support group for the families of missing people, only to meet three people mourning family members, all people of color, lost in the Mt. Hood National Forest. And not just the same forest, but the part surrounding the same *town*.

She sent Hari a quick snap of the flyer. When he had talked Erin into helping him with his true crime podcast, he'd been focused on historical crimes against people of color, cold case stuff from the fifties and sixties. But when she told Hari about Faraday and its missing people problem, he was sure she was onto something.

So maybe it had been a bit of a stretch when Erin told their boss Faraday was the next hot tourist destination, but it had given her and Hari a budget to spend a week out here. *Oregon Traveler* was financing an article about rafting and relaxing on the Clackamas River with Erin's trademark sharp writing and Hari's fabulous photos. Erin secretly hoped they'd learn enough to pitch a book.

Plus, maybe while she was out here she could finally get the closure her shrink had wanted her to find.

Erin turned away from the bulletin board and narrowed her eyes at the river that had supposedly—according to authorities—swallowed her brother. Its emerald water swirled between boulders the size of VW buses. On the far side, a dipper flashed down to the shore. Dipped. Dipped again. Sprang into the air in a startled flutter, like a secret springing from surprised lips. *Hope is the thing with feathers*, she thought, and felt a tickle deep inside her chest.

She stared after the dipper, but the bird had vanished into the afternoon shadows, another creature absorbed into the trees. She bit her lip hard enough to feel the fatty tissue roll between her teeth. It was time to get moving—check-in at the B&B started soon. She turned back toward the car.

The ground beneath her foot squelched. Not like mud. Like something tougher and wetter than dirt.

She looked down and wished she hadn't. Red leaked out from

the thing she'd stepped on, a dull red-brown like (*don't say blood,* her brain nattered wildly), like, well, blood. Erin lifted her foot and a chunk of something gristly and gooey plopped back onto the dirt. She covered her mouth.

"So, the morels?"

With a shriek, she spun around.

The mushroom seller threw up his hands as she nearly collided with him. "Whoa! You all right?"

She pointed down at the ground, her hand shaking. "I—I—"

He stepped around her and hunkered down beside the bloody patch. "Looks like part of a kidney." He looked up at her. "Deer," he added, smiling kindly.

Erin swallowed. She didn't even eat meat, let alone hunt. "Deer. Okay." Of course her mind had gone to Elena Lopez, thinking the worst. But deer made more sense. "Isn't hunting season in fall?"

The mushroom guy stood up creakily. "This area's got a real problem with poachers lately. I'll call the game warden and let him know."

"Thanks," she called back over her shoulder. Despite the man's logical explanation for the grisly thing, she couldn't get back to her car quickly enough.

HIGHWAY 224 FOLLOWED THE CLACKAMAS RIVER EAST as the waterway grew wilder and wilder, twisting into the foothills of Mt. Hood like an enormous, sinewy root. Now the occasional house and small business, shuttered for the season, sprang up on its banks. Civilization couldn't be far now. Erin slowed the car and passed a sign: NOW ENTERING FARADAY. POPULATION: 3,576.

For another minute, the town looked like more forest, and then the square bulk of Cazadero Brewing appeared on her right, its back to the river. Despite its unpretentious exterior, cars filled its parking lot. The view from its deck and back windows had to be fantastic. Beside the brewery sat a small marina with a couple of rafting guide shops and gear outfitters clustered nearby. Tomorrow, she'd check in with one called "Wy'east Wonders." Erin tried to catch a glimpse of the place in her rearview mirror, but an oversize Ford F-350 pulled out of the brewery parking lot and nearly mowed down her car. She resisted the urge to flip off the driver and instead pulled into the parking lot of the Faraday Visitor Center. The truck's slipstream rocked her Toyota on its axles as it sped by.

She turned off the engine and stared at the ugly yellow A-frame. Five years ago, her brother had walked inside this place and bought a postcard with the visitor center listed as the photo credit. The postcard had made its slow way through the post office's routing system, making a side trip to Seattle before finally finding its way to her dorm at the University of Oregon, nearly a hundred miles south of this point. She hadn't received it until well after Bryan's funeral, and the sight of his handwriting had forced her to her knees in the middle of the student center.

She'd held on to it, of course. From dormitory to co-op housing to shared house to studio apartment, she'd kept that postcard stashed inside an old journal where it slept, if not soundly, at least quietly. Then she'd learned about Faraday. It took some digging to find the postcard with its image of a little girl sitting in a canoe with her own tiny fishing pole. It was so precisely the kind of cutesy thing Bryan would pick out for her that Erin had started to cry all over again, her shoulders shaking, her gut aching. She'd thought about getting rid of the damn thing. Saying goodbye, just like her therapist had been telling her to do for years. But of course she couldn't.

Erin drew the postcard out of her tote bag and gave it a good long look. Beyond the cuteness of the kid in the canoe, there was something off about the image, something she couldn't quite put her finger on. She dug around for the safety whistle one of her running buddies had given her, the kind with a compass and magnifying glass in the body. Under magnification, details came out: the barrettes in the girl's hair, the pink seams on her fishing pole, the tiny figure on the far side of the water. Erin turned on the interior light, her skin creeping up in goose bumps. She moved the lens over the postcard again. She was right. Someone stood on the far side of the water, their figure a pale silhouette with eyes like enormous black pits. Or like eyes behind a pair of binoculars, which was just about as creepy.

She dropped the magnifying glass, her fingers trembling.

Someone had stood on the lakeshore spying on this photo shoot. Maybe it was nothing. A bird watcher. A coincidence. Or maybe this town was as fucked up as Hari believed it was.

With a deep breath, Erin turned off her car and got out. Darkness filled the windows of the Faraday Visitor Center, and a fern had sprung up from the gutter at the corner. She went up to the front door anyway and tried peering inside, making shields of her hands to minimize the glare. Clusters of algae had colonized the gap between the glazing and the frame and begun to crawl across the glass. She could just make out a customer service desk; beneath the point of sale system was what appeared to be another missing person poster—a man, this time.

"We don't open until Memorial Day weekend."

Startled, Erin spun around. A tall, silver-haired woman

stood on the graveled lot behind her, her purple silk dress revealing the bones in her chest, as starkly furrowed as a washboard beneath a classy string of pearls. A cotton tote bag had been slung rather incongruously over her shoulder, and a sprig of eucalyptus stuck out over the top.

"Do you work here?" Erin asked, although it seemed impossible a woman who wore silk to do her shopping should work anyplace.

The woman brushed a twist of her white curls off her cheek. "I run the chamber of commerce, which oversees the center." She took a few steps forward, her nose crinkling as she took in the green stain on the glass. "Every winter, it's the same. Nothing holds back the green, not once it sets its mind on the place."

"Oh," Erin said, because what else could she say? "Well, thank you. I guess I'll just go check into my bed-and-breakfast."

The woman's watery blue eyes flashed back to Erin's face. "Where are you staying?"

"The Vanderpoel Guest House?"

The woman straightened. "Excellent! I'm Olivia Vanderpoel. You can just follow me up to the house." She patted the tote bag with a beringed hand. "I wanted to get these flowers for you, but I got a late start this morning."

"That's a kind gesture."

"We get so few visitors this time of year." The woman pointed up the street, where a rectangular tan Volvo of the same vintage as her '80s wrap dress sat parked in front of a flower shop. "I can't wait to show you the house."

The line about the B&B had been a simple ploy to free herself of the woman; Erin had in fact hoped to see more of the town before settling in for the night. But there was nothing for it now. She got into her car and waited for Olivia Vanderpoel to make her way into her own vehicle. As they crawled through the streets of Faraday, she found herself dreading her arrival at the guest house. It would probably be stuffy and ancient, its chairs covered in crocheted doilies and its walls adorned with fake flowers. She set her jaw and followed the other car up Vanderpoel Road, which dead-ended in a circular driveway and a purple Victorian house just this side of being a mansion.

Erin pulled up beside the Volvo and got out. Olivia stood beside the house's wrought iron fence. The top of each fence post tapered to a tiny point, exactly like the fence in *The Addams Family*. The yard, however, looked as crisp and upper-class as Olivia herself, the green expanse of lawn outlined with a handsome array of azaleas and hydrangeas.

"Let's get you checked in."

Erin followed the spry older woman up the front stairs, trailing her fingers along the finely worked handrail, then the ornamentation along the porch doorway. The colors of the varying trims must have taken a month to paint. Olivia clicked her tongue impatiently, and Erin followed her through a handsome wooden door with a geometric stained-glass panel insert. When the door closed behind them, they stood in faintly red-and-blue-dappled gloom, and then Olivia pushed the antique light switch, and the chandelier overhead flickered to life.

She picked up a ledger sitting on a low bookshelf. Underneath the big book sat a stack of photocopied pages with the word "MISSING" emblazoned across the top. Erin caught a quick glimpse of a photo of young man before the ledger was lowered back into place, but she thought it looked like the same poster hanging on the visitors center's counter.

"Let's see, if I remember right, you paid with a credit card, in full."

Olivia began turning pages, but Erin's attention had gone to the walls. Instead of doilies or fake flowers, a series of large paintings ran the length of the hallway, their colors saturated, intense. The forms were simplified masses like Toltec sculptures flattened on canvas. Women, primarily, massive women with either enormous breasts or huge hips or both, their clothes missing or destroyed, their bodies bursting free of them. The last painting in the series, or at least the one farthest down the hall, showed only the deep canyon of a woman's bosom, vines or tree branches crawling out of her flesh like her heart birthing a forest.

"Miss Harper?"

Erin snapped her attention back to the older woman, who sounded irritated. Olivia's eyes flicked to the painting and then back to Erin's face. "Striking, aren't they?"

That was certainly one word for them. Erin made herself nod.

"My son's," Olivia explained. "His final series before he . . ." She trailed off, collapsing in on herself a little. She looked suddenly very frail and old. Then she drew in a deep breath. "Anyway, I've found your entry. If I can just see your ID, then I can take you out to your room."

Erin recognized the pain in the other woman's face: the kind of pain that hollows someone out with its mix of grief and chained hope. The man on the missing flyer had to be Olivia's son.

The newshound in Erin wanted to ask about him, but she couldn't bring herself to. Instead, she put on a cheerful smile and dug in her shoulder bag for her wallet. "Out?" she asked.

"Oh, yes, the guest room is above the garage. You'll be able to come and go with total privacy."

Erin had missed that detail when booking on the website. "That's terrific."

"It was my son's apartment," Olivia said. "It's nice that someone can get some use out of the place." She wrote down Erin's driver's license number, then took out an honest to goodness key, the kind with a plastic tag, as well as a bag of mint truffle Hershey's Kisses. "I usually put these out on the nightstand, but I forgot. Follow me."

Erin followed her outside again, passing the cars and heading around the side of the house. Beyond the garden was a cluster of small outbuildings, all of them painted the same purple as the house. They climbed the creaking flight of exterior stairs running up the side of the largest building.

"Here we are." Olivia undid a deadbolt, and the apartment door opened with a low groan. A spare studio apartment with pale wood floors and white walls gave up the smell of Murphy Oil Soap.

Olivia strode inside, pointing to the various amenities: extra bedding in the baskets under the futon, a microwave, sink, teakettle. White towels in the tiny bathroom. No television, just a plain wooden desk with a severe black office chair, a bronze statue perched on its corner. It was the most spartan space Erin had ever seen. She supposed it was an improvement over the floral wonderland she'd expected.

"Well." Olivia sat the bag of candy on the simple wooden nightstand. "If you need anything, just ring the doorbell. At least until eight—I'm afraid I'm rather an 'early to bed, early to rise' sort these days."

Erin looked around the room and shook her head. "I can't imagine I'll need anything. I'll probably walk back into town to get some dinner, though, so I'll be sure to be quiet after eight."

"Walk?" Olivia's voice quavered.

"Yes, it's not far, and I could use the exercise."

The woman put out her hand, her fingertips just grazing Erin's shoulder. "Just . . . be careful." She hesitated. "There are so many bad drivers these days," she added, a bit lamely.

"Thanks," Erin said, and waved goodbye to the older woman. She couldn't help but think Olivia had wanted to say something more just then.

She closed the door and looked back at the room. The bronze statue looked so out of place in the plain space that she reached over to pick it up. Its style was unmistakably Olivia Vanderpoel's son's—the blocky figure stared back at Erin, her body all flattened squares and points, save for her enormous mouth, puckered as if she was whistling. In her hands, she held an enormous mushroom. His style made the mushroom look nearly phallic, and the combination of mushroom and mouth gave it an unsettling sexual quality.

With a shudder, Erin put it down. She wouldn't be having mushrooms with her dinner, that was certain.

CHAPTER THREE

THE WALK BACK INTO TOWN REINFORCED ERIN'S first opinions of the place. *Oregon Traveler* expected her to paint a portrait of Faraday as the next Bend, or at least a tiny McMinnville. To do so, she was going to have to narrow her focus to the riverfront area. The real town, the parts not being offered up to tourists but where the actual residents lived, was as rough around the edges as most former lumber towns in Oregon. Erin had gotten an eye for that certain style of decay—the roofs with tarps covering rotten spots, the siding with moss chinking the gaps, the driveways with cars sitting on blocks or being swallowed by blackberry vines. If Faraday was up-and-coming, the money was still struggling to flow uphill from the river.

She hit 2nd Avenue and made a right. Here, a few bars offered up midweek specials and karaoke on the weekends; a high-end Mexican restaurant boasted tequila flights; a kitchen store with French pretensions welcomed tourists and weekend passersby. She paused in front of a promising breakfast joint and made a note to come back in the morning. The guest house offered a complimentary continental breakfast, but Erin wasn't expecting much.

Her back pocket vibrated, and she pulled out her phone. Grinned at the name on the screen. "Hari," she answered, "tell me you changed your mind and you're coming up this afternoon.

There's tons of room at my B&B, and I can't wait to start doing research."

"Are you psychic? Because that's why I'm calling," Hari answered. "Matt's meeting wrapped early, so we're driving up right now. Kayla's been helping me go through some cold cases on the Clackamas county sheriff's department page. Got some promising ones for the podcast."

Kayla? Erin didn't know the woman well, and in fact found her more than a little intimidating. Like her boyfriend, in fact. Matt had been Hari's roommate in college, and now he made big bucks doing software development. He also ran fifty-mile trail races like Erin ran 5Ks. The idea of spending a week rafting and camping with them made her distinctly uncomfortable. But Matt had been to Faraday before and was friends with one of the local outfitters. It galled Erin to admit that she needed him.

She changed the subject. "Did you get that picture I sent you? Elena Lopez. She's been missing for over a week. The flyer was at a picnic area just outside of town."

"That jibes with some of the other missing persons cases I found." An unfamiliar female voice sounded behind Hari, and he mumbled something back at her. "Hey, we're about to stop in Sandy to pick up a few supplies, so we should be there in forty-five minutes or so."

"Fantastic!" An older man walking his dog glowered at Erin, and she realized she was shouting in the middle of the street. She dialed her enthusiasm down a notch. "Are you sure you want to stay with Matt and Kayla in the RV? I'm going to be lonely in my big old guest apartment."

He laughed. "I'd say you should join us, but I'm sleeping on the floor while Kayla's sister crashes on the dinette seat. Still, it's where all the fun is happening."

Kayla shouted in the background: "Ask her where we can meet her!"

Erin looked around. She could see up Abernethy Street to the glowing light of the brewery on Highway 224. "Let's meet at Cazadero Brewing. You can't miss it—it's right on the highway. I'll be the one who's three beers in."

"Great," Hari said. She could hear more voices in the background, maybe Matt's. "Oh! Question: Do you prefer gummies or marshmallows?"

"Marshmallows?" She hoped they were talking about edibles and not just snacks.

"*Excellent*," he purred. "See you soon!"

She hung up and put her phone back in her pocket. A damp breeze crawled down the collar of her raincoat as she waited for a shiny Sprinter van to pass. Even here on the highway, she could smell the wildness of the area. Faraday was the only real town for thirty miles in any direction, and it didn't even have a doctor's office. Planning emails from Matt had warned her that cell service pretty much ended at the city limits. The Mt. Hood National Forest stretched out around the town, harboring bears and cougars and who knew what else. It was the kind of place where outdoorsy types like her brother went to unplug.

And to disappear forever, she reminded herself, like someone pressing a salt flake into a cut. It stung, just as she meant it to.

IT WAS BARELY FOUR O'CLOCK, BUT THE BREWERY WAS packed.

Erin pulled open the heavy front door and basked in a wash of oregano and grease. Yeah, this was a good choice.

She stood for a long second on the black doormat, looking

for the best place to sit. Most of the booths had been claimed by older folks in twos or fours. A family had taken one of the big center tables, the three kids covered in ketchup, the parents sharing a pitcher of beer. ESPN showed silently on the TVs above the empty bar, so she went to the counter and climbed up on a stool. An elk head looked down at her disapprovingly.

Erin returned its glassy gaze with her own fierce look. Growing up, she'd eaten in dozens of small-town joints. The Harper family hadn't been much on togetherness, but once a year, her dad would take a week off from the lumberyard and take her and Bryan out on a fishing trip. Every summer a new river or lake, a new series of campgrounds, a different batch of middle-aged waitresses slinging fried food and weak beer under the watchful eye of taxidermied animals. Those women had always seemed so much more motherly than the woman waiting for them at home.

A bottle-blond server—yes, middle-aged—waved at her. "Be right with you!" She bustled toward the kitchen. Now Erin caught a whiff of chicken wings and French fries, and her stomach rumbled.

She picked up the menu, tacky with old grease. No amount of bleach water could touch the layer of stickiness a busy fryer could spread around a restaurant. That and the worn seat of the barstool promised a place popular for all the right reasons.

The server returned, sliding a red plastic glass of water across the bar. "Can I get you a beer or some coffee to start?"

Erin glanced at the tap list chalked above the tap handles. "The Fireball red ale doesn't taste like the whiskey, does it?"

The woman shook her head wearily. "If I had a dollar for every time someone asked, I could retire. No, it's a regular red ale, just named for the meteor strike back when the town was first built." She wore a pin beneath the logo embroidered on her red polo shirt—a photo of a familiar smiling young woman, the words "BRING HER HOME" circling her face. Elena Lopez had left a big hole behind when she vanished.

The server raised an eyebrow, and Erin realized she'd been thinking too long. "I'll give it a shot, then."

"Anything else?" She was already pulling the beer.

Erin glanced back at the menu. "Can I get a mini cheese pizza with mushrooms, spinach, jalapeños, and olives? And a side of French fries? Please."

"Sure thing." The waitress flipped a coaster across the table and dropped the pint glass onto it. Foam sluiced down its side. "Be out in a few."

A white guy in a green trucker cap dropped onto a seat a few stools down. "Hey, Patty. Can I get a Moose Drool and an order of nachos? Extra sour cream like usual."

"You know it, Jordan." The server pulled a brown bottle out from under the counter and put it in front of him.

Erin did a double take. She recognized the man from someplace, she was certain of it, although with his trucker hat and scruffy brown beard, he looked like an average Portland guy. He reached for his bottle of beer, and she noticed the fir tree tattooed on his middle finger.

"Sorry to bother you," she began, and the guy swiveled in his seat to face her. "Are you TrekkinScene on Instagram?"

His mouth fell open a little, stretched into a grin. "I've never been recognized in public before!"

She brightened her smile. "I was studying up on the history of the area, stumbled onto your account. Great stuff."

He held out his hand. "Jordan. Nice to meet you."

She took it. "Erin. Nice to meet you, too."

He took a swig of beer. "So, what brings you to Faraday?"

"I'm a writer for *Oregon Traveler*. Working on a profile of the town. It's the next Bend or something."

"Or something." He shook his head. "Wish I could go back in time and tell Teen Me a travel magazine would be interested in Faraday."

She reached for her beer. "Would you have believed it?"

"Hell no!" He laughed. "This place was a shithole. We still don't have our own high school—the kids have to bus into Sandy."

Her fries appeared. She nodded at the waitress, but Patty was already moving. Erin turned her attention back to Jordan. He was maybe five years or so older than she was, her brother's age, a late-stage millennial. Worked outside, probably; the crow's feet were already noticeable around his eyes, but other than that, he looked young, fit. Cute in a thru-hiker way, if she was being honest with herself.

She bit a fry in half. "So why are you still here?"

He gave a dry laugh. "Born here. Got out for a while, but I had to come home to help my family. The Instagram stuff is just to keep me sane."

She was nodding, familiar with the story, even if she was glad she'd escaped it. Since Bryan vanished, visiting her family had gotten to be excruciating. She couldn't imagine moving back to her hometown permanently.

"Well, I'd love to chat with you for the magazine," she said. "Or even go hiking together. Tomorrow I'm on a mini rafting trip, but I'm here for a week."

"Where are you staying?" Jordan asked, but the door opened and his attention went to the door.

A redhead stood framed in the doorway, her black hardshell

jacket outlining the kind of curves any woman might covet. She caught sight of Jordan and waved happily.

"Jordan!" she called out in a smoky voice that went with her wild curls and tilted nose. She unzipped her jacket as she strode across the room. Heads swiveled as she passed by tables and booths. She wore practical hiking pants and a button-down shirt the way some women would wear a little black dress. Erin could feel the blood moving to the surface of her skin, every inch of her flesh wishing it could be touched by this delicious being.

"Hey, Dahlia," Jordan said, and Erin didn't need to know the two of them to know he was smitten with this woman and had been for a long, long time.

"So, Scene." The redhead swatted his shoulder. Not flirtatiously, just friendly. "Who's your pal?"

He pointed with his thumb. "This is Erin. She's a travel writer."

Dahlia turned her smile toward Erin. Her teeth were crooked and not particularly white, but it didn't matter. Erin felt herself sitting up straighter and pushing back her own ordinary brown hair. "Erin Harper, by any chance?"

"How did you know?"

The redhead put out her hand. "Took a wild guess." She winked. "Dahlia MacIntosh of Wy'east Wonders. We don't get many clients in April, so the odds seemed good."

Erin liked Dahlia's handshake. Jordan's, too. Solid handshakes, the hands muscular and a little rough. "Really nice to meet you."

Dahlia looked around the room. "Where's Matt?"

Of course—she was the outfitter, so that made her Matt's buddy. Erin felt a little irritated to be sidelined by him but smiled back. "He and the rest of the crew should be here in like half an hour."

Dahlia waved at a table just being vacated by a group of teens. "Let's grab that booth, then. I'm eager to get to know you all."

Jordan made a face. "I don't know, Dee—I spent the morning on the mountain, and I'm pretty wiped."

She gave him a gentle shove. "Come on, I want to pick your brain, too."

The brewery door thudded open and two men in camouflage jackets entered. Big guys, Carhartt pants, Red Wing work boots. The biggest stopped in his tracks and ran his eyes the length of Dahlia's body.

Dahlia grabbed Jordan's hand and yanked him half off his stool. "Shit, it's the Steadman brothers."

In two steps, the big Carhartt guy had them cut off. Erin nearly slammed into Dahlia's back as she came to a stop.

"Hey, Dahlia. How's business?"

Dahlia's shoulders collapsed. "Fine, Nick," she said, her voice wispy. Whoever this guy was, he had effortlessly sucked the power from her body.

Jordan took a half step forward, lifting his chin. "Hi, Nick."

He might as well have been a ghost. Nick stepped past Jordan and put his arm around Dahlia. "I was just thinking about calling you. We can take my boat out, drink a few beers." He brushed his finger down her cheek. She flinched away. "Come on. It'll be fun."

Dahlia wriggled in his grasp. "I don't think so, Nick."

His grip tightened. "Come on, Dahlia."

From behind him, a hand closed on Nick's shoulder. "She said no, dude."

Erin was relieved to see the hand belonged to Kayla. Nick

spun around to face her and his eyes went big. She looked like a sports model and carried herself like a black belt—which she was. Her mouth smiled pleasantly, but the expression didn't touch her ice-blue eyes. She looked from Nick to Dahlia. "Are you all right?"

Dahlia shook off Nick's suddenly limp arm. "Yeah, thanks."

"Hey, you've got the wrong idea," Nick said. For a second, it looked like he was about to get in her face, but his companion—*brothers*, Dahlia had said—interjected himself.

"Hey, let's just get out of here," he said. "We can get a burger with Craig at the A-Street Tavern or something."

Nick scowled at Kayla. "Sounds good, Howie." He let himself be led away, but he glanced back over his shoulder at Dahlia. "Next time, Dahl. You know you're my girl."

When the door closed behind them, Dahlia sagged against Jordan. "Jesus, that guy." He patted her back. "Thanks," Dahlia said to Kayla. "Nick Steadman and I have a lot of history."

"No need to explain," Kayla said, just as the rest of the group spilled in, laughing at something Hari said. Matt held the door, dressed in black Patagonia/Fjällräven/REI chic, same as Kayla. The smile he shot toward his fiancée glowed a nearly halogen-bright white.

"Hey, you found Erin!" he called. "And Dahlia, too!" He came up to put his arm around Kayla's waist and the pair stood in harmonious, smiling perfection.

Erin smiled and waved, but the expression felt forced. Out of the corner of her eye, she caught Jordan glancing her way, and they exchanged a knowing look. He understood. He'd grown up here, after all. Her hometown wasn't quite the shithole Faraday had been, but they shared DNA. She'd known just from glancing at Jordan's and Dahlia's teeth that they'd grown up the way she had: no orthodontia, no dance lessons, no new car when you turned sixteen. Even Hari didn't understand that, much as he tried.

"You're Dahlia?" Kayla asked. "I've heard so much about you. You should join us for some beers."

Dahlia beamed at her. "That would be terrific."

"Anyone else hungry?" Matt asked.

"I'm starving, and this place smells *a-ma-zing*," Hari pronounced.

Dahlia led them to the open booth.

"Hi," another girl said. She'd been hidden behind Matt and Kayla. She looked like a shorter, more feminine Kayla, her blond hair waving in short curls that gave her an anime-like quality. Her pink sweater only accentuated her cuteness.

For a moment, Erin forgot how to speak. "Hi," she finally squeaked.

The girl's cheeks dimpled. "I'm Kayla's sister, Madison." She extended her hand. Her nail polish matched her sweater. "I'm so excited to finally get to meet you."

They all piled into the booth, everyone smiling awkwardly but happily as they squeezed in too tightly around the table. Erin squished between Madison and Jordan, and she couldn't help noticing Hari giving Jordan occasional looks. Jordan didn't seem Hari's type, but she had to admit he was cute. She'd probably be giving him looks if Madison and Dahlia weren't so distracting.

The waitress arrived with Jordan's nachos and Erin's pizza. The second glimpse of her pin jolted Erin's brain back into functionality. "Hey, that flyer I saw—our server is wearing a pin about her."

Hari sat up straighter, shedding his flirtatious expression.

"Are you talking about Elena?" Jordan looked upset. "She's a really nice girl. I saw her just about every time I stopped in here."

Dahlia nodded and shifted the ice in her mouth so she could talk. "It's bad news for the brewery. Another waitress went missing last summer, too. Really pretty girl from up at Three Lynx. They found her car in a ravine between here and the Oak Grove powerhouse, but they never found her."

Goose bumps broke out on the back of Erin's neck. Sitting in her Portland apartment looking at old news sites, she'd known there was weird shit going on in this town, but it was different being *in* Faraday, hearing actual residents talking about this stuff. She wondered how hard she should press them on the issue, but then a basket of fries arrived, and Hari sent them around the table. An entire tasting flight appeared, every flavor of Cazadero's beers in cute little glasses, and they were all reaching to taste them and argue about which was the best.

Then Dahlia grinned, more than a little mischievously, and said: "Hey, do you all like hot springs?"

CHAPTER FOUR

THE MAN BROUGHT HIS PALMS CLOSER AND CLOSER together to feel the currents of air moving between them. He pushed until he felt the tiny threads in one hand brushing against the flesh of the other, the electrical snap when the threads touched each other. The sensation continued beneath his skin, popping and fizzing pleasantly up his wrists and arms. He smiled and then let the smile die. The Strangeness didn't appreciate such gestures, small as they were. Its threads weren't for play. He stopped before he could draw more of its attention to himself and hummed a tune off-key.

In the days before he had found the Strangeness, he had been quite good at staying at the borders of people's attention. He could walk down Main Street and feel people's eyes rolling off him like water off an umbrella. At night, he could walk past the windows of houses without causing even a dog to bark, stand with his nose right up to the glass and never be seen. It had been very lonely.

That was one good thing about life inside the Strangeness. He never felt lonely anymore.

But he did feel tired. He brushed his fingers over the scrapes and bruises on his arms, simple physical wounds from last night's rampage. The Strangeness had not condoned it, but it had lent him the power to smash plywood and hurl concrete slabs. It approved of his self-appointed work as a forest protector and perhaps even benefited from it. If it hadn't, it would have steered him away from the ruined old hotel and on to some other, more necessary work. His job, after all, was to serve.

A frog splashed in the stream, reminding him of his mission. He was once again to check on the girl in the creek. She had lain there for several days now, still and cold and quiet, but the Strangeness was patient. Days were nothing to a mind like the Strangeness's.

The thought sent pointed crackles up the back of his head, and he quickly turned his attention back to the stream. Mud and algae streaked the rocks along its edges, making the footing tricky. He could scramble up the bank to hit one of his usual trails, but his legs were tired from the long climb out of the center of the Strange, reporting on what had happened to that male coyote last week and what the man himself had done in retribution. Nothing would make the man happier than to simply sit and rest on one of the big boulders beside the stream, but if he dared take a break from this assigned task, the Strangeness would certainly reduce his will to crackling and fizzing and steer his body itself. No, it was better to keep moving, enjoying the fine rain and the cheerful yellow faces of the spring violets.

The stream rushed downhill to join with a larger one—Hillier Creek—so he followed an easy path from the water and then broke into a happy jog. Just running in the spring air, no real reason save for the pleasure of a drizzly day. He jumped over some kind of old mining equipment that his father would have known by name and startled a Douglas squirrel out of hiding. It darted into the underbrush, shooting sparks of irritation as it went. In the night he would have been able to see them, the tracks of electricity pulsing from one Strange to another, but by day, it was just another squirrel.

Something rustled off to his left and he shrank beneath a huckleberry bush. Held his breath. Very few people came here to the former Hillier townsite, and mostly only in hunting or huckleberry season. The man let out his breath, slowly, silently, and listened again. There were only forest sounds as far as his ears could stretch.

In the back of his mind, the Strangeness stirred. Prickled in the hinge of his jaw, like eating something too sour. The skin on his arms hummed and crawled. The man got to his feet and hurried to the creek bank. The closer he got to it, the more his skin strained and twitched with the Strangeness. It felt like bugs crawling on top of his muscles, a sensation that had nearly broken his mind at first. Maybe it had broken his mind. He couldn't be sure.

He stopped where his skin told him to stop, crouching on a rock beside a fallen tree. Its branches stretched into the creek, straining the water. This high up on the mountain's flank, it caught only organic things: floating leaves, little twigs, the foam of dissolved humic acids.

The pallid body of a dead girl.

She was beginning to give off a stink, but she was in much better shape than if she hadn't been in the water. Despite all the warm rain lately, the springs feeding the creek were as cold as any refrigerator.

He looked more closely at the girl. A faint electricity crackled beneath her skin despite the fact he'd never seen the Strangeness take hold in something dead this long. He knew that was why the Strangeness kept driving him out here to look for signs that she was waking up from her long cold sleep. She was a mystery, and one with the potential to change the Strangeness's entire network.

Close your eyes.

The Strangeness didn't speak, but it was hard not to feel some of its impulses as words. The man squeezed shut his eyes and let his Strange senses do their job. About a dozen different points of view: the tiny, fish-eyed glances of the Douglas squirrel; a crow's cockeyed stare; the light-to-dark gradient of plants and mushrooms he could barely understand.

Then nothing, or at least no vision. All the beings had turned their attention to their new electrical sense, and with their eyes closed (or whatever the hell a plant used to recognize light), the colors flared from one being to another. Yellow ribbons of electricity snapping and crackling between him and the squirrel. Pink connecting him to the crow. The whole damn rainbow in tiny threads at the tips of their fingers/claws/talons. Little rippling colors going into the ferns and the mosses draping the rock he knelt upon.

And down below, her hair tangled in the dead tree's branches, the creek girl: her shape beginning to fill with the purple threads of new growth.

The man dug his fingers in the mosses to balance himself as he leaned out over the edge of the boulder. *Hello!* he called, but only in his mind, where he knew she could probably hear it. If she couldn't hear it yet, maybe she would remember hearing it when she was ready.

The Strangeness pulled back its attention with a sudden snap that left him shivering and blinking, rubbing the skin of his arms with fingers that almost felt normal. He drew a few deep breaths, relishing the way the air tasted when his mouth was not full of threads.

Then—quickly, quickly—before it could return, he hurried down to the ruins of the mining town and settled into one of his favorite perches above the old mill wheel. He drew out his pocketknife and a stick of wood, the kind beavers tossed out of their winter dens. Stroking the blade over the pale alder, he watched a shape release from the wood. No one would see the statue except for him, but that was all right. No one had cared much for his art when he'd been a part of the human world, anyway.

CHAPTER FIVE

THE EDIBLES HIT ERIN AS DAHLIA PULLED HER SUBARU into a two-car trailhead parking area. Benevolent waves rippled from Erin's core, filling every cell with well-being and contentment. The trees seemed to smile down at them, and Erin found herself blinking happiness back at them as Dahlia reached across Hari and Jordan to rummage in her glove box. The light inside it made Erin squint; it was nearly twilight now, and the gloom wonderfully comfortable.

"Ah-ha!" Dahlia held aloft an orange laminated rectangle. "Northwest Forest Pass. We can at least park legally before we start the trespassing portion of the night."

"Trespassing?" If Hari had been a dog, his ears would have pricked up. He'd only found his inner rebel since he'd started his podcast last year. He'd been talking about starting parkour someday soon, but since Erin had never known him to hit the gym or go for a run, she took his claims with a grain of salt.

Speaking of salt, she desperately needed some chips. And a bottle of Gatorade. Or at least a breath mint.

Jordan must have been a mind reader. He smiled over his shoulder and stuck out a tin. Not Altoids, just similar packaging. Hopefully vegetarian, unlike the curiously strong mints. Erin took one and tasted spearmint and skunk. The night was only getting better, then.

Except for the trespassing thing. That could be bad. *Oregon*

Traveler really wouldn't appreciate it if two of their staff got arrested.

"Trespassing?" To her stoned ears, she sounded like Hari's echo.

Dahlia opened the driver's side door. The rain had stopped about an hour ago, and it smelled fresh and clean and woodsy outside. "Just Olivia Vanderpoel, and she hasn't called the cops on anybody in while." She got out, vaped her first blast of the night, and peered inside at the rest of them. "Come on, kids. The fun starts here."

"Can somebody let me out of the hatch?" Matt groaned. As the tallest person, he probably should have ridden in the front seat, but he'd been far too chivalrous. Erin couldn't decide if that made her like him more or less.

"I'm coming, Matt!" Kayla scrambled over her sister and then tumbled out of the car.

"I guess we should get out," Madison said. She'd been leaning into Erin's shoulder the whole ride, and her curls gave off a wonderful smell, like cocoa butter and some kind of fancy boutique. "Let's see if I can get the door open."

Erin, giggling madly, spent what felt like a full minute trying to find the seat belt clip. By the time she managed it, the others were already gathering at the trailhead, adjusting packs and coolers. The sunset painted the whole group so golden it almost hurt to look at them, beautiful and muscled and beaming with promise. She wasn't sure she belonged with such a crew.

Dahlia blew a cloud of white smoke and beckoned Erin over. "Doing all right?" she asked.

Erin nodded. The marijuana silliness had gone out of her. "Yeah. Yeah, just taking a mental picture."

Dahlia put her hand on the back of Erin's neck. Her palm

was warm, a little rough. "It's important to record the beautiful moments." She squeezed very gently, and then stepped forward. "Come on, people, the water is calling!"

Jordan slipped a headlamp out of his pocket and over his head, while around him the others did likewise. "Erin in the middle since she doesn't have a headlamp. It's going to be dark in the woods."

Erin wished all her gear wasn't locked up in the back of her Toyota, still parked in front of the Vanderpoel guest house. She felt like the odd one out, neither the local nor the outdoor addict. The darkness of the forest ahead felt suddenly very dense, the trees downright judgmental.

Hari tapped her shoulder, covering his headlamp so as not to blind her. "Have you ever been night hiking before?" he whispered.

"Nope. You?"

"Does walking through Old Town at two in the morning count?"

They spent a few moments of silence, the trail steep enough Erin was nearly panting. Apparently, there was a difference between running on city streets and hiking up actual mountains. She made herself concentrate on her feet, although her brain felt so light and wiggly it was a struggle. If twilight still lingered, the forest now blocked it out. The darkness shrank the world to the path under Erin's feet, the white beams of the other's headlamps roving over the ground and the underbrush. She tried not to think about her brother or the missing girl.

"The missing girl you were talking about—Elena Lopez." Hari, apparently psychic, kept his voice low.

The trees leaned in around them. Erin rubbed her arms. "You think she's podcast material?"

"All kinds of people go missing in this place," Hari said, "but people of color are more likely to just vanish. Last summer, a thru-hiker got off the PCT for some Portland-area tourism. Met up with friends, then they come out here for a rafting trip, stayed in the campground on the east side of town. The group gets up, starts making breakfast, but the hiker, she's not stirring. Not a peep. So the friends unzip her tent, and there's no sign of her. Her pack, her phone, her sleeping bag, it's all zipped in there, but she's gone. They look everywhere. Her folks are *still* looking for her. Not a single clue."

"Latinx?" Erin asked, her reporter's sense tingling.

"Yep."

"That's fucked up." She reached for her phone. She had to make a note of this.

"Right?" Hari's voice rose with excitement. "How many stories have you read about hikers or climbers getting lost on Mt. Hood? But none of them mention Faraday."

"Hari," Matt's voice cut in, "remember the rule: no work on the river or the trail."

"You're harshing my mellow!" Kayla called, and then burst into giggles.

The laughter spread down the line until even Hari was chuckling a little.

"Are we really up for this, Hari?" she whispered. "This isn't like a trip to a winery vineyard. What do we really know about investigative journalism?"

He hopped over a tree root and pushed a branch out of their way. His face was all but invisible in the darkness, his headlamp blazing from his hairline. "I wouldn't be here if I didn't believe in you. The introduction you showed me for our book? It's the real deal."

Tears prickled her eyes. "That means so much."

"You're welcome. Now let's hurry up before we get lost in the freaking woods," he said, urging her back out in front of him into the beam of his headlamp.

As Erin moved through the darkness, Hari's words and the softness of the spring night drove away her uncertainty. The bob and dance of the headlamps made the ground beneath her feet recede and advance, recede and advance, the land become sea, a tide of stone and tree roots. Above her head, branches wove the sky into a plaid of alternating darkness, the stars metallic threads bursting from the fabric. They pierced the dome of her vision and sent it sparkling, swirling.

No one spoke. Their footsteps synced into a shared rhythm.

Sometimes Hari touched her shoulder, not as if to urge her forward, but perhaps to reassure himself that she was still there, an ordinary person and not some luminous star being. She found herself reaching ahead of her to touch Kayla's shoulder a few times herself. *There could be anything out here,* she thought, but instead of feeling fear she felt only wonder. She laughed and liked the sound of her own voice.

They had all started laughing again now, an echo of the creek that was gurgling in the distance. She tried to guess how long they'd been walking and came up blank. An hour, maybe? She found herself climbing over a split-rail fence, and now the path descended, not so steeply she feared falling, but enough to make her concentrate on her feet again. People bunched up and got out of order. She had no idea who she walked beside; someone's hand touched hers and stroked it. She thought she smelled cocoa butter.

"These trees are amazing," Hari said, his voice hushed, reverent.

"They have to be old growth," Madison said, running her fingers along the massive ridge of bark on the nearest giant Douglas fir.

Erin stared up into the treetops, enjoying the way the group's lights rose up them, reflecting warmly on the trunks and vanishing into the darkness of the upper branches. Perhaps it was just the edibles, but she thought she could see their souls, gold and green and eternal, patiently watching the hikers below.

"The Vanderpoels never logged this area," Jordan said. He was staring, too, his face as awed as Erin's must have been. She reached for his hand and squeezed it. "It seems out of character for them, though. Maybe it was some kind of agreement with the tribes? But thank goodness they didn't."

Madison put out her arms to a tree, measuring it with her body. It would have taken at least two more Madisons to go around it. "You know they're connected, right? Especially in ancient forests. The soil is full of fungal organisms, all of them sending out threads of mycelium. Some of the mycelium taps into the roots of trees, trading sugars for minerals. The fungi help the trees grow, and the trees help the fungi grow, and all of it's woven together into one enormous net of life."

Erin thought she stood at the edge of comprehending that connection. It was probably just the edibles, but her heart felt swollen with everything around her. She had to imagine this was how Bryan felt when he went into the woods. So much awe, and joy, and wonder. She wondered how he had lived like that.

"Awesome," Matt breathed, and then they were walking again, the moment fading as the light ahead grew stronger.

The forest broke open and the moonlight nearly shocked Erin with its brilliance. The creek spread out shallow and broad except where its windings cut deeper pools in its clay banks. Slabs of stone broke up ground and water as if some giant hand had emptied out its dice bag and then decided it no longer wished to play such a chancy game.

In the moonlight, swirling wisps of steam shone silver above the nearest pool. The sharp stink of sulfur hung in the air.

Dahlia flung out her arms. "Behold: Vanderpoel Hot Springs!"

"They named it for themselves?" Erin asked.

Dahlia yanked off her tee shirt. "There have always been Vanderpoels in Faraday, and they've always wanted to remind people about it." She wore a black bralette, her skin redhead pale in contrast. She wriggled out of her pants. "Let's bring the coolers down by the water. I'm starving."

Everyone else was starving, too. And no one needed urging out of their clothes and into the water. Hands touched above containers of hummus. Water sluiced down bodies as smooth and perfectly curved as cellos. Someone passed Erin a cider and she drank it too fast as the steaming water lapped the tightness out of her shoulders. Madison leaned against her shoulder, warm as the water.

"I like your butterfly tattoo," Erin whispered, and then hoped she didn't sound too cringe. The collarbone sporting the butterfly was the real piece of artwork, but she suspected that would be an even worse line.

"I like your tattoos, too." Madison traced her finger down the feathers on Erin's forearm. Her touch made every inch of Erin's skin tingle.

Then Dahlia moved closer to them, interrupting the moment. "I can't thank you enough for helping me back there, Kayla," Dahlia said, her head tilted toward the stars. "When I see Nick Steadman, I'm like a different person."

Water splashed as Kayla shifted to rub Dahlia's shoulder. "It's all right. That's what guys like that get off on."

"Not on Kayla's watch," Madison said, all sisterly pride. "She looks out for the people who can't look out for themselves."

"Our parents raised us to help," Kayla said. "So, I'm in development at a nonprofit helping women leave their abusers, and Madison builds parks for inner-city kids. We're lucky we can do the work."

"'To whom much is given, much will be required,'" Matt said, and Erin could hear the quotation marks around it.

"That's something from the Bible, right?" Hari asked.

"Luke 12." Jordan took a drink from his can of cider. Erin shot him a surprised look. He seemed the most likely to be an atheist. He took another longer drink, sighed. "My mom's born-again."

"At least she's not an Indian mom." Hari pointed one finger to the sky, his face puckered lemon-sour. "'If you're going to take photographs for a living, why did you even bother going to university?'" He dialed his parents' accent to cartoon level so that Madison burst into giggles. "'Your father and I did not sacrifice ourselves so you could gallivant around town wearing purple trousers and getting fancy haircuts!'"

Everyone was laughing now. He sank back down into the hot water and stole Jordan's cider. "It only *sounds* funny," he grumbled.

"Your parents don't know you're gay?" Dahlia asked.

"Nope," he admitted, face to the quiet stars.

The group gathered closer, letting the water embrace them and warm away the pains of the world. The stars watched them without judgment.

Madison held Erin's hand, tethering them to each other and the basalt banks of the murmuring river.

DAHLIA SUGGESTED THEY HIKE A LITTLE FARTHER SO she could show them one more cool spot. After the hot springs, everyone was amenable. Who wanted the night to end? So they packed up and followed her farther up the trail. Madison walked in front of Erin, putting her hand back now and then to squeeze Erin's fingers. Every time her skin brushed again Erin's, glitter exploded in Erin's capillaries, crackling throughout her body. She felt like a teenager again, back at summer camp and stealing touches under the craft table.

The whole night had that feeling—the instantaneous friendship that came out of being pushed into someplace radically different from normal life. In the dark, Dahlia was their camp counselor, leading them from one adventure to the next, older and wiser but somehow more fun.

"We're actually on the hotel property now," Dahlia called from the head of the group. "The Vanderpoels owned it, too, before it burned. Still do, I guess, although they don't do anything with it."

"They're the ones who own the hot springs?" Hari asked. Erin could just about see the gears turning in his head, the notes he was making for the podcast. If one family built a town, and the town was a hotbed of racist crime . . .

Dahlia stopped by a fence post, her headlamp lighting up rusty strands of barbed wire sagging between the moss-covered posts. "You got it."

Erin looked around herself. There were so many trees it was

hard to believe there'd ever been anything else here. The wind stirred their branches toward the group, the arms of the trees reaching out for her. She wrenched her eyes from them and back to Dahlia's face. "How long ago did the hotel burn down?"

Dahlia looked at Jordan expectantly. "1947? I think? Something like that. Anyway, there's not much left now except the old bakery." He dug his thumb into the fence post, pulling off a swathe of moss to reveal the pitted metal beneath. "This post marked the original horse paths. The place was enormous, the whole package—even another hot springs feeding into the swimming pool at the hotel."

"Tennis courts." Dahlia grinned. "Pool boys."

"The hotel had its own electricity with power lines running from a private dam on the Clackamas." Jordan turned off his headlamp to walk backward like a tour guide. "Their own brewery and laundry. A lot of people sheltered here during the big fire after the meteor strike in 1907."

"Meteor strike?" Kayla asked.

"Biggest thing that ever happened to this town," Dahlia laughed. "Anyway, the hotel is mostly gone now." She waved a hand to her right. The moonlight was just bright enough to cast the landscape in shades of gray, and her headlamp sent shafts of brightness between the trees. "Those are the old stables there."

If she hadn't said anything, Erin would have hiked right by the small heap of bricks covered with ferns. She couldn't help wondering if Dahlia and Jordan were just making all of this up, trying to add some excitement to the end of the night. But the trail beneath her shoes was hard-packed as if people regularly came and went. Beer cans winked in the light of the headlamps, little twinkles beneath the ferns and salal shrubs. People were obviously drawn to the area.

As if reading her mind, Jordan said: "The bakery is in much better shape. I've been thinking about shooting one of my videos up here, but I'd want to get OVP's permission first."

Matt had to duck his head beneath the overhanging elderberry branch that hadn't come close to scraping Jordan's hat. "OVP?"

"Olivia Vanderpoel," Jordan explained. "She's still a pretty big force in Faraday, and I don't want to get on her bad side."

"I asked for her advice before I started Wy'east Wonders," Dahlia admitted. "It was terrifying, but she signed me up for the chamber of commerce and put our brochures in the visitor center. I think deep down she's okay, but I wouldn't fuck with her."

"So why are we trespassing on her property?" Hari asked, but Dahlia was already sweeping her arm in front of her like a maître d'.

"Et voilà," she announced.

The building hulking at the end of the trail exceeded Erin's expectations. Two enormous rhododendrons framed the doorway, their winding trunks as sculptural as bonsai. She couldn't help putting out her hand to touch the smooth wood. She could see the lowest flowers floating pink above her head, but she almost couldn't believe them.

"I didn't know rhododendrons could get so big," she whispered.

"These are just amazing," Madison said. "I wonder what varietal they are?" She squinted into the canopy as if she studied them long enough, she might figure it out. Erin felt even more smitten.

"You're really into plants, huh?"

"Yeah, I guess so. It started out with houseplants, then kind of spread. Plus, I work for Portland Parks, so I'm surrounded by nature nerds."

"That's how I got into them—my brother was a botanist. He really loved native northwest plants, and he was always showing me some cool fern or another when we were in the woods together."

"Was?" Madison took a step closer to her. She still smelled good, even after swimming and hiking. "Did he lose his job?"

"He . . ." She wasn't sure what to say. Didn't want to share too much, too soon. It was easy to open up when you were high, hard to hide your baggage when you weren't sober. "He died," she said, and felt those hope feathers struggle against the word, no matter how much her parents and the government believed it.

"I'm so sorry. I didn't mean—"

"It's okay. Come on, let's catch up with the others." Erin hurried toward the lights, now almost vanished into the dark depths of the ruined building.

Madison stayed close, her headlamp shining over Erin's shoulder, and Erin was glad for the light. It would have been easy to trip or worse—the place had obviously been a place to party and camp for decades. Empty liquor bottles lay everywhere, the occasional beer can or forty sticking out from under trash and abandoned gear: a lawn chair someone must have put their foot through, moldering cardboard boxes, shredded tents and rotting tarps. The air congealed with the stink of rotting wood and scorched brick.

Near the walls, things scuttled.

"What the hell is that?" Madison grabbed Erin's arm, turning her toward a heap of junk.

"What?" Erin began, but then saw the slumped figure propped up against one of the ancient, rusting cabinets. "Is that . . . Madison, do you think she's dead?"

The blonde on the ground didn't move. Erin took a tentative step toward her, Madison still gripping Erin's arm. The woman looked strange, her hair too perfectly coiffed, her legs too pink.

Erin could barely make out the others' chatter, their lights faint flickers in the cavernous gloom. The biggest sound was the hammering of Erin's heart inside her chest as she forced herself to stoop beside the woman.

"Are you okay?" she whispered.

The woman stared down at the ground. Madison hunkered down beside Erin, her headlamp lighting up a dark, horrible hole in the bottom half of the woman's face.

Madison stumbled backward with a stifled shriek, her light flickering across the too-shiny surface of the blonde's pink face. Pink mildew crawled across scratched pink vinyl and blue-painted eyes, and seams showed dingy along the blond plastic waves of hair. The hole was the round O of an artificial mouth.

Erin clutched her chest. "It's a blow-up doll, Madison."

"Oh, Jesus." Madison forced a laugh. "That scared the shit out of me."

"Me, too." Erin gave Madison a hand up. "Let's find the others, quick."

They rushed out of the dark piles of junk. Up ahead, moonlight lit an open expanse where time and weather had taken out part of the roof and the stars smiled benignly upon a litter of cigarette butts and beer can tabs. The others stood beside the stone circle of a fire pit. Beside it slouched a rusting hulk that seemed to combine an industrial hopper with gears. Up close, she realized it was some kind of industrial bread mixer with a hood for funneling flour. She tried to imagine how much bread the hotel must have been making.

"Erin! Can you help me with this groundsheet?" Kayla called.

She shook out a big tarp, and Erin caught the far corner. They worked for a second to lay it flat in the smooth center of the building.

"My sister seems to like you," Kayla said.

"Yeah, I guess."

"That's great." Kayla smiled, but Erin thought there was an edge to her voice. The protective big sister. But if Kayla wanted to say something, she didn't get a chance. Matt appeared behind her and tackled her to the ground in a flurry of kisses and giggles.

More food, and Dahlia found a pop-up lantern she'd forgotten in the bottom of her pack. Erin sat cross-legged on the tarp. Jordan sat down beside her, unpacking the last of the food: more hummus, veggies, cheese, salami. Erin's stomach growled just looking at it. Hari stretched out across from them, looking up at the moon, smiling quietly to himself. He stretched his foot sideways and nudged Jordan's knee, and then went back to stargazing.

Madison leaned into Erin's shoulder, her breath warm on Erin's neck. "I'm really sorry about your brother. What was he like?"

Erin felt Madison's hand close around hers, and she squeezed it back, looking for the right way to distill her favorite person into words. "He was kind," she began. "He couldn't talk about something like climate change without crying. He made you want to be a better person."

Her throat clenched around all the other things she wanted to say: that he was the reason Erin had gone vegetarian in high school, that when it rained he would pick the worms out of the puddles so they wouldn't drown, that he had taken a job in the Forest Service to protect the forests and had grown progressively more disenchanted every year he'd worked there.

"Hey, Scene!" Dahlia shouted, a merciful distraction. "Any apples in there?"

He held up a red globe—"Heads up!"—and tossed it her way. She caught it with ease and bit into it dramatically.

Reaching for a cherry tomato, Erin glanced over at Jordan. "'Scene'? Is that for your channel?"

"What?" He laughed. "No, she's been calling me that forever." Madison nuzzled into her neck, making it hard to keep her gaze on the man's face. "Dee and I were best friends in high school, and we were both really . . . oddballs. We'd take the bus into Portland and see all these bands and hang out with street kids all night. I was really into the whole thing. Wore eyeliner. Let Dahlia give me crazy bangs and neon green stripes in my hair."

"You were a Scene kid!" Madison laughed.

"Guilty as charged."

Erin mulled that over for a minute. "I never thought of Scene kids as outdoorsy."

"Life happens even when you're wearing skinny jeans."

Matt dropped onto his belly beside them to unwrap the cheese. "So you're the expert on the area, Jordan. You know how to get to the hotel's old pool?"

Kayla knelt beside Matt, rubbing the back of his neck. "I'd love to check out the grounds."

They fixed their smiles on Jordan, Matt revealing movie star–worthy dimples. The lantern lit his face gold, and once again, Erin was reminded of fine art. A bronze statue, maybe.

Erin remembered the statue she'd found in her guest house and felt a sudden prickling on her arms. She didn't want to associate her friends with any of the missing Vanderpoel's creepy art.

"It'll be cooler in the morning," Jordan said. "You'll really be able to see everything."

"But the moon is so bright!" Matt protested. He nearly spilled a bag of chips onto the tarp in his excitement. "Just think how creepy it will be out there. This place has got to be haunted."

"That's a good reason *not* to go out there," Madison argued.

"Scaredy cat." Kayla elbowed her in the ribs.

"Fifteen people died when the hotel caught fire," Dahlia said. She stood still in the shadows, so her voice floated, disembodied, through the dark space. She sounded less like the camp counselor now and more like the kid telling ghost stories beside the campfire.

"Yeah, it's definitely haunted." Matt was grinning as he got to his feet.

Jordan sighed. "Dahlia, you're not helping."

Hari sat up. "It'll probably just be a stupid walk in the dark, but at least we can pee while we're out there."

He was such a voice of reason that Jordan had to nod. "Okay, fine."

Matt gave him a high five. "I knew you were cool, Jordan! This is going to be awesome!"

CHAPTER SIX

IVY AND TRAILING BLACKBERRIES COVERED NEARLY every inch of the ground beyond the bakery, swallowing up the trees and shrubs at the edge of the path. The brambles clawed at Erin's sneakers, gripping even the rubbery midsoles. Even carrying the pop-up lantern, she was glad there was some moonlight as well as the others' headlamps.

"Jesus," Hari hissed. "It's a jungle out here."

"A sure sign people used to live here," Madison said. "Invasive plants colonize abandoned lots more easily than native plants."

She sounded so much like Bryan it made Erin's chest squeeze. Had Bryan come out here when he'd visited Faraday? She couldn't imagine him finding this place. He would have been drawn to the river and the mountain trails, not this patch of private forest, shabby and ill-maintained.

Her toe caught on something hard, and she nearly fell. Madison's hand caught her elbow. "Easy, there!"

"Thanks."

Madison nudged at the obstruction with the toe of her Keens. "Looks like an old bicycle handlebar."

They stepped carefully, but the rest of the bike must have rotted away. Erin thought about what Madison had said about her job, and about plants. "So have you always been outdoorsy?"

Madison laughed. "Not really. I was more of a book kid. When my parents took us to Yosemite, I stayed in camp reading while everyone else went hiking." She snorted. It somehow sounded cute. "But my—*our*, Kayla started there two years ahead of me—college had all these outdoor requirements, and I really liked them. Kayla, too. She actually minored in outdoor education, if you can believe it."

"Is that what brought you to Oregon?"

Madison looked back over her shoulder. "Are you one of those natives that hates new arrivals?"

"No, I'm used to it. I mean, I'm usually the only person who isn't from the Midwest in any given group."

Laughing, Madison held back a branch for them both to pass by. "Don't hate us, but we're from California. And yeah, I got an internship with a nonprofit when I was a junior, and it wound up turning into a full-time job. I'm getting my master's in public administration at PSU now."

She stopped because they had caught up with the others, who were standing beside a pair of stone columns. They must have once formed an arch, but time or vandals had brought down the middle stones.

"The pool and hot springs are just there." Jordan sounded uncertain.

"I don't see anything," Madison said. "And I'm hungry. Can we just go back now?"

Hari took a step closer to Jordan, squinting out into the night. His headlamp bounced off a few pale trees and what looked like an overgrown field. "This swamp?"

What she'd thought was a field was actually a wetlands, Erin realized. The bushes were willows, the few trees the long white streaks of alder—both water-loving species. She had the sudden thought of Bryan stepping off the path and into some unmarked pool of stagnant water, weeds and algae gripping his legs while he flailed to get out. She hugged her arms against her chest and tried to focus on Dahlia's calm and smiling face.

"They had a diving board!" Dahlia laughed, pointing beyond the trees to a bizarre geometric shape Erin supposed could have been a diving platform. "The pool house is still standing, right, Jordan?"

"Yeah," Jordan said. "I mean, it was the last time I was here, like three years ago."

"And it's cool?" Kayla asked.

"Really cool," Jordan admitted. "A lot of neat old statues and stuff. It's just on the right-hand side of this swamp."

"We've got to check it out," Matt urged.

"Just stick close to me, okay? The ground feels pretty squishy."

They all followed behind Jordan, weaving between the trees. In places, open water still showed, winking up at the moonlight between clumps of willows and yellow flag iris. The ground squelched beneath Erin's feet, and in spots where an animal had perhaps been rooting around in the eighty-year-old layers of leaves and moss, Erin thought she could make out the turquoise of the old, tiled patio. It must have been beautiful when it was new and fresh. She tried to imagine the pool sparkling in the sunshine, women in their old-fashioned bathing suits sunning themselves in lounge chairs, men paddling about impressively in their trunks. But a scorched stone bench reminded her all of it was long, long gone.

Back at the bakery, a trip to explore the pool and the ruins of the old hot tubs had sounded exciting. Now it only felt sad. Like an expedition to an apocalypse or visiting a crime scene.

The others must be feeling it, too. There was none of the laughing and joking from earlier. Even Matt had gone quiet. Maybe they were all getting tired, or maybe it was the ripe stink of the hot spring–fed swamp, but a seriousness had fallen over the group. Erin rubbed her arms. Through her rain jacket, the air felt colder, too.

"It smells bad," Kayla complained.

"The hot spring can get really hot," Jordan said. "So maybe an animal—"

Dahlia cut him off. "Do you hear something?"

They stopped, listening to the night. Nothing. It was too late for frogs, too early for birds. Maybe it was the quiet that had made Dahlia whisper. Maybe it was the quiet that made Kayla grab onto the back of Matt's hoodie.

"There it is," Jordan said, his voice softer, too.

The structure just ahead was still very recognizable as a building. A tree grew up and through the far side of it, but the walls still stood square, and the sloped roof looked surprisingly intact.

A noisy rustle made Erin jump into Hari's back. He grabbed her arm with a squeak.

"That was the sound," Dahlia whispered.

Matt let out a soft laugh. "A tarp! It's a tarp in the breeze." He pointed at the roof. The smooth expanse Erin had noticed gave a tiny waving wriggle as the breeze moved over it again. The accompanying rustle was softer than the one a moment ago.

Hari took a step forward. "Why would somebody patch up the roof of an abandoned pool house?"

Jordan shook his head. "Homeless people, maybe?"

"Nah," Dahlia said. "Probably somebody's just using it for their hunting camp." She strode confidently toward the building. "Come on."

"Oh," Jordan said, his voice immensely sad. "I think you're right. Look."

Beside the pool house stood five life-sized statues, two men and three women in various states of losing their togas. Whoever had carved them had taken great pains to make them look happy, but the water stains on their cheeks and the algae growing in their seams turned their smiles tortured, full of warning. Someone had draped a gray raccoon pelt over one of the women's heads in a parody of a coonskin hat.

Erin's feet slowed. She remembered the deer kidney she'd stepped on by the river. Hadn't the mushroom guy said the area had a problem with poachers? How pissed would a group of illegal hunters be if a group of idiots just wandered into their secret hunting camp?

"You guys—"

But Dahlia was already pushing aside the makeshift door, the others on her heels. Erin could only run to catch up with them.

"Wait," Matt said, stopping them in the doorway, passing his fingers over the plywood—splintered and gouged, as if someone angry and incredibly powerful had slammed their fists against it, over and over. "What do you think happened?"

"Oh God, it stinks." Madison covered her nose with her sleeve. "Why does it smell so bad?"

Kayla moved to pass Erin and hissed, "Ouch."

"You okay, babe?" Matt asked.

Kayla backed out of the doorway to study the back of her hand in the high beam of her headlamp. "Just a scrape, I guess. Madison, do you have any Band-Aids in your jacket?"

"You guys, check this out." Dahlia turned to face them, her headlamp nearly blinding Erin. She beckoned them in. "It's definitely somebody's hunting camp. Jordan, come see."

"I don't want to," he said, but he squeezed past Erin anyway.

Erin trudged after him. She had to see now, even if she didn't want to.

In the soft light of her lantern, she could make out a long streak of dried blood trailing from the door to the center of the room, where a bent spike of rebar had been hung like a meat hook from the ceiling. Her knees wobbled as she tried not to step on the blood. As she looked around the filthy space, she wished she could turn off her nose.

Everywhere, there were bloodstains. Against the wall at the far end of the room stood a table that even Erin could see had been made from a door balanced on two sawhorses, and where the knob used to be now served as a drain. Beneath the drain, a black-and-brown clotted stain spread across the pale stone floor.

Erin's eyes prickled with tears and her stomach squeezed tight around itself. It was like one of those awful murder houses from a torture-porn movie. The air was thick with the stench of rancid meat and old blood. She could almost hear the sounds of all the animals who had been cut apart here, the screams and the whimpers. Her legs threatened to give out on her, and she caught herself on Jordan's shoulder.

"This is awful," he whispered.

"Yeah."

Kayla stepped past them, pointing to her left at the wall of the former changing area, where faint pink, white, and blue shapes suggested variants of Venus on the half shell. Half of the tiles were smashed and broken, lying in shards at the base of the wall.

Kayla put her bandaged hand on Jordan's shoulder. "It's like somebody saw what these hunters were doing and got super pissed."

Madison slipped past Erin, moving toward the bloody make-shift workbench. On the bench, someone had left an empty box of gallon-sized Ziploc bags and half a roll of freezer paper. A bloodstained coyote pelt had been tacked up on the wall beside it. "What did they do to this animal? It looks like it was tortured."

Erin forced herself to go to Madison and look at the pelt. The stench was even worse here; she covered her nose with the back of her hand. Up close, she could see the slashes along the sides, the skin blackening with rot. "How old do you think it is?"

"No idea. A week maybe?"

"Let's get out of here," Dahlia said. "We've got to report this to the sheriff's department." The others moved faster than Erin. Her lantern flickered and went dark, leaving her alone in the fetid blackness.

"Oh, shit." She slapped the side of the lantern, but nothing happened.

The pale gray rectangle of the door stood a few feet away. She forced herself to take a step toward it and then felt something run over the top of her foot.

She screeched and leapt forward, skidding on something slick. Her lantern hit the floor and flared into light, shining a white beam into the corner.

Underneath what had once been an elaborately mosaiced pink countertop lay a seeping mound of—what to even call it?

Parts?

Offal? Scraps of fur and stringy tails and bones with meaty bits. A crow's wings. A shriveled deer head stared out from the pile with pits for eyes, the fur gone black with mold, the nostrils and eye sockets crawling with maggots. The rustling came from maggots, everywhere maggots, twisting and turning their tiny bodies with the sound of Rice Krispies hitting milk.

Erin's brain stopped communicating with her legs. The rustling filled her head, stole her ability to think. Her mouth opened and closed, but all her words were gone.

"Erin!" Dahlia's voice penetrated Erin's brain, but even Dahlia's hand on her shoulder couldn't make Erin's eyes turn away from the horrible mound.

The lantern flickered back off. Dahlia's headlamp tilted crazily around the room as she looked for it on the ground. The mound blazed blue-green in the darkness, a faint stream of rainbow light wafting away from it, like powdered glow-in-the-dark paint stirred by the wind.

The very weirdness of it finally brought Erin to life.

"Dahlia!" She stretched out her hand to her friend and caught her elbow. "Get me out of here!"

They ran out of the pool house and stood gasping in the fresh forest air. Dahlia put the dead lantern in her pack.

Matt stepped out from behind a tree, wiping his mouth. He looked pale and shaky. "You guys, what if the poacher comes back?"

And just as if his words had summoned someone, a twig snapped somewhere in the woods behind them.

"Let's get the hell out of here!" Kayla whispered, and they broke into a run.

AFTER FIVE MINUTES OF HARD SPRINTING, THEY HIKED in silence for almost half an hour. Erin found herself stumbling, the darkness, the weirdness, the lateness of it all turning her limbs wobbly and lifeless. She couldn't remember the last time she'd pulled an all-nighter. Even in college, she'd avoided them. Now all she wanted was to lie down on the trail and close her eyes. But Dahlia pushed them hard enough they were all panting.

At the front of the group, Jordan stopped, and everyone stumbled into each other's backs. Erin heard her teeth click together as she smacked into the back of Madison's head.

"Did you hear that?" he whispered, his voice barely louder than the breeze ruffling the branches overhead. Erin held her breath.

Silence. And then, somewhere up the hill, the unmistakable sound of a cough.

"Run," Dahlia ordered.

They bolted downhill, slipping on rocks and skidding on tree roots. Erin found herself in the dark for a second, too far behind the others to make out their headlamps. A twig snapped again, closer, and she put a burst of speed into her legs and half fell, half tumbled after the others, trying not to whimper in fear.

The pounding of their feet was thunderous. If there was some- one behind them, whoever it was knew exactly where they were.

"Slow down!" Erin hissed.

But no one listened. She screwed up her face and picked up her legs. All those miles she ran every day, and her brain was more tired than her glutes. She didn't want to fall. Didn't want to, but did, and came down hard on her wrist.

"Motherfucker!" She clutched her hand to her chest, flexed her fingers. The muscles burned, but the fingers still worked.

She hurried down the trail. The others were slowing, their energy draining away. At some point they'd passed the turnoff to the trail to the hot springs; Erin hadn't noticed.

As the group picked their way down the last steep slope to the trailhead, every muscle, every tendon in Erin's body groaned. She could barely keep upright any longer.

"Jesus Christ," Dahlia said, staring at the driver's side door. "This night just doesn't stop."

Erin and Hari came around the front of the car to see what she was looking at: a red smear on the door panel. A red smear like blood.

"We've got to call the sheriff's office," Jordan said.

No one said anything in response. Erin pulled her phone out of her pocket and took a picture of the smear. She'd put it in the book pitch for sure.

CHAPTER SEVEN

MOONLIGHT ILLUMINATED THE BODY IN THE CREEK, the mostly smooth expanse of pale bare skin, bloated and sloughing after so much time in the water. The dead girl had reached the mill wheel now, and floated high in the water. Crows had come, but perhaps they smelled the Strangeness and knew not to taste that flesh.

By night the Strange coyote passed through the ghost town to and from her den. She would deliver pups any day now, the first Strange infants of their kind. When she stopped to check on the body, the creek girl twitched with each of the pups' kicks and hiccups, the threads binding the unborn creatures into their placental sacs winding through the wall of the coyote's uterus and burrowing through the muscles and skin of her abdomen to spark at the air outside.

Nighttime was the Strange ones' time. In a land without fireflies, lights flickered and danced all across the Salmon Huckleberry Wilderness, the steadily expanding domain of the Strange. In the folds of the hills and the runnels of the deep ravines, the lights rippled and connected. To the eyes of the Strange, the landscape glowed like the Vegas Strip. An attentive human being might have noticed a few sparks and tracers and assumed they were simply seeing things.

The body bobbed in the creek's current. Rigor had come and gone, the creek girl's arms now bending when a tree branch nudged them, now waving as the branch was sucked beneath the blade of the water wheel and found its way downstream. Algae slicked the submerged places of her body, the waterline along her thighs, the furrows between her toes, cultivated itself in the dark outline of her pubic hair. The algae stayed well away from the grated flesh on her ankle, where the coyote had dragged her from the adit. To the other Strange, that place glowed a brilliant yellow, thousands of tiny threads stitching the flesh close around themselves. A smudge of electric orange crust had begun to grow along her Achilles tendon, the strip of injured flesh that stayed above the water the most time.

The crust felt the moonlight and transmitted a dull pulse up the threads in the ankle and then carried along a fibrous cord that thickened as it ran beneath the skin of the leg. When it hit the hip, that tracer of connective tissue sent out shoots, their fine tips worming between the beads of fatty tissue and the deepest layer of the creek girl's skin. If she had been conscious, the itching would have made her scratch herself raw.

When the shoots found the big nerves, the ones linking the pelvis to the spinal cord, they dove deep, drawing glycogen and protein out of the body's muscles to thicken themselves and braid their way up the spinal cord. The cold of the creek made every chemical process work at a crawl, but the Strange continued, unfazed by the softening of the tissues around it, the waste products building up in the body's cells, the gradual loss of the hair and skin. The Strange had a use for the girl.

It had never successfully colonized a human female before. The ones it had discovered were always too dead or too broken to be of real use. After its experiments with the coyote, it was very excited about the girl in the creek.

The moon shifted its face behind the tall line of trees as if it did not want to see the Strangeness at work within the girl's body. It kept moving westward, away from the mountains, away from the woods that ought to be filled with darkness but instead trembled with the suggestion of light. Soon the sun would rise, and the Strange would rest.

Rest, but still grow.

CHAPTER EIGHT

ERIN AWOKE ON THE COUCH IN DAHLIA'S LIVING room to sun patterns dancing on the ceiling. She envied Hari, snoring softly on the love seat across the room. Her body felt dull with exhaustion.

A door creaked somewhere inside the house, so she sat up. Dahlia's house was sparse, the decor and furniture either inherited or poached at a thrift store. The only thing giving off any sense of her personality was the framed photo of a kayak going over a waterfall.

Erin folded the blanket she'd been using and hung it over the arm of the couch before following the soft sounds of motion out to the backyard. A picnic table sat beneath an aged apple tree, tiny nubs of green fruit already crowding its branches. In true Oregon fashion, the sunshine had already switched to drizzle.

Dahlia looked up from her phone. "There's coffee in the kitchen."

"I smelled it," Erin said, sitting opposite the other woman. "Thanks." She nodded toward Dahlia's phone. "Any word from the sheriff's office?"

Dahlia tapped her screen as if that might hurry a response. "Not yet. But I know Deputy Duvall. She's good people."

Erin noticed a black three-ringed binder on the table, the thick kind like her aunt used to organize genealogical material. "What's that?"

"Pictures from Wy'east trips," Dahlia said, focused again on whatever app had swallowed her attention. "You're welcome to check it out."

Erin slid it across the table and folded back the cover. Mandatory whitewater shots filled the first page: people laughing, rubber rafts bouncing over big rocks, exactly what Erin might have expected. On the second page, camping setups, more people laughing, somebody posing with a big fish. She kept turning. The activities looked the same, but the gear looked newer. Dahlia posed with her arm around a guy with a big mustache who also wore a Wy'east Wonders tee shirt. Erin hadn't thought about the fact Dahlia probably had employees. She didn't seem bossy enough to be a boss.

Dahlia's phone rang, and she answered it tersely. Erin flipped another page. Here a page of kayakers. There someone SUPing. Here, a camp with several beached kayaks, a group dancing and drinking, Dahlia kissing one of them on the cheek.

Erin pulled the binder closer. The guy Dahlia was kissing looked familiar. Too familiar. Her breath caught in her chest. He looked so happy here, a beer in his hand, his arm around Dahlia. Erin had no idea how Bryan had known all these kayakers, but he was clearly having the time of his life.

Dahlia hung up. "Deputy Duvall should be here in half an hour to get our statements," she said, standing. "We better wake up the others."

"Great," Erin said. Quickly, before Dahlia could leave the porch, she asked: "Hey, Dahlia? Do you know when this picture was taken? I know this guy."

Dahlia leaned over Erin's shoulder. "Oh, about five years ago, I think. This group of Australians wanted to kayak the Clackamas, and they met this guy on the river. Owned his own stuff, didn't rent anything from me. Bryan. Great guy." Her voice changed, went sad. "He went missing right after we got back. I went out with Search and Rescue for a couple of days, but he just vanished into the forest. I still have his kayak, actually."

"What?" Erin twisted around to stare at Dahlia, unsure she'd heard her properly.

"Yeah, he left it tied up at my dock," she said. "I guess his family didn't want it or something."

Erin followed Dahlia into the kitchen, her head spinning. Dahlia had known Bryan. And weirder than that: somehow, in the time it had taken him to get from Seattle down to Faraday, he had acquired a kayak. It wasn't impossible, of course, but Bryan had been a die-hard environmentally motivated minimalist. He was the last person on the planet who would have purchased an item as carbon-intense as a kayak if he was planning to kill himself.

Erin's hands moved on autopilot, pouring coffee, stirring the pancake mix that Dahlia handed her, waving at the others as they crawled into the kitchen after their brief morning naps. She knew she ought to be feeling things, sadness or confusion, maybe, but instead her brain was drawing up lists, making notes. She wished for an hour alone with her laptop. This would be the opening chapter of the book, she thought, this moment when she'd discovered the photo of her brother with Dahlia. That surge of feeling could propel the storyline forward, giving readers something to really latch onto.

A hand on her shoulder made her jump. Madison chuckled. "Sorry to scare you."

She was even more adorable in daylight, her gap-toothed smile and pointed chin making her look like some kind of nature sprite who tended plants and sang with bluebirds. Erin felt an absurd desire to tap the tip of Madison's nose, and contented herself with grinning like some kind of lovestruck tween.

"Hi," she said, sounding as idiotic as she must have looked. Somehow, she could hold her own interviewing people all across the state, but having a cute girl smile at her melted her brain.

"Thanks for making pancakes." Madison picked up the plate Erin had been filling. She wasn't precisely batting her eyes, but her eyelashes were so long and deerlike, she might as well have.

Jordan stuck his head around the corner of the doorway between the kitchen and the living room. "Deputy Duvall is here."

And just like that, Erin felt serious again. She turned off the stove and joined the others around Dahlia's coffee table.

Deputy Duvall sat down in a brown leather recliner and balanced her hat on her knee. Raindrops dripped off its plastic cover, soaking into the beige carpet. She was a big woman, her blond hair bound back in a ponytail, her face square and honest. Even if Dahlia hadn't vouched for her, Erin would have gotten a strong "good people" vibe off her.

"We went up to the old Lumberjack Hotel site," Duvall began. "Smelled the smoke when we were half a mile off."

"Smoke?" Kayla leaned forward.

"I'm pretty sure the fire marshal will say it was arson," Duvall replied. "The whole place stank of gasoline. But the old pool house was pretty damp, so the fire wasn't as thorough as the poachers would have liked. Lots of evidence left—enough to open a case with Fish and Wildlife, that's for sure."

Hari caught Erin's eye, his eyebrows shooting up on his forehead. The skin on Erin's arms prickling with gooseflesh. These poachers had been willing to risk burning down the woods to cover their asses.

"Are we safe?" she blurted. "If they know what we saw—"

Deputy Duvall raised a hand. "Try not to panic, Miss . . ."

"Harper," Erin said. "Erin Harper."

Duvall frowned. Erin wondered if the deputy recognized the name, was connecting it back to Bryan. "I'm sure you're fine," Duvall said. "There's no reason to think this was anything more than criminals covering their tracks."

"What about the blood on Dahlia's car?" Jordan asked.

"Definitely animal blood," Duvall said. "Probably a deer. And again, not a sign that you're being targeted—probably just something that rubbed off when the poachers were coming and going from the site."

Her words weren't particularly comforting. After all, if someone had been behind the group when they'd left the pool house, it made no sense that they could have made it back to the trailhead ahead of the group. But when pressed, Deputy Duvall simply urged the group to stick together and not to go back to the old hotel site. Then she left.

Erin ate two pancakes and a vegetarian sausage patty, thinking about her brother, the poachers, the missing girl on the flyer. The other missing person flyer she'd seen inside the visitor center. On the couch beside her, Dahlia and Matt were already talking about taking a short stand-up paddleboard outing as a replacement for the initial day-long rafting trip they were supposed to be taking. It was like listening to people from another planet.

"Jordan, man, you want to come with?" Matt asked, clapping him on the shoulder.

Jordan's face flashed with irritation, which he quickly concealed. "Naw, not my scene," he said. "But thanks," he added, although his voice didn't sound particularly grateful.

"What about you, Erin?" Madison asked.

Erin held up her hand. "Oh, my wrist is still sore after that fall on the trail. Maybe paddling isn't such a good idea today."

Madison frowned. It was hard to tell her no, but Erin needed to get back to the guesthouse and her laptop. She wondered if Dahlia would let her borrow the photo of Bryan, and felt a surge of adrenaline.

She was getting closer to figuring out what happened to him, she could feel it.

WHEN ERIN CLOSED HER EYES, THE NAMES OF DEAD girls scrolled across her retinas, the green tinge of overexposed film. She rubbed her eyelids, the tissues hot and swollen, the pressure of her knuckles setting off fireworks like the puffs of glowing spores that had hung above the poachers' scrap pile. Someone had crammed her brain full of nightmares and then took away her power to wake up.

She squeezed her shoulders and forced open her sticky eyes. She sat cross-legged on the bed in the guesthouse, the laptop still resting on her lap. She'd been making notes all through the lunch hours. The next time she saw Hari, she'd need to get some citations for the case he'd been talking about from last summer. Her own Google search had brought up the missing waitress that Dahlia had mentioned, who was white but had the same dark hair and bright eyes as Elena Lopez. Searches for other missing women had brought up one other potential match, a girl from the Warm Springs Reservation who had passed through Faraday on the drive into Portland. She'd vanished three years ago, and according to the Facebook page someone still occasionally updated, her absence had never been adequately investigated by the Clackamas County Sheriff's Office.

She shoved aside the laptop to lean against the bedroom wall. A lot of these cases came back to the efforts of the sheriff's office—or lack thereof. Deputy Duvall seemed helpful enough, but Dahlia knew her personally, and the incident at the pool house involved a couple of locals. Erin didn't know how hard the department had looked for Bryan; Erin's parents had admired the team and accepted the decision about his case as if it were gospel. Erin liked to think that if she'd been there, she would have pushed harder, but she couldn't really know.

At the time Bryan had gone missing, Erin had been a junior in college, prelaw and working both a work-study job and a part-time job in a secondhand store to make ends meet. It had all been very confusing; none of Bryan's coworkers had known about his trip to Faraday, and he hadn't mentioned anything to their parents, either. If someone hadn't reported his car vandalized at a trailhead, no one would have ever known he'd gone into the woods at the edge of town.

Erin rubbed her arms. She'd never gotten the name of the trailhead from her parents, she realized. She wasn't even sure they knew.

Erin yawned. She ought to try to take another nap before she met up with the gang for dinner, but she'd been pounding Rockstars since she left Dahlia's house, and even her fingers had jitters. Her mouth tasted like an artificial flavor factory.

She jumped to her feet. A run would suck, but it would give her a second wind. It didn't have to be very long to do her good.

After college, she'd found running. She'd started a 5K program on a total whim after finding herself in a bar with a vodka tonic in one hand and a second one waiting next to it. For a moment she'd looked at her hand on her drink and thought her fingers looked just like her mother's, the same plumpness, the same freckles, the same death grip on her alcoholic beverage of choice. So the next day she put on two bras and went for her first run. She'd made it half a block before she had to throw up.

Now she bounded down the guesthouse stairs, her blue ball cap jammed over her hair and her sneakers flashing pink on her feet. She still wasn't fast, but she was hooked.

The hill felt steeper in running shoes, the houses bigger. She jumped over a mud puddle, imagining herself some forest creature, a fox, a deer. She took the first right and picked up the pace through a middle-class neighborhood, basketball hoops on the garages, the occasional RV parked in the driveway. Here it was easy to forget that 80 percent of the town barely made a poverty wage, or that in the nineties the population had dropped by nearly a quarter. This was the part of town that went with the article *Oregon Traveler* wanted her to write.

The road curved left hard, and she found herself running toward the Faraday K-8 School, "Home of the Meteorites!" The mascot, a smiling rock with a colorful tail, waved at her from the sign in front of the building. The school grounds connected to a small but thickly forested park. She cut into the park, where the temperature dropped a welcome few degrees. She brushed sweat off her forehead, unsure whether the trees rustled in a welcoming manner or a suspicious one. "I'm friendly," she whispered to a moss-swagged maple.

Then she noticed someone farther ahead of her strolling along. Hoping she hadn't been overheard talking to a tree, she casually leaned into a lamppost to stretch her calves and watched the figure crouch beside a clump of ferns. A cardboard flat of mushrooms sat beside them, mostly empty now. The Mushroom Man.

She jogged up to him. "Hello."

"Hi!" He straightened up and gave her a double take. "Do I know you from somewhere?"

"We ran into each other yesterday," she said. "By the river. Did you call Fish and Wildlife about the organ meat we found?"

"Ah, yes," he said. "I left a voicemail, but who knows what will come of it. I heard from Deputy Phillips that they found a poacher's hunting shack up on McIntyre Ridge. Real nasty stuff."

He reached for the cardboard flat he'd set on the ground. "Oof." He rubbed his lower back and rolled his shoulders. "Threw out my back just getting out of bed this morning," he complained.

"I can get that for you." Erin squatted to grab the flat and stopped in mid-crouch. In the bottom of the flat lay a small wooden statue. "Where did you get this?"

"That ugly thing?" The mushroom hunter snorted. "Out by Hillier. The ghost town," he clarified. "You think one of those artsy-fartsy places downtown would buy it from me?"

"Maybe," Erin said, but she was already trying to think of how she was going to find this ghost town. The wooden figure was recognizably the same style as the art in Olivia Vanderpoel's house.

CHAPTER NINE

B Y THE TIME ERIN GOT A HOLD OF JORDAN AND explained what she wanted to do, it was a little after 3:00 P.M. She half expected him to say no, but he jumped at the chance to take her to Hillier. When he pulled up in his battered white pickup, he had even picked up coffees for both of them.

"I love ghost towns," he explained as she climbed into the passenger seat. "There's so much to learn, even from buildings that are mostly rotten." He used his hands while he talked, barely keeping a grip on the steering wheel. They had turned off the highway and onto a graveled Forest Service road, so for safety's sake, she wished he'd dial down his enthusiasm.

On last night's hike, Jordan had been reserved, less talkative than the others. Erin got the impression he wasn't sure if he belonged with the group. But today she saw why he and Dahlia had been friends for so long. There was something charismatic about his nerdiness, something that reminded her of Bryan.

"So what do you know about this place?" she asked. "Was it historically significant?"

"I don't know a whole lot," he admitted, gripping the steering wheel a little more tightly as they jolted along a particularly rough stretch of road. "Back in the 1920s, it was just a little mining town on the bank of Hillier Creek. Started shrinking in the fifties, and I think the last resident finally left in 1978 or '80."

"You sure know a lot of details for a place you don't know a whole lot about."

Jordan flashed her a grin. "Okay, so I maybe know a little." He hesitated. "It's going to sound dumb, but I've been working on a book about the area. Like a hiking and history kind of thing, something I can self-publish to go along with the You-Tube channel."

"Sounds pretty cool," she said. "How long have you been working on it?"

"The last year or so." He slowed the truck to skirt a pothole that could have easily swallowed a Vespa. He glanced down at the odometer. "Just about half a mile farther," he said.

One thing Erin had learned on the job was that sometimes people who most wanted to talk about something needed plenty of time to spill their thoughts. She folded her hands in her lap and waited for Jordan to circle back to his book.

"I'm not a historian, right? Like, I went to community college and got certified to be an arborist. I'm not the kind of guy people expect to be writing a book."

"In my experience," Erin said, "those people don't know anything about writing."

Branches screeched against the truck's roof as Jordan eased into a wide spot on the side of the road. He turned to undo his seat belt and smiled at her. "I had a feeling you'd understand," he said.

"Me?"

"Yeah. I mean, you're a writer. And you're one of those quiet people that watches a lot. Somebody like me."

"Yeah, I guess you're right." She smiled back at him, although she didn't really think of herself that way. Of course, she hadn't talked much yesterday—there'd been so much going on, and she only really knew Hari. But she guessed compared to people like Matt and Dahlia, she must seem like a blazing introvert.

"Well, come on," he said, opening his door.

As she reached to unbuckle her seat belt, she noticed a spray of gray speckles along the hem of her rain jacket, like mildew, but with an odd sheen. She scowled at the offending dirt and scrubbed it against her jeans. It was a brand-new jacket.

"You waiting for Christmas?" Jordan called.

"Coming!" She jumped out of the truck and hurried to catch up with him. She wouldn't have noticed the trail if she hadn't been following someone who knew where they were going. There was a slightly worn quality to the flank of the hill, more like a game trail than a path made for human feet. As she scrambled up the steep and crumbling ground, she found new appreciation for the friendly mushroom hunter, who had to be pushing seventy. She grabbed onto the branches of the firs as she passed them, wishing she had worn shoes with better traction.

Jordan looked over his shoulder. "It's not far," he assured her.

The trail widened as it leveled out. Jordan strode through the ferns with confidence, holding back branches for her and pointing out hazards in the trail like tree roots and fallen tree limbs. At one point they had to clamber over a fallen tree, and he offered her a hand like a gentleman from an old-fashioned romance novel. She wondered if he was like this when he hiked with Dahlia, and immediately decided Dahlia would have never tolerated such treatment.

He pointed out a jumble of rocks off to the left. "There used to be a road connecting Hillier to Faraday, but it washed out back in the nineties. You can still follow it in places, at least on foot, but it's really rough going."

The news surprised her. "I guess I just imagined this place quietly rotting in the woods."

"Well, it is," he said, "but like I said, at least one old geezer lived out here up to the seventies. That's not so long ago, not really." He pointed out a shape so covered over with blackberry vines and branches that it took her a second to recognize it as some kind of antique pickup. "My mom and my dad used to drive up here sometimes. Pick huckleberries, hang out. I guess they were sort of friends with the dude."

He hadn't mentioned his dad before. She wondered if she ought to ask about him, but the trail took a steep downturn and in between trying not to slip in the mud or get clawed by a tree branch, she realized they were walking next to an old building, its brick walls tumbled down in heaps so overgrown she hadn't recognized them as man-made. Only the regularity of the shape, a straightness so out of place in the woods that it tugged at the back of her mind, had clued her in.

"Is this it?"

Jordan pointed ahead, where a house was still sort of upright. "That's the last building standing."

They'd dropped down over the edge of a ridge, and now she could hear a small stream gurgling behind the cadaverous old house. The stream must have been larger at one time; she could see how the town had built on what must have been the bank of a medium-sized creek. A little farther downhill, the remains of a fallen mill wheel lay across a gully. It seemed to mark the end of town.

"What did they mine up here exactly?" she asked, looking around, trying to picture the place as it had looked a hundred years ago. The mill wheel suggested a sawmill more than a mine.

"I'm not sure," Jordan admitted. "They were probably doing a mix of logging and mining. Those were the two big industries out here. Except for dam-building, I mean."

Erin tried to think about the place the way the Mushroom Man would have been thinking about it. He would have been looking for mushrooms, of course, and she knew next to nothing about those except that they liked damp, dark places. And rot. A sudden image of the pool house with its maggots and glowing fungi rose in her head. She shook it off.

"So, why'd you want to come up here?" Jordan asked. "You said it might be some kind of lead on your missing persons project."

"Oh." She hesitated. It had seemed like such a reasonable idea, back in Faraday: the Mushroom Man had found a statue made by a missing guy, so she ought to go where he'd found it. But now her logic just felt like jumping to conclusions. "Maybe it was a dumb idea," she said. "I had a lot of energy drinks today."

Jordan just looked at her. Using her own waiting game to get her to keep talking. Which she did.

"I was talking to a mushroom hunter," she began.

"White hair? Pointy nose?"

She nodded.

"Ray Hendrix. Good guy. Not crazy. Used to be a sheriff's deputy."

That made her feel better. "Anyway, he had this weird statue with him today, and when I asked him about it, he said he found it up here in the ruins. The statue looked a lot like one I saw at the B&B where I'm staying—Olivia Vanderpoel's place."

"Oh," he said. He started walking toward a concrete embankment that supported the old mill wheel. The concrete must have supported the sawmill, fifty or a hundred years ago, but now the forest had taken back the building, leaving only the gray footprint running along the top of the stream bank. "You know, her son Scott disappeared almost a decade ago."

She followed after him. "Yeah, but the statue looked so much like the stuff he was making, I just thought . . ." She felt too stupid to keep talking.

"I had him for art class in high school," Jordan said. "Really nice guy, super encouraging. But, like, odd. He was obsessed with Native American stuff, especially their monsters and myths."

"Monsters?"

"I don't know, like giant troll women and raccoon-eyed watchers. He would bring out paintings and photos of these things and encourage us to get inspired by them."

"Sounds like his art," she said, bracing herself against a tree get a better look at the top of the water wheel. Most of the paddles were broken, but enough were still intact that she could easily imagine it in motion. The water wheel stood at least twelve feet tall, and the creek felt very far beneath her. She tightened her grip on the tree branch as she looked down. Over the years, people had used the creek and its ravine as a dumping ground. Vines and brambles had overwhelmed the bank on the opposite side, but she could see the rusted-out curve of an old wheelbarrow, a couple of tires, tin cans, chunks of wood, lots of old metal things she couldn't have identified if she wanted to. A bitter smell hung in the air, but also a rancid stink, like maybe an animal had gotten caught in the trash and died.

Suddenly, Jordan grabbed her shoulder. "Erin, look."

He pointed into the bottom of the creek, and it took her a second to see what had caught his eye amid the rocks and debris.

Something pale floated in the water, something long and

grayish, like a waterlogged tree limb with its bark peeled off, but even as she thought it, she knew it was wrong—knew it by the constriction of her gut and the bubbling panic rising in her head.

"Is that . . ."

She couldn't make the words come out. She was frozen, staring at the thing in the water, which she might never have recognized as a body if one of its feet hadn't gotten jammed between a rock and the water wheel, the pale toes outlined against wood and stone. A spot of pink glitter nail polish still twinkled.

Tears welled up in Erin's eyes as she forced herself to take in the purple-red streaks around the ankles, the gray mottling of the flesh, the awkward angle of the arms, their shape becoming more and more recognizably human as she stared. The body bobbed in the foam of the creek, jammed up and over the junk that had built up at the bottom of the stream. This body, which had once been a girl, dumped here like the rest of the trash.

Behind her, Jordan dry-heaved. Erin thought she should be repelled or sad, but instead she set her jaw. She wouldn't stop observing, cataloging; she would remember every single horrible detail. This poor girl had gone through god only knew what, suffering all the wrongs Erin could see written across her cold, gray flesh. Erin could at least look, and make notes, and plan to write something in her honor.

"Jesus Christ," Jordan said, his voice hoarse and hollow. "I think that's Elena Lopez." He gagged again.

On the far side of the creek, a flicker of movement stole Erin's eyes away from the body—a flash of blue far too large to be a scrub jay.

Erin reached behind her, grabbed Jordan's wrist hard enough to feel the bones compress. "Shh."

Jordan went so silent she thought he might have stopped breathing. She lowered herself into a crouch, pointing across the river. The flash again, a broad shape—a jacket, maybe?—swinging behind a tree. And now gone.

"I saw . . ."

"Me, too," he breathed. "Come on." He stayed low, duckwalking under the salmonberry brambles and behind the ferns.

Her heart felt too big for her chest. Any second now, she expected it to come out of her mouth, dragging her lungs with it. She gave up on duckwalking and pulled down the sleeves of her jacket to protect her hands as she crawled behind Jordan. They weren't headed back into the ruins of Hillier, but following beside the creek on what had to be an animal trail, rough and overgrown. Her eyes hurt from scuttling in their sockets, trying to catch another hint of blue creeping up on them.

"Do you think it's the poacher?" she whispered. "Or Elena's killer?"

"What if they're the same person?" Jordan looked around them, anxiously. The tangled branches of a fallen maple blocked the way forward; the way down to the creek was all rock, steep and exposed. "Fuck, Erin, we're in the middle of nowhere and nobody knows we're out here."

She leaned closer to him, keeping her voice barely above a breath. "We have to stay hidden. Under cover."

"Maybe we can loop around the old house and get back to the trail." He pointed to his left. They'd have to climb up an exposed slope of boulders to get back to the level of the townsite.

"Okay," she said. The thought of it made her breath come even faster in her throat.

"Just go fast," he said and launched himself forward, scrambling around the first big boulder.

Erin forced herself to her feet and charged after him. The air smelled powerfully of the dirt Jordan had kicked up, old stone and patchouli. It was almost fun for a second, and then a shot rang out, shattering the top off the nearest boulder.

Erin threw herself down to the ground, her ears ringing. She was breathing so fast gray spots rose up in her eyes, and her limbs buzzed with shock. Someone was fucking *shooting* at them.

"We see you, Jordan McCall!" someone bellowed.

"Fuck!" Jordan swiped blood from his cheek. "New plan!"

"What?" Erin gasped, but he was already pulling himself up to the top of the hill. She forced her trembling fingers to grab at a nearby vine maple and urge her frozen body after him, but felt the soft earth digging out beneath her feet. For a second, she thought she'd slide backward, tumbling downhill to her death, but then her toe found purchase on something hard, and she pulled herself up. A second shot rang out, splintering a stump just inches from her head.

She couldn't help the scream that burned out of her throat.

"They must not want to hit us," Jordan said, yanking her into the brush.

"What?" She couldn't make sense out of anything.

"The poacher!"

They crashed through a stack of bricks that might have once been a wall, the shock of it ringing up Erin's shins, and she stumbled after him, cutting uphill at an awkward angle.

Uphill? Away from the path, the truck, the fucking world?

She shoved Jordan in the back. "Where the hell are we going?"

He shot an angry look over his shoulder, miming zipping shut his mouth. She could only follow after him, her arms over her face to keep the branches from slicing her eyes. They crept along a tiny stream whose channel followed the folds of the hill, a deep and narrow slot so overgrown they had to slither on their bellies beneath fallen trees and overreaching brambles.

Behind her, she thought she heard a shout of surprise, and then nothing. The forest had gone so quiet every snapping twig or falling pebble made her flinch. She imagined pulling the undergrowth over the stream like a blanket, imagined burrowing deeper into its mud and slime like an enormous salamander. A coolness and quietness filled her as if she had called the forest down into her bones.

She squeezed shut her eyes, vertiginous. Overcome by that feeling she'd had last night, walking in the woods, the trees and sky and herself all one. She could hear her pulse in her ears, but instead of pounding, it rustled. Green. Everything inside her was going green.

Somewhere far away, a foot splashed in the water, calling her back to normalcy. Jordan cursed very quietly. Erin dug her elbows into the wet, rocky ground and slithered after him as quickly as she could. Overhanging branches dug at Erin's back. Devil's club bit into her scalp. The cold water soaked through her layers, chilling her belly.

The stream vanished at the base of the rocky bulge that made up the summit of the hill, where a spring seeped water from the very rock. Jordan risked getting to his feet and then darted along the hillside to shelter behind a fallen log. She followed him. In the streambed, she hadn't felt the rain start up again, but now a steady drizzle sifted down on them, turning to diamond drops in Jordan's brown hair.

"I don't hear anything," he whispered. A swollen gash on his cheek marked where the rock shard had hit him. An inch higher, he would have been blinded.

"Me, neither."

He licked his upper lip. "Wish I'd brought a water filter."

She made a weak almost-laugh. A water filter was probably only tenth on her list of things she'd wished she'd brought on this misadventure.

"Where the hell are we, Jordan?"

Wincing, he got to his feet. "Remember I said there used to be a road back into town?"

"You said it got washed out."

"It's gonna be a bushwhack," he said. "And possibly some Class 3 rock climbing."

"What?"

He nodded at the rock stretching up above them. "We've got to go around that thing."

In the distance, a group of crows sent up a volley of alarmed caws. Erin looked at the jutting crag and restrained a whimper. After all, whatever Class 3 rock climbing involved, it had to be safer than getting shot.

"Let's haul ass."

CHAPTER TEN

Whan ERIN AND JORDAN STUMBLED OUT OF national forest land into the middle of a clear-cut, the sudden blast of light and open space made her stand blinking and confused. A crew of tree planters packing up after a hard day's work rushed to their side to make sure they were okay. Between the planters' broken English and Jordan's broken Spanish, their situation got explained. Head spinning a little, Erin climbed into the back of a pickup and held herself in place as it jounced down a pitted road back into town.

The crew dropped Erin and Jordan off in front of Faraday's tiny outpost of the Clackamas County sheriff's department. The pair dragged themselves inside, where Erin was so tired that the desk sergeant's questions sounded like the nonsensical honking adults made in Peanuts movies. Somehow, she and Jordan were given granola bars and cups of coffee, and were packed into a cramped office where they sat on folding chairs waiting for something to happen. The room smelled of wet things that had never dried thoroughly and the warm fug of reheated dinners. The smell did not make the granola bar more tempting, but Erin gulped it down in about ten seconds.

She was starting to feel a little more human when Deputy Duvall came into the office and took in the pair's battered appearance. "Looks like you two have had a heck of a day."

The deputy squeezed between the pair of ancient metal desks

and took a seat behind the tidiest. She drank from her Ducks Unlimited mug and then put it down beside a yellow legal pad.

Erin took another glance around the room. The messy desk was piled high with file folders and cardboard boxes. Beside it stood a big Rubbermaid container being used for the hybrid tasks of filing and storage. Duvall followed Erin's gaze to the plastic tub and shoved it backward so a beige rain jacket hanging from the cubicle wall nearly covered it.

"We got attacked by the Steadman brothers," Jordan blurted.

"We were shot at," Erin added. "Near Hillier Creek."

Duvall sighed and pushed back a strand of hair that had come free of her ponytail. A piece of moss had caught in the top of her hair, and there was a scrape just above her eyebrow. It had clearly been a very long day for her, too. "You're sure it was Nick and Howie, Jordan? Hillier's a long way from Steadman Automotive."

"I did cross-country with Howie, Claire, and you know it." He folded his arms across his chest and set his chin mulishly.

"No need to get prickly, I'm just trying to get all the details sorted out." Deputy Duvall rubbed the corner of her eye, which was twitching a little. "About an hour ago, we got a call saying someone had seen you, Jordan, and 'some girl'—I'm guessing you, Erin—up in the woods with a dead body."

"There's definitely a dead body up there," Erin said. "I'm pretty sure it's Elena Lopez. I think her murderer dumped her in the creek."

Duvall sighed. "And why were you two in that particular part of the woods? Not exactly a tourist hot spot, and technically trespassing on the property of Vanderpoel Minerals."

"Vanderpoel? Do they own everything in this town?" The question was rhetorical but both locals were tiredly nodding at her. Erin cleared her throat. "I'm writing an article about the area for *Oregon Traveler*. We have a lot of readers who are interested in history."

"Mm-hmm." Deputy Duvall wrote this down, her expression impossible to read. "A minute ago, you said you thought the body you saw in the creek belonged to Elena Lopez. Do you know Elena? And do you have any reason to believe she was murdered?"

"No, but . . ." Erin looked to Jordan for help, but he was busy with his cup of coffee. "Jordan recognized her. When I saw her body, I just figured—"

"Just figured what?"

"That somebody killed her and dumped her body up there."

"This isn't downtown Portland, Miss Harper. I've seen people die in a thousand different ways out here." Deputy Duvall's voice was not unkind as she said this, continuing: "We've got bears and cougars. We've got rough terrain and alpine weather conditions. People fall into mine shafts. People drown while they're fishing. You don't need a murderer to explain a girl going missing in these woods."

"So, what killed Elena Lopez?" Erin shot back at her.

"A detective will figure that out once the department can send one from Oregon City." Erin made a disparaging sound, and Duvall sighed. "Hey, I care about Elena Lopez as much as anyone else in Faraday. I was at her first communion. But my team here in Faraday? We're just the folks who secure the crime scene."

"What I want to know," Jordan said, "is who called about the body."

"I'd like to know that, too," Deputy Duvall said. "The call was recorded, but no one in the whole station seems to recognize the voice." She looked very pointedly at her notepad. "But maybe your information about the Steadman brothers might lead me to the caller, Jordan."

He tossed his coffee cup into the nearly full garbage can. "I'll never forget the day Howie Steadman left that dead rat in your locker."

"Neither will I." Deputy Duvall glanced at the clock. "Well, I've got a meeting with Fish and Wildlife in five minutes. You two are free to go."

Jordan immediately jumped to his feet. Erin waved at him. "Hang on." She leaned over to retie her shoe. The lace was gummy with mud and plant juices. But, bent over like this, she could see the hem of Deputy Duvall's raincoat. Beside a long swipe of mud, she could clearly see a pattern of glittering speckles like a constellation of dark stars across the nylon. It reminded her too much of the sparkling gunk on her own rain jacket to be a coincidence.

"Done yet?" Jordan snapped.

Erin stood up. "I sure am."

Out in the hallway, a pair of deputies were frog-marching a woman shouting slurs and flailing toward what appeared to be an interrogation room. Erin squeezed against the wall to let them pass by, and then had to half-sprint to catch up with Jordan.

The sound of her feet racing across the linoleum must have caught his attention, because he stopped at the front door and held it open for her. Outside, the rain had ended and the sun was low behind the hills. Erin's stomach grumbled.

"Dead rat in her locker? Sounds like some story."

"Fucking Steadmans." Jordan jammed his hands in his pockets. "I've been dealing with their shit my whole life. And there isn't a woman under forty in this town they haven't harassed."

"Those guys are in every town."

A pair of enormous blue-white safety lights big enough for a football stadium lit up the group of small cinder-block buildings that made up the sheriff's office. Erin's eyes ached from the brightness, or from being completely exhausted, or maybe both. But cortisol and adrenaline were kicking in. She needed to find Hari and tell him about Elena Lopez. And then learn more about Hillier, like why the place would attract someone dumping bodies. She ought to go back and talk to the Mushroom Man again, find out what he knew about the area.

"Hey, what did you say that mushroom picker's name was? Ray something?"

"Hendrix," Jordan said. "Why? Do you want to interview him for your article?"

Maybe it was time to come clean with him about the real project. "It's kind of complicated," she began. "Can I buy you a beer while I explain?"

"You just want me to guide you to the Cazadero because you're lost," he laughed. "But I've got time for a beer."

CHAPTER ELEVEN

DARKNESS. TOTAL, HEAVY DARKNESS.

The Strangeness thrummed softly, cut off and alone. The only sensations: cold pressing up from below, the damaged tissues surrounding it giving way here and there, the threads exposed, electric against a bitter material, a human material. The kind of stuff humans brought into the forest with them, but thicker, nearly impermeable to air and light. Only the tiniest seepage of air where the—*plastic*—had been connected to a thin ribbon of fibers and tiny metal teeth.

A zipper, I can feel a zipper going over my cheek. My eyes! I can't see anything! Why is it—

The Strangeness tightened its tendrils, raised the volume of its humming to cut off the panic hurtling through the creek girl's body. Pleased, though, at the way the hormones had begun working again inside her organs. She had been in the water so long, it hadn't been sure she would come back with such things. Inside the girl's heart, the Strangeness allowed the muscle to contract a little, stirring the sludge that had replaced her blood.

The heart moved slowly, one beat, another. The threads inside the spinal column sent a few microbursts of electricity, encouraging the nerves to connect again. The creek girl's toes twitched inside their shroud. A few neurons connected again, her inner voice activating. *I'm dead, aren't I. I'm dead and this is Hell. Mamá was right about skipping Mass.*

Something connected in a different area of the brain, memory sparking. The man leaning across the seat of his pickup to open the passenger door, the light inside spilling out onto the wet pavement. The rain soaking her hair and running down her neck.

Her legs stiffened; heart rate spiked. The man. The man with the smile. If she could rip it off his face, she would. Her lips curled back from her teeth.

The Strangeness drew gently on the protein stores of her muscles, broke them into energy, sent a soothing stream to the girl's brain and used the rest to hum a little louder. The threads in the girl's palms flickered against the black plastic encasing her body, sending out a compound that would in time dissolve it.

I'm going to find him. I'm going to find him and make him pay—no matter how long it takes.

Not understanding the girl's thoughts, the Strangeness hummed its warm support. Words did not have meaning for the Strangeness, only the chemicals that bodies created in response to them. It had never found a body whose chemicals it couldn't eventually subvert. It only took time, and for the Strangeness, this world was made of time.

CHAPTER TWELVE

A T THE CAZADERO BREWERY, ERIN AND JORDAN managed to snag a table and order both food and beers. She left him uploading photos from Hillier to his socials and headed toward the restrooms. It was the kind of place where the bathrooms occupied a long hallway with doors labeled "Bucks" on the left and "Does" on the right, a community corkboard filling the wall at the far end. Erin somehow hadn't noticed earlier the way Elena Lopez's missing poster sat in the direct center of the corkboard, the plain black-and-white paper stark in a sea of missing pet fliers and babysitting ads.

Elena. Had that really been her body back in that creek? Did that gray, soggy face really belong to the beautiful girl smiling at Erin?

The Does door swung open and a white woman came out, wiping her hands on the back of her pants. She stopped in front of the corkboard, her frizzy brown-and-gray hair obscuring Erin's view of Elena's face. Intarsia kittens danced a conga line around the midpoint of her pink sweater.

The woman reached for the pushpin holding up the corner of the missing poster.

Inside Erin, a cord snapped. She rushed forward. "Hey, what do you think you're doing?"

The woman turned around. Pink-framed glasses magnified

watery blue eyes. "Hello." She turned back to the poster and finished unpinning it.

"You can't take that down," Erin said. "People are looking for that girl."

"I collect them?"

Erin reached for the poster, her fingers closing around the woman's hand. "Stop. Do you know what her family is going through right now?"

"Erin, it's okay." Dahlia's voice came from the hallway behind them. "Annie," she added, easing Erin away from the other woman, "it's all right. They found this one."

The woman's lower lip wavered. "They never found Melissa."

Dahlia put her arm around Annie's shoulder. "I know. And we're all so sorry about your sister." She steered the woman away from Erin, murmuring to her quietly.

Erin blinked hot tears from the corners of her eyes. Her whole body was trembling.

Dahlia returned. She leaned against the wall, folding her arms across her chest. "What was that all about?"

"I . . ." Erin scrubbed her palms down her face. "My brother Bryan went missing out here five years ago."

"Bryan . . ." Dahlia winced. "Bryan Harper. I should have made the connection."

"It's a pretty common last name."

"Yeah but . . ." Dahlia shook her head. "He was . . . He was a good guy, and I really liked him."

The tears spooled down Erin's cheeks, unrestrainable. "He was so, so good."

Dahlia pulled her in for a hug. "I'm so sorry, Erin." She stroked her back for a moment, and Erin sagged into the hug.

Some part of her that had been holding the world at arm's length for the last five years relaxed.

Sniffing, she gave Dahlia one last squeeze and pulled back. "I'm really glad you knew him."

The redhead was blinking away tears. "Is that the real reason you're here?"

"Yeah," Erin admitted. "I started hearing about other missing people in Faraday, and I realized I needed to come out here and see what I could find out. And then Jordan and I found a dead girl in the creek."

"He just told me." Dahlia paused as a middle-aged Black man passed them to use the Bucks room. "Hey, Fred." She turned back to Erin. "When we got back from SUPing, the whole town was talking about the body. Somebody on the force leaked that it was definitely Elena Lopez. Probably Norm Phillips—he's sleeping with Gwen at the A-Street Tavern." She made a face.

"I can't believe we found Elena Lopez."

"Me, neither. I honestly can't believe she's dead. It's so unfair."

The stress of the day after the terrifying night settled over Erin. Her bones felt heavy. Her heart ached. And underneath all that was something jittery and tight that had planted itself back in the pool house and stayed with her all day.

"Dahlia," she began, and then stopped to let Fred go by again. She cleared her throat. "Hari once told me that serial killers often start out by hurting animals. It's like . . . practice before they get to the real violence."

"What are you saying?" Dahlia's voice was tight.

"Those poachers using the pool house were clearly fucked up. What if torturing animals was just the start?"

The jittery feeling surged inside Erin's chest, and she let herself name it: fear.

She grabbed Dahlia's arm. "The Steadman brothers were up at the creek when Jordan and I found the body. They shot at us. What if *they're* the ones who killed Elena?"

Dahlia looked like she was going to be sick. "We've got to go talk to the others."

WORRIED FOR HER SAFETY, KAYLA AND MATT WALKED Erin the mile back to the guesthouse, bickering the entire time. Kayla wanted to dive right into investigating the Steadman brothers. Matt thought her vigilante instincts were more dangerous than BASE jumping. Erin dragged herself along after them, her legs tired enough that each step felt like a 5K. The couple kept stopping to kiss and make up, only to restart the argument in a few steps.

At the end of the long walk up Vanderpoel Road, the lights of the Vanderpoel house twinkled like Christmas. Kayla stopped so quickly to stare at them that Erin collided with her back.

"Is this where you're staying?"

"Yeah. There's a whole apartment above the garage."

"I kind of wish I wasn't staying in Matt's parents' RV," Kayla said. "This looks swank."

"Hey, the RV is cozy." Matt wound his arm around Kayla's waist and kissed her cheek. "I'm sure this entire place smells like potpourri."

Erin laughed to hear her own expectations uttered in his voice. She waved good night to her friends and headed toward the beautiful old house. A few minutes later, the soft rumble of an engine took her by surprise, and she stumbled as a Volvo crept by. The car stopped in the driveway, and the woman emerged, the scarf over her hair and a belted trench coat straight out of Hollywood's glamour years.

"Mrs. Vanderpoel!" Erin blurted, surprised to see the older woman out this late.

"Please, call me Olivia. You missed breakfast this morning."

"Oh." Erin tried to imagine telling the older woman that she'd stayed up all night trespassing at scenic locations while baked out of her brains and then running from possibly psychotic poachers, and couldn't even scrape up a decent excuse. "I'm sorry."

Olivia stepped toward the house. "Why don't you come in for a hot toddy? You look like you could use one."

Erin paused for a second, tired and not especially eager to hang out with a rich old woman, even one who had so far been perfectly pleasant. "That would be nice," Erin lied, and followed her into the house.

Once again, the Victorian weight of the house settled over Erin, the smells of beeswax and old dust, the strangely intimate feeling of the engraved doorknob against her palm as she closed the front door. This luxurious house felt light-years from her family's three-bedroom ranch with aluminum window frames and vinyl flooring. A twenty-year-old duct tape patch still marked the spot where her brother had accidentally stuck a hole through the screen door with his butterfly net.

Olivia walked briskly through the front hallway and into the kitchen, stripping off her scarf and coat and hanging them on the hook on the back door. Her dress was a mustard-colored variant of the wrap dress she'd worn the day before. Erin stopped in the kitchen doorway and looked around. The lavish textures and overpowering artwork ended in the hallway; the black-and-white checkered linoleum and battered green cabinets of the cramped kitchen suggested that whoever had built the house had never intended to set foot in this room. It wasn't exactly grim, and the stove and refrigerator were newer, stainless-steel models, but charm had clearly been a low priority.

"Let me hang up your coat." Olivia put out her hand. Her fingers were very long and slim, with no sign of arthritic knotting. Erin found herself wondering just how old Olivia might be as she hung up her rain jacket.

The woman took out a pair of Fiestaware mugs. "I had one of those instant hot water faucets put in a few years ago," she said. "Lousy for tea, but it will do for a toddy."

She assembled them quickly, reaching for the whiskey, not over the stove, where Erin's dad kept his amaretto liqueur for special occasion tippling, but in the cabinet beside the glasses, where Erin's mom kept the vodka—and the whiskey itself was not some fancy import, but plain old Jack Daniel's.

"Can you bring that cookie jar?" Olivia asked, carrying the mugs and a couple of saucers through the kitchen's third doorway into the dining room.

Erin hoisted the stoneware crock and followed her back into the Victorian era. An enormous sepia-toned map hung above a vast sideboard and, facing the windows, a mirror in a gold-leafed frame that probably could have financed Erin's college degree. The simple table and chairs looked dwarfed by the space. Olivia sank into a chair and put Erin's mug across from her.

"My grandfather used to have very large gatherings," she announced, looking into the shadows of the farthest corner of the room. It struck Erin that Olivia had left all the lights on while she was out of the house. It seemed like a very lonely thing to do. "He was the first Mitchell Vanderpoel. Mitch Jr. didn't follow in his footsteps, though, and I've never been much of an entertainer."

"Was he your husband?" Erin asked, more to be polite than out of true curiosity.

"I never married."

"Oh." What had it been like to be a single mom in rural Oregon in the 1970s or '80s? Erin looked for something to add to the conversation, but her brain was too busy rewiring everything it thought it knew about this woman.

The woman jerked her chin toward the crock. "Could you pass me a cookie, please?"

Erin pried open the crock and found a paper sack of gingersnaps inside. Olivia pushed a saucer toward her, and Erin piled three on the fiery orange plate. She took three for herself, as well, because even though she'd eaten several slices of pizza, her stomach had started rumbling again.

"I'm sure I can seem old-fashioned to people your age," Olivia continued, and then bit into a cookie with a sharp snap. She chewed rapidly, the creases around her mouth forming into new canyons and ravines as her teeth moved. "In the 1970s, I was considered quite progressive. Forward-thinking, in fact. After my father died, I steered his company into new ventures. Reinvested our holdings from petroleum and minerals and into things like biotech. Dismantled the sawmill instead of selling it to some enormous corporation."

Erin put down her cookie. "Wow."

"Yes. People in town called me a tree hugger. Blamed me for the demise of the local economy. But after Scott—my son—was born, I had to focus on things closer to home, and they started to forget about us."

From the sound of it, the town was still very conscious of

the Vanderpoels. Erin took a sip of her hot toddy. The whiskey vapors made her blink.

"I heard you were up in that ghost town when they found that girl's body."

"Yeah." There was no way to sugarcoat it. "I was hiking there with Jordan McCall, and we saw the body first. Then some guys showed up and started shooting at us."

Olivia leaned forward, cupping her toddy to her heart. "Why were you up there?"

Erin hesitated.

"My father was obsessed with that place," the older woman said. "My grandfather owned the mine there, you know. Quicksilver. I'm sure the ten years they were smelting poisoned the entire watershed for decades."

"Quicksilver? You mean, like, mercury?" How toxic was the ground there these days? Had she and Jordan poisoned themselves?

"Yes." Olivia took a long drink from her toddy. "So. Why, with all the beautiful places within driving distance of this town, did you want to visit a tumble down toxic-waste dump like Hillier?"

"Your son, actually," Erin blurted.

Olivia flinched away from her. "What?"

"The Mu—" Erin's journalistic training kicked in before she could name her source. "Someone found one of your son's carvings up there."

"That can't be."

"I could have been wrong," Erin said, "but it looked like the statue in the guest room. Like those paintings in your hallway."

The older woman knocked back the last of her hot toddy and put down the mug. "Do you want to see more of his work?"

"Sure."

Olivia led them into the hallway and toward the stairs. "You'll probably think I'm a fool for keeping so many of his things after all these years," she said, glancing back at Erin. "It's been nearly a decade, and I'm still putting up flyers."

"It's not my place to judge." Erin's legs were protesting the climb, but her heart was pounding with excitement. Ever since she had seen the carving in the Mushroom Man—er, Hendrix's—basket; her intuition had been urging her to look into Scott Vanderpoel's disappearance.

The staircase ended in a narrow hallway with dark wainscoting below and rose-dappled wallpaper above. It smelled more ancient up here on the second floor, as if time, like warm air, rose toward ceilings. Olivia opened the first door on the right and flipped a switch. A blazingly bright light snapped on, its color a harsh white matching the small room's decor. Paintings leaned against the far wall, stacked by size; the biggest canvas stood at least six feet tall and stretched nearly as wide. She couldn't make out any details on the red, densely patterned surface.

"Scott left art school," the woman said, simply. "They didn't really understand what he was doing, I think. A lot of people called his work 'derivative.'"

She took a few steps deeper into the room, allowing Erin to see more of the display.

The right side of the wall held floor-to-ceiling bookshelves packed with books, boxes, and more of the figurines like the one in the guest apartment. Several had tremendously exaggerated mouths, puckered as if they were whistling, some had grotesquely pointed breasts, others monkey-like ears, but they were all sturdy women shaped in a nearly geometric style. Erin stepped closer to study the one nearest to her eye level and realized the pointed breast held a strong resemblance to a beaver-chewed stick, the material even chipped to accentuate the chewed quality.

"Scott adored Emily Carr," Olivia said. She slid a book off the shelf far enough that Erin could see a picture, swirling shapes in green and blue, a black bird. Nothing she'd ever seen before. "When he was a teenager we saw her work at the Vancouver Art Gallery. I think it transformed Scott. After that trip, he became only and thoroughly an artist."

"Why her?"

She shoved that book back into place. "He once told me Carr understood the light and shapes of the Pacific Northwest in a way that no one else ever had. I guess, growing up here, that hit him somehow."

Erin noticed a framed postcard of the same black bird painting and squinted at it. The heavy forms of trees, the simplified shape of the raven—she could see how the work had deeply influenced Scott's style. And yet, there were differences.

"Scott's work seems more realistic, though."

"It became that way." Olivia turned to the other wall, where a large portrait of a dark-haired, blue-eyed woman stared sternly down at them. It took Erin a minute to recognize her as a younger Olivia Vanderpoel. "He spent a great deal of time hiking." She folded her arms around herself, but kept staring at the harder, younger version of herself. "Scott never really fit in with the other children. For him, nature was always a refuge. I think that these days he would have been diagnosed with—what do they call it? High-functioning autism?"

Erin nodded, letting her silence encourage the older woman to continue.

"He liked Indians," she said. "And I guess I encouraged him.

They seemed so much better than the men in this place. Clean, kind. They never hurt anything or ruined anything."

Erin restrained a wince at how problematic that sounded, and then tried to imagine what it had been like for this odd young man, growing up alone in this house with just his mother and no friends. A gentle outsider raised to love nature in a place that had been founded on destroying it. It must have been so hard. She looked up at the portrait of Olivia. That stern face. Those cold eyes.

Hard? It must have been nearly impossible.

"So that's why I say I can't imagine Scott at the Hillier ruins," the older woman said. "It was the opposite of everything that called to him. He knew what kind of a place it had been. He wouldn't have wanted to spend time there."

"Maybe someone found the statue and left it there," Erin said. "After all, Scott's been gone a long time."

Olivia bit her lip. Erin took a step closer to her. She could smell the sweetness of honey and whiskey on the older woman's breath.

Olivia turned to look at Erin. "Sometimes, I've seen someone. In the woods behind the house. The first time, he was wearing a blue fleece jacket just like the one Scott was wearing when he disappeared."

"Do you think it was him?"

"He didn't answer when I called," the other woman said. Her eyes drifted off, like she was looking into the past, into the woods in the back of the house. "So I thought, well, there are a lot of people around here who own jackets like that." She thrust out her hands, catching Erin's in her own frail grip. "But about a year ago, I found something."

"What?" Erin's voice was barely a whisper.

Olivia turned to the bookcase, looking to the far-left side, where a black-and-gold plaque commemorating five years teaching at Sandy High School stood. Then Erin noticed the little piece of wood, an inch, maybe two inches tall. Whittled awkwardly, as if by someone with the most remedial tools, into the rudimentary shape of a woman. Where the mouth should be, the artist had bored a round hole.

Olivia's hands closed more tightly around Erin's. "If he's out there," she said, "why doesn't he come home?"

Erin could not count the number of times she had thought the same thing about her brother, and she wanted to say so—but she couldn't stop staring at the little figurine. The carved woman looked like she was screaming. And in the dark pit of her tortured mouth, something glinted like glitter, or like the strange spores sparkling on the hem of Erin's rain jacket.

CHAPTER THIRTEEN

A N OWL FLITTED OVER THE DARKENED MAIN STREET
and up Sawmill Drive, landing in the fir tree beside the
group of buildings making up the Faraday sheriff's station.
When the door opened and the girl from the creek staggered
out, the Strangeness sent a jolt of electricity coursing beneath
the owl's skin that puffed up all its feathers like a winter's storm
had struck it. Inside the girl, the Strangeness echoed back at
itself.

There were no Strange within the town's limits, but the owl
had a nest above an entrance to an old mine nearby, a tunnel
the Strangeness had been colonizing with tiny lives for decades.
The creek girl's eyes had begun to work again now that she had
freed herself from the duct tape binding her wrists, the body bag
she'd been zipped inside, and the chest freezer that served as the
town's makeshift morgue. Even turned to its warmest setting,
the cold had damaged her extremities. The fingers and toes the
Strangeness had mostly repaired, but the tops of the ears were
beyond saving. The girl gave off a rank, spoiled smell as she wobbled down the stairs.

The Strangeness augmented her vision with its Strange kind,
all shimmering lights and whirling colors. A group of crane flies
twinkled yellow to grab her attention and spur her onto a deer
trail. The Strangeness did not notice that the trail had been widened, the brush cut back, a boot print sunk into the mud here

and there. It was focused on the warm purple glow of its tunnel, uphill from the town and across several property lines. The girl splashed through a creek, rubbing off the blackened tip of her toe on a sharp rock. She slithered under a barbed wire fence, the barbs tearing out chunks of her long dark hair. Threads of the Strangeness showed in new gaps and tears in her skin, a color the human eye would recognize as phosphorescent blue.

When she stumbled out onto a driveway filled by three multiton pickups, the voice in her head—subdued now by the Strangeness's growing net throughout her brain—began to whisper again. It knew pickups.

It hated pickups.

The Strangeness sent a more powerful jolt of electricity, but its message went unnoticed, the voice's rage stirring chemicals in the creek girl's body that the Strangeness had never felt before. It could only watch as the creek girl, lit softly by the sun's earliest rays, walked to the back door of the house at the edge of the woods and went inside.

The screaming began within a minute.

CHAPTER FOURTEEN

ERIN LAY ON THE BED IN THE GUEST ROOM, STARING at the sloping ceiling. In the light of the nightstand's lamp, shadows collected in the angles of the room, gray and darker gray against the white-varnished surfaces. She could see how Scott would have liked this spare environment, the white space like a gallery. It must have hurt him to be shut out of the greater art world, left to teach uncaring high schoolers in a town miles from the nearest cultural hub.

Or maybe it hadn't bothered him in the slightest. She rolled over and stared at the statue on the desk. She had no idea what it was made from. For all she knew, it could have been Sculpey or actual cast bronze; the details about it, like the tools Scott must have used, had been removed from the room. She wondered if Olivia had kept them, or if they'd held no interest for her.

At some point Erin must have accidentally turned the statue so it faced the bed. She couldn't imagine knocking into the heavy thing without noticing, but it had definitely moved. Unlike the figures she'd noticed in Olivia's collection, this statue was entirely smooth. The breasts were simple mounds without sign of tooling, and the divot between the legs was only the slightest of indentations. The focus had clearly been the face.

It looked at Erin and she looked back at it. The longer she looked, the stranger and more alien the face became. It wasn't just the pursed lips that felt off, but all its angles. Beneath the surface of the skin around the eyes, a faint network of lines spread like veins or roots.

Erin shuddered and tore her eyes away from the thing. She rolled back onto her back, her body heavy with tiredness but her mind too pumped full of curiosity and cortisol to slow down. In some ways, Scott reminded Erin of her brother. Not the art thing—Bryan's interest in art began and ended with the illustrations in books about birds and plants, and he could barely draw a recognizable stick figure. But they were both quiet men pulled keenly to nature and the care of the natural world. They might have even been friends, if they had ever had a chance to meet each other. But Scott had disappeared nearly five years before Bryan went to Faraday.

That was their biggest shared characteristic, of course: they had both vanished into the Faraday woods, and nobody knew if they were dead or alive. The difference, of course, was that Olivia Vanderpoel was still putting up missing person's flyers and looking for her son.

A tear ran down Erin's cheek, cooling until it dropped into her ear canal with the sting of ice water. She jammed her finger in her ear and angrily swiped it away. She forced herself to take a deep breath and unball her other hand from its fist. She was looking for Bryan even if her parents had given up. That counted for something, didn't it?

Erin's breath began to move more slowly in and out of her chest. Her mind went back to the figurine Olivia had found— the one that looked like Scott's work, and her breathing began to speed up again. This time, it wasn't anger stirring, but another feeling, a much more dangerous one. She tried to push it (tiny, feathered thing that it was) out of her mind.

A knock on her door nearly launched her out of bed.

Rubbing her neck, she crossed the room and pressed her cheek to the door. There was no peephole. The knock came again. She reached for the knob and hesitated.

"I can see your feet," Hari said.

"Hari!" She flung open the door. "What are you doing here at eleven o'clock at night? You didn't walk alone, did you?"

He pushed past her. "I am a grown-ass man, Erin. Remember when we worked on that whale-watching article and I had to rescue you from smugglers?"

"They were fishermen selling pot," Erin reminded him, locking the door. "But thank you for convincing them I wasn't a cop."

"The worst weed I ever bought."

Erin's nose crinkled as she registered the smell of clove cigarettes wafting off his clothing. "Cigarettes? Really, Hari? I thought you quit smoking."

He perched on the edge of the bed and slung his messenger bag off his shoulder. "Some sweet young thing left his pack at my place last weekend, and I brought it in case of emergency." He made a face. "Which there was. Seriously, this place is stressing me out. I need the nicotine."

She pulled the chair out from the desk. The statue's bulging eyes glowered at her, and she spun it around to face the wall. "And why are you here and not asleep in the RV with the rest of the gang?"

"The sisters have been fighting." He reached for the bag of Hershey's kisses on the nightstand and began unwrapping one. "Since the poacher business, Kayla's gotten really serious about helping with our little investigation, but Madison's not into it. I think you guys finding a dead body was kind of the last straw for her."

She reached for her own piece of chocolate. "What do you think she'll do?"

"I don't know." He kicked off his shoes and crossed his legs underneath him. "I spent a lot of time online today."

"I thought you were SUPing."

"I thought you were recovering from a sprained wrist, but I guess we can both multitask." He folded his arms across his chest. "Seriously, Erin, I can't believe you went off with Jordan. I thought we were a team."

"I'm really sorry, Hari. I should have called you the second I saw that carving in Ray Hendrix's basket. It just seemed like such a good lead, you know?"

He wasn't meeting her eyes.

"This is all really personal for me, you know?"

"Yeah." He reached out and squeezed her hand. "I do."

Erin recognized she was being forgiven. She reached for another Hershey's Kiss. "So what did you find out today?"

He puffed out his cheek. "This place is bad, Erin. Worse than I thought. I found Elena Lopez's older sister on Facebook. She knew of two other Latinx people who vanished from Faraday in the past three years. One was a twenty-year-old woman taking the bus from Portland to visit her family. She got off the bus at the end of the line, but she never made it to her parents' house."

Erin tucked her own feet underneath her. "Shit."

"Yeah. The other was just thirteen. She was supposed to meet some older kids to go skateboarding at the park. Her friends found her skateboard just sitting beside a bench. No sign of the girl."

"Just thirteen?"

"The sheriff's office told the parents she'd probably run away. Apparently, all kids who skateboard are 'wild.'" His mouth twisted like he'd tasted something terrible. "She had a little brother that she babysat while her mom worked the night shift at the grocery store in Sandy. The mom had to quit after that.

The family got evicted from their apartment and lived in their car until extended family could take them in."

"Jesus." She rubbed her eyes. "It's like this place is so far from the rest of the world the cops don't even care."

"The cops everywhere don't care, at least when brown people are involved." He slid sideways until he was lying on his side, his dark eyes, enormous and suspiciously bright, drilling into her face. "Erin, you've got to help me show people that the sheriff's department is half-assing these cases. The podcast, our book—people have to know."

"Yeah," she agreed. She got up and sat on the bed beside him. She was starting to feel tired again, her body overriding her scrambling brain. "I just wish I knew how all the cases were connected."

Hari rolled onto his back, blinking up at her. "What do you mean?"

"Like, serial killers have a pattern, right? So the missing girls make sense."

"Exactly. They're all dark-haired girls, mostly Latinx."

"But that kind of killer isn't going to go after somebody like my brother or Scott Vanderpoel." She gave an exasperated sigh.

He propped his head up on his elbow. "So maybe they're not connected to missing girls."

Erin thought of the glittering spores in the pool house and on the figurine Olivia had found. They seemed like a connection, but then again, she didn't know anything about mushrooms and spores. She wished she could call up Bryan and ask him for advice. A frustrated sound creaked in her throat.

Hari sat up. "Hey, we'll figure it out. I believe in us."

"I don't know why," she said. "You're brilliant, but I'm just a travel writer, not a real journalist."

Hari clapped his hands on either side of her head, pulling her face closer to his. "Who knew those fishermen were up to something in the first place? You!" He gently tapped his forehead against hers and then fell backward onto the pillow. "I am very good at research, but you're the one with the killer instincts."

She lowered her head onto the pillow. "You always know the right thing to say."

"Damn right." Hari's eyes fluttered closed. He had been blessed with the kind of luxurious eyelashes a girl would pay several hundred dollars for. "Can I sleep here?" he murmured. "I'm too tired to go all the way back to Dahlia's house."

Erin had forgotten they'd parked the RV there. "Sure. We'll just sneak you out in the morning."

"Mean OVP," he mumbled.

She lay down beside him. She'd left the lamp on, but she felt too tired to turn it off. Too tired, and maybe too unsettled. The more she learned about Faraday, the more fucked up it seemed to be.

It would probably make their book sell like hotcakes.

AT SOME POINT IN THE NIGHT, SHE WOKE UP TO PEE. Hari snored softly, not even stirring when she turned off the light and crept as quietly as possible around the side of the bed. She reached out to turn back the comforter and noticed blue sparks in the darkness.

For a second, she thought her eyes were tweaking in the change from light to dark. But as she slowly slid under the blankets, she felt more and more certain that the tiny motes of light were really there, pinpoints sprinkled across Hari's cheek like stars trapped beneath his skin. She closed her eyes, and reminded herself she was exhausted. Before she could think more about it, she was asleep.

WHILE ERIN JOINED OLIVIA FOR HER COMPLIMENTARY breakfast, Hari crept down the driveway to find something with fewer carbs. One cup of coffee and three cinnamon muffins later, Erin set out for Dahlia's. When she arrived, she found Madison sitting outside on the front porch stoop, a purse and a backpack leaning against her leg.

"Hi, Madison." Erin put her hands in her pockets and then quickly took them out again. It was the first time they'd been alone together since they'd gone into the ruined bakery. She couldn't have felt more awkward if she tried.

"Hi," Madison said. Her eyes looked red.

"Can I sit down with you?"

"It's a free country."

Erin dropped down beside her. "Everything all right?"

Erin waited, and like it did for everyone, the silence pushed the words out of Madison's depths.

"I like you, Erin," Madison said. "I was really hoping we could spend more time together this week and actually get to know each other."

"Yeah." Erin lit up. "I'd like that, too. You're really great, and you smell good, and you're . . ." She trailed off, looking at Madison's face and remembering what Hari had said the night before. "Are you leaving?"

"Yeah." Madison looked off in the distance and picked at the cuticle at the base of her thumbnail. The one on the other hand was bitten and bloody. "You've got to understand my sister. My real dad beat my mom, and Kayla never got over it. I think that's why she works where she does. She's kind of a crusader."

"Okay?"

"Now Kayla's really into this whole project with the missing girls." Madison looked back at Erin, her eyes sparkling unhappily at the corners. "But Erin, you got *shot at* yesterday. You can't stop guns with a black belt and running shoes. This investigation is too dangerous."

"We'll be really careful—" Erin began, but Madison cut her off.

"'Careful'? We've been chased through woods, you twice, and somebody left blood as a warning on Dahlia's car. 'Careful' would be leaving this for the cops."

"What's going on?" Hari called from the sidewalk, clutching a to-go cup of coffee. "Madison, why do you have all your stuff?"

Madison stood up. "Hari, I can't believe you didn't tell Matt and Kayla the real reason you were interested in Faraday. We never should have come here."

"Madison—" Erin began, but Madison cut her off.

"Erin, you should come back to Portland with me. It's Hari's podcast, not yours."

Erin slowly got to her feet. "I have to figure out what happened to my brother. And I'm part of Hari's podcast, too."

Madison shook her head. "I don't think your brother would want you to put yourself in danger. And I don't think a *podcast* is worth risking your life for."

Hari threw down his coffee cup in anger. "If I don't stand up for people like Elena Lopez, who the fuck will?"

A blue SUV pulled up in front of the house, the purple Lyft logo glowing bright. Madison hoisted her pack onto her shoulder. "I'm done trying to talk sense into you people."

Kayla burst out onto the front stoop. "Madison!" she shouted. "Don't leave like this!"

Without turning around, Madison shot them all the bird.

"Madison!" Kayla shouted again, but Madison was already getting in the car.

Hari put his hand on Erin's shoulder. "Let's get to work."

ERIN PICKED UP THE COFFEEPOT AND STARED AT THE cold dregs inside, unable to stop thinking about what Madison had said. She turned to face the others settling around the dining room table, snacks in hand. Dahlia looked exhausted, Matt confused. Kayla's mouth was pulled tight, her eyes red-rimmed. Only Hari smiled back at her, but his smile didn't reach his anxious eyes.

She put down the empty pot. "Madison's not wrong, guys. Things have been a lot more dangerous than Hari and I expected."

"I'm really sorry. I thought I'd just be meeting people and setting up interviews," Hari interjected. "I didn't think we'd get involved with any actual criminals."

"I don't want to put anyone in danger," Erin said. "I'd rather never know what happened to my brother than be responsible for one of you getting hurt."

"You're the one who almost got shot," Matt pointed out.

"That's true," she agreed. "But I'm the one on a mission, not you."

Dahlia stood up. "Hari and Erin are right about the people who disappear around here. Every summer, somebody asks if they can put up a missing persons flyer in my shop window. I don't want to get shot, but I am tired of seeing those flyers and never finding out what happened to those people."

"I want to help." Matt looked around the group. "None of this is connected to me. But I have two skill sets in life: I am really good at running fast on trails, and I can do a hell of a lot with a computer. If I can use either of those skills to support Hari, then I want to."

"Dude," Hari began, and then choked off. He tried to clear his throat.

Matt tapped his shoulder with a fist. "Roomies for four years, brothers for life."

"Where Matt goes, I go," Kayla said. "Plus, if those douche-bag Steadman brothers are involved, I want to see them go down. Guys like that are the reason I even have a job."

Erin didn't know whether to laugh or to cry. She wanted to hug each and every one of them. "You guys are all crazy. I can't thank you enough."

"Thank us by making more coffee," Dahlia suggested. She took a map out of a cupboard and began spreading it out on the dining room table.

Erin couldn't help smiling as she started the coffee maker. It felt different, knowing she was part of a real team. Everyone's voice sounded more cheerful: Hari's laugh as he ribbed Matt for getting a second fried egg sandwich. Dahlia's humming, punctuated by the clatter of cereal hitting the bottom of a bowl as Kayla refilled her Lucky Charms. It all reminded her of the sounds of her brother and dad getting ready for a camping trip, a thought that made her heart give a funny squeeze.

She took a seat at the table as Dahlia shoved a roll of paper towels toward Matt. "Don't get yolk on my table, man."

He shook his head, mouth too full to make promises.

"So what's the plan?" Hari asked.

"We should explore the area," Erin said. "Maybe hike around

the perimeter of the town, see if there are any unofficial trails people might be using. Stuff the police might not think about."

Kayla scratched at the Band-Aid on the back of her hand, studying the map. "Where all did we go Friday night?"

"We started at Vanderpoel Hot Springs," Dahlia said, tapping a spot.

Kayla put the salt shaker, a yellow ceramic mushroom, on the spot. "Where's the hotel?"

Dahlia drew a line with her fingertip. "About there, I think."

Kayla slid the matching pepper shaker into place. The red ceramic mushroom stood out on the green expanse of the Mt. Hood National Forest like blood. The comparison was an unwelcome one this morning. Kayla caught Erin's eye. "And the town of Hillier?"

Erin leaned in over Dahlia's shoulder, following the forest road she'd taken with Jordan until she found where two creeks connected a few hundred feet above. "There-ish, I think," she said. She dug in her pocket for a nickel to mark the spot. "Jordan would know for certain."

"Jordan takes his mom to church in Sandy on Sunday mornings," Dahlia said. "You know, I've got Post-its."

Matt shifted his last bite of sandwich into his cheek. "I wouldn't have taken him for a churchgoer."

Dahlia went into the kitchen and returned with a stack of yellow sticky notes and a pencil. "He gets brunch while she churches." Dahlia wrote the word "Hillier" on the yellow square and replaced Erin's nickel with it.

Kayla used her fingertip to circle the locations. "All of these sites are on the east side of town."

Matt wiped his mouth on a paper napkin. "Where do the Steadman brothers live?"

"Here." Dahlia ran her thumbnail down the white line of Cemetery Road, past the cemetery and out to its terminus, nearly a mile northeast of Faraday's city limits. "Bill's got a junkyard on the other side of the road from the house. Plus, he owns about eighty acres of forest. Logs an acre or so every year just to keep his hand in."

"Where's the nearest major hiking trail?" Hari asked. He had his phone out and was making notes.

"Maybe here," Kayla said. "This one on the south side of town. It eventually goes into the Clackamas Wilderness. Great trail. Backpacked it in college."

Hari raised his head. "Lots of traffic?"

"Fair," she said.

Matt was nodding and looking excited. "So they're probably avoiding that. At least for the poaching stuff. Nobody wants their hunt getting interrupted by overzealous hikers."

"So that narrows the area we want to focus on," Kayla said, taking Dahlia's pencil. "Can I use your napkin?" She didn't wait for Matt to offer it to her but took it and pinned it down on top of where Dahlia had marked the Steadmans' compound. "Let's use a three-mile radius for our search." Thumb on the napkin, forefinger and middle finger pinching the pencil, she drew a wobbly circle on the map. "This is the area we suspect the Stead-mans are working in."

"Looks like Cazadero Brewery falls neatly inside it," Hari said.

"The whole town does," Kayla said. "The place probably looks like a giant feeding ground to these guys."

"Wait a second," Erin said, remembering the blue flicker she'd seen by the mill wheel. She couldn't imagine a poacher wearing anything besides camouflage. "Do we for sure believe the Steadmans have something to do with the missing people?"

"Erin," Kayla said, her tone acerbic. "You don't really think it was a coincidence that they showed up where there was a dead body and started *shooting at you*? These guys are definitely involved."

"So what should we do about it?" Dahlia asked. "Go around asking people if they've seen Nick or Howie kidnapping girls?"

"No," Erin said, thinking back to the fishermen selling marijuana. "No, we have to figure out what their pattern is. Find out what their normal routine is like and see where it might intersect with the people who've disappeared."

"Good idea," Hari said, making notes on his phone. "Where do you think we should start, Dahlia?"

"Umm," Dahlia said. She shifted in her chair, looking uncomfortable. Erin remembered the way she'd been so anxious around Nick Steadman and wondered what exactly had happened between them. From the concerned look Kayla was giving Dahlia, Erin suspected Dahlia had told the other woman—which might explain some of Kayla's anger toward them.

"What about this municipal dump?" Matt said, leaning over the map. He rested his finger on a site just off Cemetery Road, an easy walk from the Steadmans' place.

Everyone looked at him.

He shrugged. "What? Assholes love dumps. In sixth grade, those guys probably went out there with Alka-Seltzer and blew up seagulls. They probably still go out there to do target shooting and stuff."

"I guess that makes sense," Kayla agreed. "Let's go check out the garbage."

Everyone in agreement, they got into Dahlia's Subaru and drove toward the north end of town. Without Madison, everyone easily fit inside the car. Maybe that fact weighed on the others, because nobody said much. Dahlia turned on the radio for noise. When an ad for Steadman Automotive came on, Dahlia flicked the radio back into silence.

They turned onto Cemetery Road, passing unprepossessing houses and a field where two horses grazed. It looked peaceful, charming, even. The kind of place people dreamed of retiring to, not someplace a serial killer operated.

The road twisted around a sharp corner, and Dahlia slammed on the brakes. A police cruiser blocked the road, lights flashing, and beyond that, a long row of emergency vehicles filled the lane. Erin craned forward in her seat. Beyond the police car, she could see the sign for Steadman's Scrap and Recycling, and past it, a big gray house with an ambulance in its driveway.

A lean blond deputy with an enormous mustache strode toward them.

Dahlia rolled down her window. "Hey, Norm. What's going on?"

He stooped his head in through the window. "Hey, Dahlia." He looked at the rest of the group, crammed in like fish sticks. "Leading a trip today?"

"Yep," she said simply, although he was almost certainly fishing for more information.

"Oh." He glanced back up the road—there wasn't another car in either direction—and then back at Dahlia. "Housekeeper called it in about an hour ago," he said. "Bill Steadman's dead, and the boys aren't anywhere to be found."

Hari's fingers dug into Erin's arm. She had to admire the way he otherwise didn't bat an eye; Kayla was even cooler, focused on tightening a screw in her sunglasses.

"Bill's dead? Was it . . . something criminal?"

"I'm not allowed to say." The deputy's mustache twitched as

he clearly struggled with the desire to tell her more. He leaned farther in the window. "But the cleaning lady was so freaked out they sent her to the clinic in Sandy."

"What did she see?" Dahlia asked.

He put his hand on her shoulder. "You don't want to know. Something like this is nothing a civilian should ever see."

While he spoke, Deputy Duvall strolled up behind him. She put her hands on her belted hips. "Phillips."

The blond deputy was staring at Dahlia's chest.

"Norm," Duvall repeated, sternly.

The blond deputy pulled his head back so swiftly that he hit the back of his head on the doorframe. "Just telling these civilians the road is closed, ma'am."

Duvall looked into the vehicle and met Erin's eyes for a second. Her eyebrow rose. "Interesting."

Dahlia waved out the window. "See ya, Norm. I'll just turn around here."

Duvall stood in the middle of the road and watched them turn around in the nearest driveway. She touched the brim of her trooper's hat, her eyes never leaving the car until they were out of sight.

CHAPTER FIFTEEN

YOU CONNECT THE STEADMAN SONS TO A DEAD girl in a creek, and then Papa Steadman kicks the bucket?" Kayla shook her head. "This can't be a coincidence. Especially since Nick and Howie flew the coop."

"We don't *know* that." Dahlia held up her hands in a classic "slow down" gesture. "They're pretty shitty guys, but they wouldn't hurt their dad."

"We can't jump to conclusions," Erin warned.

"It's not jumping," Hari insisted. "No one innocent would run away like that. At the very least, they would have gone for help. He's their *father*."

They pulled back into Dahlia's driveway, but Kayla raised a hand to stop them before they got out of the car. "Okay, so we don't know what happened at the Steadmans' place," she said, giving Erin and Dahlia mollifying smiles. "What we do know is that we have a plan to catch some killers, and we should stick to our plan."

Dahlia nodded. "On this, we agree. What should we do next?"

She looked around the group as she said it, but Kayla was already answering. "We get our gear together and we spend the day checking out trailheads, like we discussed." She hopped out of the back seat, glancing back at the others. "I bet we find one of the boy's trucks."

Matt opened the passenger door. "I can't wait. You and I can do a speed run up by the hot springs while the others tackle some of the closer areas."

As they followed the couple toward the house, Hari was shaking his head. "Wait up," he said. "These guys are local big cheeses, right? They probably have lots of friends they can tap to hide them."

"So?" Matt asked.

"So, you're the computer genius. You might be more useful helping me scrape up information. We ought to at least compile a list of addresses for the ladies to follow up on after their trail-head search."

"That's a good idea," Dahlia agreed. "I'll text you a few names I can think of. You might be able to find records about the company's employees, too. It's a small business, and Bill Steadman ran it like a family dynasty."

"I want to get some more information about Hillier," Erin said. "But I can help when I get back."

"Okay," Kayla said. "Text as you go, though. I wouldn't trust anyone in this town."

"Oh, I'm just going to talk to that mushroom hunter guy I met on Friday. He's not dangerous."

"Ray Hendrix?" Dahlia shrugged. "Yeah, he's a former sher-iff's deputy, and a real good guy. You couldn't be safer."

Matt brushed Kayla's cheek. "I worry about you being by yourself, though. Those guys . . ."

"She won't be alone, and I've been hiking this area since I could walk." Dahlia patted Matt's arm. "And don't worry. We're not going to chase anybody through the woods. We'll be very careful."

"*Everybody's* going to be careful," Erin said. "And we can meet up here later this afternoon, right?"

Hari pulled her aside. "You should stick with me, Erin. Last time you went off investigating, you got shot at."

She stifled a sigh because she knew she deserved his concern. "Hari, you're right about the need for more research online. But if we want to get to the bottom of these cases, we need to really understand the area. I can't understand why the Steadman brothers would have gone up to that ghost town. Maybe Ray Hendrix can give me some better insights." She had already decided not to mention Scott Vanderpoel and his carvings. If they were tied into the missing girls, then everyone would be glad for the extra information. And if not, at least she could learn something to help Olivia.

"I don't like it. Not even a little."

She socked him in the shoulder. "I'll be fine. Plus, maybe I can pump this mushroom guy for more information for the article I'm ostensibly writing. You know, for our job."

"Oh, god, I forgot." He stuck out his tongue for a second. "Do you want to take the Nikon?"

"Do you honestly trust me to use it?"

"Not in the slightest."

At least they were laughing as they said goodbye. She felt bad, not telling him everything. But he was the one focused on the missing girls. She had to keep the bigger picture in mind. Her palms felt clammy on the steering wheel of her car as she pulled away from the curb. If Scott Vanderpoel was still alive, then anyone could make it out there in the woods. Even Bryan.

She stopped at a stop sign and covered her eyes for a second. Told herself to breathe deep. She was getting ahead of herself. Letting hope fly around in her chest like it could break loose and shower her with feathers. She rubbed tears from her eyes and forced her attention on the road. One step at a time, and this step was talking to Ray Hendrix.

The drive took longer than she expected. She was glad Jordan was able to text her incredibly detailed directions, because GPS would have gotten her lost for sure. Hendrix lived on the west end of town, far enough outside the city limits that the houses dwindled to about one every mile. The road started out paved, but by the time she passed the midpoint on Jordan's directions ("when you pass the house with the planter made out of a partially detonated naval mine"), the pavement was more a suggestion than a smooth surface.

The trees leaned in closer over the narrow road, filling the car with gloom. She had a feeling that if she stopped to check her phone, she'd be lucky to see even a bar of signal. Living in Portland, it was easy to forget how isolated these little mountain towns could be. She was miles and miles away from the land of Google Maps or even 911. Her fingers hurt from gripping the steering wheel too tightly.

She slowed as she passed a boulder the size of a small pickup, Jordan's landmark for the end of her journey. And sure enough, just past the geological oddity, a chainsaw-carved wooden mushroom marked the entrance to Ray Hendrix's rutted driveway. When the driveway made its final switchback, she could see Ray Hendrix's house, red-painted cedar shakes and white trim around the windows, his old pickup parked beside the front steps. As she got closer, she could see the cracks and chips in the house's white trim. She hesitated for a moment.

"He was nice," she reminded herself under her breath, and stepped onto the porch steps. The wooden railing, worn with age and so swollen with rain it felt slimy, wobbled in her grip.

She knocked on the wood frame of the screen door. No response, so she pulled it open, its hinges screeching loud enough to frighten a sparrow out of a nearby tree. She rapped on the actual door.

"Mr. Hendrix?"

Still no answer. She backed down the stairs, frowning up at the chimney, which gave off a trickle of white smoke. She couldn't imagine that he would just leave without putting out his fire. Maybe he was in the shed on the side of the house.

Erin put her foot on the muddy path leading to the shed and stopped. The path ran between the house and a tall fence, obviously put in to protect the flower bed in the side yard. She bit her lip as she studied the massive rhododendron bush standing at the corner of the house, its glossy leaves so densely packed together the side yard was completely blocked from sight.

There could be anything on the other side.

Why had she come out here without even the canister of pepper spray she kept with her running gear? She was a woman alone in a town where lone women went missing.

"He was nice," she repeated, but the words only stirred up memories of news story after news story about friendly serial killers.

Erin balled her fist around her house key and forced herself forward.

The rhododendron's branches clawed at her sleeves and dew soaked her pants as she squeezed between the plant and the deer fence. Her rain jacket caught tight around her throat and she flailed for a second before realizing a branch had caught her hood. Her heart pounded as she broke free and stumbled out of the rhododendron's embrace.

Someone else stood in the side yard, puttering in front of a window and humming a cheerful tune.

Relief lightened Erin's shoulders. "Good morning, Mr. Hendrix!"

The humming broke off, and the tall man turned away from the window to stare at her. He was most certainly not Ray Hendrix, the Mushroom Man.

Despite the alarm bells screaming in her brain, her legs forgot how to run.

The big man blinked once, long and slow. His hands, enormous, blunt paws, still held on to the sill of the window he'd been looking through. His mousy brown hair had been pulled back in a ponytail, and a light beard fuzzed his cheeks, but that was the extent of his civilized veneer. His zip-off hiking pants, probably khaki at one point in time, looked nearly camouflage-print, the layers of dirt and vegetation stains overlapping each other so densely. Patches of moss had worked so tightly into the blue fabric of his fleece jacket that it seemed to be growing the stuff.

A blue fleece jacket. She took a step backward and felt a branch dig into her neck.

He looked back at the window, and then back at Erin. "He has one of my statues," he explained.

The breath she hadn't realized she was holding seeped out. "Scott? Scott Vanderpoel?"

He pressed his forehead to the glass. "I don't think he should have one of my statues." There was something almost childlike about his halting speech.

She took a step toward him, holding out her hand. "Are you okay, Mr. Vanderpoel?"

At the movement, he stumbled backward. "No!"

She threw up her hands, palms out. "It's okay! I'm not going to hurt you. I . . . I know your mother," she managed. "And I like your art," she thought to add.

"You shouldn't get too close," he said.

"I won't."

He risked a glance at the window, and then fixed his gaze on her face. "I know who you are."

Erin's mouth went dry. How far away was the nearest house? A mile? More?

"You're staying in our guesthouse," he said.

"Oh!" Relieved, she nodded. "Yes. I am. Did you see me there?"

He raised a warning hand. "Don't get any closer," he warned her again. "It's not safe."

She hadn't felt herself step forward, but she must have. "I won't. I'm so sorry."

"I saw you at the ghost town," he said. "I was worried something bad would happen to you there."

"You were watching me at Hillier?" Her voice sounded too high.

A twig broke somewhere behind them. Scott started, and for a second she thought he would run. But after a quick glance over his shoulder, he faced her again. "You shouldn't be here," he whispered. "It's not safe."

"I need to talk to Mr. Hendrix," she said, stalling, looking around for a way to get past him. "About Hillier."

He shook his head wildly. "No! Definitely not."

"You don't want me to learn about the old mining town?"

He shook his head again. "No, you shouldn't talk to Ray Hendrix. He's even more dangerous than I am."

His speech had gotten better as he talked, she realized. His first awkward sentences had eased into the confident tones of a high school teacher.

She had to know more. "Is being dangerous the reason you can't go home? Your mother misses you."

He squeezed his eyes shut. "You should go."

"But—"

He covered his eyes with one long hand. "You should go. Now! Before it sees you again!"

"'It'? What are you talking about?"

With a shriek, he spun around and began running toward the forest. "No!" he bellowed. "No, no, no no no!"

Branches snapped and crashed and then the big man was gone, absorbed into the woods. Erin took off after him, but beyond the little stream at the back of Ray Hendrix's property, there was no sign of Scott Vanderpoel, not even a footprint. The trees had closed themselves behind him as if he had never been there at all.

The thought made her grind to a halt. Was it really that easy to vanish in these woods? All you needed was to step off the path and you were gone? What a place for predators and poachers to play. A sense of deep discouragement—no, despair—overtook her. No wonder Search and Rescue had given up on Bryan.

A breeze caught the leaves on the alders beside the creek, lifting their branches, making them dance. The white trunks flitted and flickered. For a second, she thought she saw Scott's blue jacket moving in the distance, but then the branches closed again, and she was left alone with the dancing trees.

The rain began again, with heavy, sodden drops. With a sharp, cold strike, one landed on the cowlick at the top of her head. Ice raced through her nervous system, and she shuddered. She might not see anyone, but she didn't feel alone. She didn't feel alone at all.

Erin whirled around and hurried away from the creek. She

didn't want to stop, but she forced herself to check the shed. The door was locked, and no light showed in its window. For a second, she thought she heard something scratching inside. When she pressed her ear to the door, she heard nothing but the wild pounding of the blood in her ears. The thought hit her that if anyone came up behind her, she would neither see nor hear them.

She bolted for the driveway. If she really wanted to talk to Ray Hendrix, she'd come back with her friends.

STILL SHAKEN, ERIN PARKED IN FRONT OF A TAVERN. IT took her a minute to get out of the car, her legs tired and aching from hiking and running and moving too fast on steep paths in the woods. She stood on the sidewalk of Main Street, wondering at the stretch of trendy eateries and cute cafes. It was hard to believe such things existed in the same town as missing girls and mysterious hermits, murder cases and poachers on the run, but the pedestrian needs of both stomach and bank account reminded her that the world went on, mystery and horror be damned. And if she didn't turn in her tourism-friendly article by Wednesday, she'd have a very pissed-off editor.

A bell chimed as someone left Cleo's Cafe, and the irresistible perfume of French toast and hot coffee reeled her in like a talented fisherman. It was time for lunch.

Inside, the place was almost too cute. Yellow gingham curtains turned the late-morning sunshine golden, and tiny bud vases of daisies brought life to each of the six small four-tops. Erin's inner food writer was already making notes about the charming little jars of jam on the tables.

The waitress caught her gawking. "You mind sharing a table,

honey? We're packed." She nodded her chignon toward a table in the back corner where Deputy Duvall sat reading the newspaper.

"Sure. Are you still serving breakfast?"

"Always." The server was already leading her to Duvall's table. She handed Erin a laminated sheet. "Specials are above the coffee station, and coffee is self-serve."

Erin put her raincoat over the back of her chair and beelined for the coffeepot. Not an air pot, but an actual glass carafe. She carried it back to the table and turned over the white stoneware mug. "You need a warmer, deputy?"

Duvall didn't look up from *The Oregonian*. "Thanks."

Erin filled both their mugs, glad to see the coffee looked as thick and black as Stumptown's finest. A sip proved it was some kind of complicated roast, lots of berries and chocolate, just a touch of skunk. She pulled up a blank Google Doc on her phone and made notes. Whoever Cleo was, she really knew her coffee.

The server reappeared, took Erin's French toast order with a side of biscuits and vegetarian gravy, and left the table to settle into silence. At other tables, people laughed. A preschooler spilled a jug of maple syrup. Joni Mitchell sang about tree museums. Deputy Duvall took a bite of her bacon, and Erin heard it crunching with perfect clarity.

Erin started a to-do list. *Oregon Traveler* gave her a fifty-dollar meal budget, which would let her try at least one more restaurant, but she ought to explore some of the shops as well. She figured she could knock out enough research in the next hour to get most of her article done, and then she'd check in with Hari and Matt. After her encounter with Scott Vanderpoel, she was almost looking forward to visiting ordinary shops like—she glanced out the window—Chocolates on Main and Kitty's Knitting Kaboodle. She thought she remembered that Kayla liked knitting.

"Could you pass me the jam?" Deputy Duvall asked.

Erin slid the jar across the table to her. "How are you doing this morning, Deputy?"

The French toast appeared. The waitress leaned across Erin. "Claire, you want your regular to-go order, too?"

Duvall squinted at the specials menu. "Any of those apple muffins left?"

"Just blueberry, sorry."

"Cleo, you know I can't resist the blueberry. I'll take two. It's gonna be a long day."

The blond woman, Cleo, hesitated. "Is it true what Norm said? About that girl's body?"

Duvall shot her a look. "You know I can't answer that."

Cleo glanced over at Erin. "Sorry to talk over your head. Just local gossip!" She forced a titter. "I'll be right back with that side of biscuits and gravy."

Erin twisted in her seat so she could look Deputy Duvall in the eye. "Did something happen to Elena's body?"

Duvall scowled. "I'm not telling you anything, Nancy Drew."

Erin studied her. The deputy looked even more exhausted than the last time Erin had seen her; her hair was limp and un-washed, climbing free of its ponytail. Dark smudges stood out beneath her eyes. The last few days had to have been shitty for her. Faraday might be the kind of town where people went miss-ing a lot, but Erin couldn't imagine it got two murder cases a year, let alone in two days.

She shifted tactics. "Hey, do you know how the town got its name? I like to weave a little history into my articles."

Duvall knocked back the last of her coffee. "Sure. It's named for the scientist Michael Faraday. It was a tent city for work-ers building the Faraday dam. When the first Faraday burned down, the postmaster proposed rebuilding out here. Vanderpoel Lumber was already building a sawmill on the site, so it seemed like a good idea."

"Wow." Erin leaned in like this was the most fascinating thing she'd ever heard. "I'm surprised they didn't name it 'Vanderpoel'!"

Duvall slid her chair back. "Don't think they didn't try."

The deputy who had stopped Dahlia's car the day before threw open the door. "Claire, you won't believe whose prints they found at the site." His large blond mustache trembled with excitement.

"God damn it, Norm, not in public!" Claire threw down her napkin and got to her feet. "Cleo, can you put this on my tab?" Cleo was already rushing forward with a to-go cup and a white paper sack. "Oh, you are an angel."

Erin got up like she was making space for the woman to get around her. "Thanks for the information, Deputy."

Duvall ignored her, moving toward Deputy Phillips at top speed while shooting out smiles at the concerned faces of the other diners. Erin followed behind with her empty coffee mug, just an ordinary person getting a refill. She really felt like Nancy Drew when she heard the other deputy whisper: "But Claire, they belonged to the girl! How the hell did she get from our basement to Steadmans' place if she was dead?"

The bell chiming over the cafe door covered up any response Duvall might have made, but it didn't matter. Erin had heard enough.

CHAPTER SIXTEEN

THE CREEK GIRL LAY ON HER SIDE INSIDE THE PITCH-black tunnel. The Strangeness had urged her to push on-ward, to continue deeper into the cool darkness that wound up into the hills, but she had collapsed on a heap of old sacking just beyond the fern-covered tunnel door, clutching her middle. The protein bar she had discovered back at the house churned in her stomach, the acid too diluted to break down the peanut butter–flavored thing. She hugged her knees to her aching belly and shivered.

The Strangeness sent tendrils out through the skin in her knees and ankles, dissolving microscopic holes in the moldy canvas on the ground and soaking it back up into the creek girl's flesh. Cellulose reworked into carbohydrates, saturating her cells. The shivering eased. The Strangeness sent a wave of tension through the girl's skin. *Go, walk, move.*

She sat up. Her eyes could make out nothing in the darkness, but other senses had grown stronger since the Strangeness had taken hold. She could feel the long strands weaving their way up the wooden girders around her like electrical cables strung all the way into the heart of the mountain. The strands here felt the new-est, fresh young purple threads connecting to older blue ones, still older yellow ones, the orange and red so far away she could barely sense the flicker of them somewhere far up in the Mt. Hood foot-hills.

The girl rested her chin on her knees and plucked a tiny brown mushroom off the back of her hand. It felt like pulling off a loose hair, a sensation registered by the Strangeness with unease. Whatever that small fruiting body had been, it was not Strange. It sent a surge of proteins and carbohydrates into the girl's hand to fortify its own threads against Earthly fungal invaders.

She registered all of this as only the faintest of irritations. Her stomach began to unknit as the protein bar settled. She stroked the skin of her legs and registered the electric tickling of the Strange threads waving from her pores. She did not mistake them for hairs and possibly couldn't. When concepts appeared in her mind, they were like pre-recorded transcripts of thoughts she had once had but now could not string together into sense. Being strangled had caused a certain amount of trauma to her brain, and her three days floating in the creek caused more. The man she had torn apart inside his kitchen had screamed out the word "zombie" over and over.

But certain synapses kept flashing, memories so vivid they defied both death and the goading of the Strangeness. She slowly pushed herself to her feet and turned back toward the doorway. When she got a little closer, the green light of day seeping in around the doorframe stung her eyes.

She pulled the door open and stepped outside. She was looking for a man.

CHAPTER SEVENTEEN

ERIN SAT IN HER CAR FOR A MOMENT OUTSIDE Dahlia's house. The information she'd overheard at the diner—the discovery of the dead girl's prints at the Steadmans' house—roiled in her brain, as undigestible as a deep-fried shoe. Of all the strange things she had encountered in Faraday, this had to be the strangest. She squinted at the lights in the front window, wondering what kind of progress the guys had made. She hoped they'd discovered something in their research to help untangle some of the knots this town had created in her head.

She reached for the bag of saltwater taffy she'd picked up at Chocolates on Main and picked out a brown one. The smell of caramel filled the car as she peeled the sweet off the waxed paper and popped it in her mouth. As kids, she and Bryan had ridden their bikes to the waterfront almost every day, burning their allowance on the saltwater taffy Mrs. Thompson sold by the pound. Erin had even worked for Mrs. Thompson one summer, scooping ice cream for Californian tourists, and she'd come to hate the spoiled-milk stench of the stuff, how it stuck to her skin no matter how much she washed. How in the sunshine her hair gave off the smell of butter. But taffy never stopped tasting good.

The candy softened enough to turn stretchy against her tongue. She pushed it against her palate to fill the roof of her mouth and let the caramel sweetness unspool memories both sweet and sour.

Bryan had loved caramel. Anything caramel flavored: taffy, toffee, popcorn, chocolates, ice cream, ice cream sauce. On her occasional good days, their mother would sometimes make a batch of her homemade butterscotch sauce and they would pour it hot over scoops of vanilla, waiting for it to turn into a thick, cold stew of sugar. Erin couldn't remember the last time they'd done that. Couldn't remember the last time her mother got up off the couch, really. Even before Bryan had vanished, she'd turned mostly immobile, except when she needed to refill her glass.

Erin rubbed her fingertips against the denim of her jeans, scraping away the faint sugar tackiness. Her mother, the first big absence of her life, and then Bryan. The first loss hadn't mattered so much, because her mother had always been absent, and her father had tried to compensate for it. He took them fishing. He took them hiking. He was busy with work, but he tried. Maybe she'd never learned to expect anything from her mother, so the failure never hurt so badly.

But Bryan? He'd been her world. Their dad had only been around so much. He had to work, had to take extra shifts at the mill when he could. When it was just the two of them, Bryan had taught her to make macaroni and cheese and how to sound out the instructions on her homework. They'd stay up together watching horror movies with Joe Bob Briggs and then stay up longer, comforting each other through the bad dreams that often followed. They had each other.

They had each other.

She supposed that was why she was sitting here, staring at a house that had been one of the last places her brother visited in his too-short life. Why she could not, could never believe her brother committed suicide. He wouldn't leave her. He just wouldn't.

She grabbed the bag of candy and went inside.

ERIN UNWRAPPED ANOTHER SALTWATER TAFFY—THIS one cinnamon—and listened to Matt's end of the phone conversation. "Definitely truck tire tracks? And fresh?"

"How does Kayla know what fresh tire tracks look like?" Hari whispered, taking a green taffy out of the bag.

Erin shrugged. She was impatient for Matt to hang up so she could tell them the news about the fingerprints.

"I didn't quite catch that, Kay." Matt shifted in his chair, pressing the phone more tightly to his ear. The faint stubble on his cheeks made his face look sharper, his eyes more tired. Erin had never seen him looking less than perfect.

Now he was shaking his head. "Wait, those guys know what Dahlia's car looks like. I don't think— Hey, don't cut me off like that, I'm trying to—" He slapped his phone down on the table. "God damn it. They're going up to the old hotel."

"What?" Erin spat her taffy back into its wrapper. "Are they insane? Do they want to get attacked?"

"Right?" Matt got up, stretching his back. "We've got to go after them."

Hari made a face. "I told Flora I'd be there to interview her in half an hour." He caught Erin's confused glance. "Elena Lopez's sister. For the podcast."

"Ah." She looked back at Matt, who had begun doing lunges. "I'm no trail runner, but I'm not going to let you go alone."

He brightened. "That's a good idea."

"Great, so you grab your rain gear, and then you and I head out to the old hotel. We can text Kayla and Dahlia to let them know we're gonna be their backup." She turned to Hari. "You can walk to your interview with the sister?"

He hesitated. "I have a lot of recording equipment."

She wished Kayla was here. She would have solved these logistics before anyone even thought of them. But instead, Erin was in charge. "No problem." She made herself smile. "Matt, why don't you also tap Dahlia's kitchen for snacks, because who knows how long we'll be out? I'll drop off Hari and be back in fifteen."

"I'll get my stuff." Hari darted out of the room to grab his podcasting gear.

Erin found a couple of water bottles in the kitchen, filled them, and snagged a banana off the counter. First thing that morning she had tossed her day pack in the back of her car, as well as her hiking shoes. She sat in the driver's seat with the door open, switching sneakers while she waited for Hari to finish up in the RV. The thought of going out in the woods again made the taffy turn over in her stomach. At least it wasn't raining.

Hari slid into the passenger seat and plugged the address into his phone. "Thanks for the ride, Erin." He popped the phone into the holder on her dashboard, and she turned into the street to follow the directions.

They were quiet for a few minutes while she maneuvered them through a couple of intersections. Then, just as Erin was about to say something about what Deputy Phillips had mentioned at the diner, Hari blurted out: "I was hoping to talk to you about this guy we found."

"You found a guy?"

"Well," he amended, "we dug through the Steadman Automotive Facebook page and cross-referenced the people we saw in pictures with the state's list of sex offenders."

"Sex offenders?" Her head whipped around to see him nodding seriously. She nearly missed the next turn. "Jesus."

"The Steadmans' main mechanic is a guy named Craig Martin. He served eighteen months for statutory rape." He held up a finger for dramatic emphasis. "Every woman who's vanished out here has been between the age of fourteen and twenty-two."

"So the killer likes them young." They pulled up in front of a small house whose blue paint was so weathered and chipped the house looked gray.

"And so does Craig Martin." He opened the car door. "I think we should check him out after we've gotten everybody back from this stupid trip to the hotel."

"Good idea," she said, neither agreeing nor disagreeing with his description of the hotel hike, although she honestly agreed with him. They weren't going to find the Steadmans in the woods, not if they were the poachers who'd killed all the animals they'd found in the pool house. The Steadman brothers might be misogynistic assholes who depended on their daddy for their livelihood, but they had to be good outdoorsmen—better, certainly, than any of Erin's friends, except maybe Jordan, who seemed pretty capable out there.

She wished he was coming with her instead of Matt. Matt might be extremely fit, but he was a city guy. She'd feel a lot better prowling around in the hotel's ruins with someone who had experience in the wilderness.

"Text me nonstop," Hari urged. "I'm going to worry, and you know it."

She leaned in for a hug. "Good luck with the interview. Take a Lyft or something when you're done, okay? I don't think any of us should be wandering around alone in this town."

His nose crinkled. "Do they even have Lyft out here?"

She laughed as Hari got out of the car. He turned around at the house's front door and waved goodbye to her. She waved back, then glanced at her phone again. Nothing from Kayla or Dahlia, and double nothing from Jordan, who was probably ferrying his mother around. And maybe he wasn't even interested in joining them in their poacher hunt. Not that she could blame him: she had her brother, Hari had the podcast, and Dahlia and Kayla had their own personal axes to grind. Jordan had no vested interest in any of it beyond curiosity and his long-burning torch for Dahlia.

Which Erin was just guessing at, she reminded herself, pulling into Dahlia's driveway yet again that day. Matt waved at her from the front porch and jogged down to the car.

"Found a whole box of granola bars," he announced as he tossed a day pack into the back seat. "I can't believe Kayla and Dahlia didn't take any. It's a good thing we're meeting up with them." He climbed into the passenger seat.

"Yeah, good thing you grabbed them." She hoped she didn't sound surprised. In the half-dozen times she and Matt had hung out together, she had never noticed his thoughtfulness. Maybe she'd just been so focused on his swagger and perfect teeth. It wasn't like Matt was a jerk, but he carried himself with a superhuman amount of . . . charisma? Self-confidence? She had a hunch there'd never been a door Matt had been worried about walking through, a place he had felt unwelcome, a task he hadn't felt up to tackling. She wondered what it was like going through life full of rizz instead of self-doubt.

". . . You think?"

"I'm sorry, I was a little distracted," she said. She had no idea how long he'd been talking. At least she'd gotten them onto the right road.

"Well, there's a lot going on today," he said, kindly. "I was just saying that I think the Clackamas is one of the most beautiful rivers I've ever seen. At least in the places that aren't dammed. It's such a shame so much of the river has been tied up with hydroelectric production."

She let herself nod along. The river raced beside the highway, a turquoise ribbon threaded between basalt walls. "I wonder what it was like before us. Settlers, I mean."

He had turned in his seat to better see out the window. "Whole, I guess."

"Whole. It's hard to imagine." Erin couldn't help but think of Bryan, crying on the phone that fucked-up Tuesday in 2016. *The whole world is broken, Erin, and no one even cares. Fuck, most people want to make it worse.* When the sheriff had told her about the journal they'd found in his car, her mind had flashed back to that conversation and all the others they'd had during the long years of the first Trump administration. Hadn't everyone who loved animals and trees and the free, wild places of the world felt their hearts break in those days? Hadn't they all wished to die, even just a little bit?

Matt faced forward again. "I love my job, but sometimes I wish I'd gone into something that helps the environment. Then sometimes I think about it, and I'm glad I didn't. Some fights feel too big, you know?"

"Yeah." She wondered if he knew she'd originally planned to go to school for environmental law, in the long-ago time before Bryan died. She felt glad they had something in common. A part of her—no *several* parts of her, like the part that had grown up with no money, the part of her with buckteeth, the part of her that got picked on in gym class—had always tried very hard not to like him.

They sat in silence a few minutes. Erin tapped her fingers on the steering wheel and noticed an osprey launch itself over the sun-sparkling river. It would have been a great day to be out for a casual hike.

Which it actually felt like, once they finally parked at the trailhead beside Dahlia's Subaru and began scrambling up the trail they had taken just a few nights ago. Erin sucked in a deep breath of trail air, smelling gloriously of freshly unfolding leaf buds, the tender tips of new growth on the firs, the brighter mineral smell of mud when it was beginning to dry. It smelled better than it had Friday night or on Saturday's desperate crawl in the rain. It smelled like summer would arrive soon.

Matt broke the pleasant spell. "No service."

Erin checked her phone just to be sure. She put it back in her coat pocket and trudged on, her shoulders a bit more bowed. They had passed out of the information age and into the realm of luck.

And when the man with the rifle stepped out in front of her, she knew their luck had run out.

CHAPTER EIGHTEEN

IN THE ALMOST-DARK OF THE RUINED BAKERY, ERIN sat on the hard-packed dirt floor, her nearly numb hands and ankles bound tight with the same blue nylon line she'd put in her camping gear when she packed for this trip. Her brain kept circling back to that idea, the presence of the cheap blue cord shifting this moment from horror to something almost surreal. She'd been so excited when she'd bought the gear, ready to hang her food from a tree, to paddle the river, to delve into the secrets of the place that had swallowed her brother whole. Somehow, she'd never worried the same thing would happen to her.

That's probably why the first thing she'd thought when Howie Steadman pointed his rifle at her and Matt had been, *This can't be happening.*

While she stood there like a frozen turkey, Matt had charged Howie. Matt had moved faster and better than she could have expected, but Howie had been faster as he swung the stock of his rifle into Matt's face. There'd been a horrible crunching sound, and Matt had dropped to his ass in the dirt, clutching his nose. Erin couldn't stop hearing that crispy crackling sound replaying in her head.

And yet Howie hadn't shot either of them. For that matter, neither she nor Jordan had been hit when the Steadmans shot at them at Hillier, either, and if the two brothers were the same people successfully killing all those animals back at the pool house, then they had to be excellent shots.

Maybe shooting was too easy for whatever the Steadmans had in mind.

A whimper bubbled up in her throat. The fear had been there since she'd seen Howie on the trail, but now after hours tied up in the stillness of the ruins, her brain finally began to accept what was happening.

"Erin?" Matt whispered.

He didn't sound like himself with his nose mashed to shit. She twisted around to see him hog-tied on his side beside the ashes of the old fire pit their captors had left them near. She wanted to answer, but she could still make out the brothers murmuring to each other somewhere in the dark half of the ruined bakery.

She forced a tiny nod.

"Can you see anything to cut us free?"

Tears welled up in her eyes. The bakery wasn't that big, and the Steadmans only left to pee. They could be back any second. If they saw her, she could wind up like Matt, or worse, Kayla.

She glanced at Kayla's still-immobile body sprawled beside the chair where Dahlia had been tied. If it weren't for the soft wheeze of Kayla's breathing, Erin would have thought she was dead.

When Howie had brought Matt and Erin into the old bakery, Dahlia and Kayla were already there, their hands tied and their faces bruised. Nick had been standing over them, his own rifle in hand. But at the sight of Matt, Kayla had leaped to her feet and thrown herself at Howie. Even with her hands tied behind her back, Kayla was ready to fight.

Nick had smashed her in the side of the head with his rifle, and the dull, hollow thud had been even grosser than the sound of Matt's nose breaking and louder than Dahlia's screams.

The moment repeated itself in Erin's brain: the screaming, the crunching, the thud when Kayla collapsed. The way the brothers had argued with each other as they reworked everyone's bonds. Nick was nearly unintelligible, jumping at every possible sound. He looked strung out and sick, with four swollen gashes running down his face. When he caught Erin looking at them, he had thrown a can of beer at her head.

He was so on edge; the slightest thing might push him over.

"Erin?" Matt repeated.

Erin's body began to quake. To move meant to risk setting off another chain of violence. But as the person with the least-limiting bonds, she was their only hope of escape.

She looked around herself for a rock, a scrap of metal, a shard of glass. She wasn't tied *to* anything, just bound, her mobility limited to scooting inchworm-style. This moment was her best and only chance. Later—if there was a later—it would be too dark to see anything. Already the daylight had moved away from the stove-in roof, and shadows made the heaps of trash look larger and more ungainly. The ruins of Friday's abandoned picnic had been kicked aside, apples and empty cracker boxes everywhere. The giant mixer looked bigger than ever.

"The fire pit," Matt hissed. "Hurry!"

Scooting awkwardly, Erin made it to the fire pit. For a second, she saw nothing except the stones outlining the ashes, and her heart sank. She could never lift one of them with her hands tied so tightly. But Matt was making excited sounds, so she kept looking, digging her fingertips in the cold ashes, finally feeling the top of an old can bite at her skin. Squeezing the jagged lid tightly between her pointer and middle finger, she levered the can out of the ash.

In the back of the bakery, the door creaked. Erin scrambled back to the spot where Howie Steadman had left her, hiding the can behind her feet. She could hear the men swearing to themselves as they made their way through the darkness, and she forced herself to breathe more lightly, as if she'd never moved.

Dahlia made a pained sound, tipping her head in the slightest of warnings—the only part of her she could really move. Erin risked cutting her eyes in the same direction. Nick looked even worse now, the gashes on his cheek leaking yellow fluid.

Howie led Nick back beside the fire pit. "It's okay," he whispered to his brother, propping up the bigger man with his shoulder. Even three feet away, Erin could smell Nick's stink, like meat and mildew and something even worse, something strange and bitter she thought she'd smelled somewhere else, but couldn't place.

And Howie looked anxious. All of his attention was on his brother, his mouth compressed into a tight, worried line as he handed his brother a half-filled Nalgene water bottle and a sandwich.

Nick dropped down onto their cooler with a grunt. "Not hungry." His speech sounded thick, slurred a little.

The cord around Erin's wrists was biting into her flesh. She shifted a little to ease the pain and Nick's dull eyes went toward her. She felt her elbows shrinking closer to her ribs, her spine collapsing to make herself smaller. Like being smaller would somehow help.

Howie reached out his hand, hesitated, laid it lightly on his brother's shoulder. Nick jerked as if burned, his attention flicking away from Erin.

"You gotta eat," Howie urged.

"Feel sick." Nick wiped at his forehead, his own hand thick, red, puffy, the joints too swollen for a man his age. "Hot." He looked down at the water bottle in his other hand, empty already. "So thirsty."

"I'll get us some more," Howie said. He picked up a backpack from beside the cooler and withdrew a water filter.

"'Kay." Nick slid off the cooler, rested his back against it. "Thirsty."

Howie shot Nick a worried look and went back outside. Erin watched Nick's face from the corner of her eye. His eyelids sagged, blinked, sagged, and then stayed closed. She pulled her knees tighter to her chest and pushed the tin can out from beneath her legs. She twisted and scooted, forcing herself to keep her breathing quiet as she moved herself and the can toward the abandoned fire pit. She braced the can against the largest of the rocks. Its top looked jagged and sharp. Not knife-sharp, but sharp-enough-sharp.

She sat for a second, making sure Nick hadn't noticed anything, and then turned around so she could bring her wrists down onto the lid. It felt impossibly awkward, and the rope snarled softly as she moved her body against the metal. But Nick didn't move.

She risked looking at him straight on. The scratches on his face looked like claw marks; perhaps Kayla had scratched him when they'd captured her. But the skin around the scratches was purple with inflammation, the welts themselves red and puckered and almost seeming to bubble. They had to be older than today. Erin couldn't take her eyes off the puckered welts, tiny wet mouths in his skin spitting out yellow slime, opening and closing, opening and closing, the lips twitching as if some kind of string tugged at the flesh. She felt herself leaning sideways, looking harder, even though in the lengthening shadows it was harder to see. Because there *was* something in there, something like string wiggling in the folds and puckers of his scratched skin.

The tin can toppled over, tinging against the rock, and it took her a few seconds to maneuver it back into position. Her back already ached from the awkward angle she was forced to lean up and sag down. She strained her wrists against the cord and felt no change. She had to keep sawing.

A shadow flickered overhead, and she snapped her eyes up to the gap in the ceiling. Nothing. She glanced across to Dahlia, who was also looking up. Erin tightened her lips against the pain in her hands and, still sawing, looked back at the hole in the roof.

And saw the figure peering down at them. Not an animal—a human.

Erin's eyes met Dahlia's, and she knew they were both weighing the danger of waking Nick versus the ache to call out for help. But wouldn't anyone who saw three injured people tied up realize they were in trouble? She looked up at the roof again and mouthed: "*Help.*"

The shape leaned closer to the edge of the hole in the roof, and with a burst of surprise she recognized the blue fleece jacket. "Scott!"

The whisper made Nick jerk, but his eyes stayed closed. Erin stared at the man on the roof, begging him with her eyes, with her mute and desperate pleas. "*Help,*" she mouthed. "*Please help us!*"

He raised his finger and put it to his lips.

The can slipped out of place again, and she nearly burst into tears. How long could it possibly take to filter a bottle of water?

Howie could return at any second. Back muscles trembling with exhaustion, she turned around and inchwormed back to the place where they had parked her, can as hidden behind her feet as she could make it. It felt pointless. She might never get another chance to try cutting the rope.

Erin pressed her forehead to her knees and tried to take a few deep breaths. Her jeans stank of dirt and moss.

She remembered the smell then, the bitter smell coming off Nick. She'd smelled it at the site where she and Jordan had found the dead girl. The dead girl whose body was now missing, whose fingerprints had been found at the Steadmans' house.

Her eyes went back to Nick. The whole left side of his face looked wrong now, bumpy, wriggly. The skin beneath his eye had begun to bulge.

"Nick, buddy? You okay in here?"

Scott's shadow vanished.

Howie half ran to his brother's side, crouching next to him. "Hey, wake up, man." His hand shook as he tapped and patted the unwounded side of Nick's face. "Come on, wake up."

Nick's eyes flickered open, although the left one looked nearly swollen shut. "'S wrong?"

"There's something out there," Howie whispered. "It was watching me at the stream. Fucking coyote or something."

"The girl that got Dad?"

Howie shook his head. "I saw its eyes, man. Glowing. No girl has glowing eyes."

Nick made a pained laugh or a cry, a desperate noise that defied categorizing. "The fuck we know, anyway?"

Howie wrapped his arms around himself. "We gotta get out of here." He repeated it to himself, rocking now, scared back to childhood comforts.

From the corner of her eye, Erin saw Matt slithering a little farther into the dark. She looked away. She didn't know what he was up to, but she wasn't about to draw any attention to it.

Nick pushed himself upright, panting at the exertion. Felt in his pockets and pulled out a bag of cotton balls and a lighter. "Fire."

Howie shook his head. "We shouldn't call attention to ourselves."

"Fire," Nick insisted. "What's out there won't come near."

"Okay," Howie said, and Erin thought it was more a giving in than an agreement. At least a fire meant light, warmth, civilization. It had to feel better than rocking yourself in the dark. But a fire meant she couldn't brace her can against the rocks in the fire pit.

She risked a look back up at the ceiling again, but there was no sign of Scott. She stifled a sob. If she'd had any hope of escaping from this bakery, it was winging away.

Howie Steadman set to work assembling a fire. Nick's eyes blinked heavily, but he didn't go back to sleep. The cotton balls sent up a twist of gold light, and the little bits of kindling caught quickly. For a minute or two, the snapping and popping of the wood gave the ruined bakery a campground feeling, summoning up the coziness of s'mores and folk songs. The heat only intensified Nick's stench.

And then his eyes shot open wide, wide enough she could see a pale thread wiggling and twisting in the bottom half of his left eye, like a worm crawling out of rancid meat, and he was on his feet, roaring: "That son of a bitch!"

Erin twisted to see what he saw: Matt crouched beside the rusted hulk of the giant mixer, sawing frantically at the ropes around his wrists. Her heart rose up into her mouth, but Nick was already rushing toward him. The ropes snapped and Matt shot out a fist meant to connect with Nick's solar plexus, but Nick merely snatched the fist out of the air and launched Matt sideways.

"Matt!" Erin shrieked, but Nick was already stooping.

The big man grabbed the ropes still binding Matt's ankles and hoisted him off the ground. Matt bucked and flailed, but it was like watching a fish wriggle on the line.

"Nick, stop!" Howie shouted.

At the same time, Nick let out an inhuman roar and swept Matt through the air like a baseball bat swinging for a home run. Matt's head hit the mixer with a wet crack. The room filled with the stench of blood and something richer and meatier.

Dahlia screamed.

Matt fell from Nick's grasp and lay utterly still, his head spilling out blood and chunks.

With a shriek of rage, Kayla leaped up from the fireside. For a second, her face looked like an animal's, her eyes flashing blue-green in the firelight, but then she landed on Nick's back. The ropes dangling from her wrists and ankles looked somehow melted.

Then Erin saw the white threads twisting out from Kayla's blood-soaked hair, wriggling and writhing like the string that had come out of Nick's eye. Erin felt her back hit a pile of garbage as she scuttled away from the two fighters.

Nick's eyes bulged half out of his head as Kayla squeezed his neck. Howie was screaming, and then he was firing his rifle into the air, and there was nothing but noise and chaos.

Erin knew she ought to be moving, ought to be trying to escape or protect herself, but the threads in Nick's left eye had come out, more and more of them, the mass tangling in front of his face into one big white snake-thing. The thread-snake gripped Kayla's arms.

But she didn't let go. Growling, snarling, Kayla rode Nick's shoulders, biting and clawing as he howled and lurched, trying to shake her loose.

And then Nick stumbled into the fire. His hiking pants instantly began to melt and his screams filled the room.

With a crow of victory, Kayla ripped one hand free of Nick's worm-strings and drove her thumb into his eye. His voice rose in pitch and he rushed forward, hitting the mixer and bouncing off it. Deep beneath the bakery, something groaned, and for a moment everything went quiet in Erin's head, even though Nick was screaming, and Kayla was howling, and the flames were climbing up Nick's clothes and into Kayla's, rushing everywhere.

It was all quiet in Erin's head, all thought, all reason swallowed up by the stink of burning skin and a wave of roasting mushrooms and metal.

A hand on Erin's shoulder. "Shh," Scott whispered. The soft whisper of a sharp knife through nylon, and her hands were free. "Shh," he repeated, leaning down and freeing her ankles.

When he looked up, his eyes glowed. She swallowed a scream.

"You've got to get out of here," he said.

"Dahlia's tied—"

"I'll come back for her. You run."

Howie's rifle went off again, and in the muzzle flash she caught a glimpse of something that had once been Nick Steadman, had once been Kayla, and had fused into something else entirely. It towered over Howie like a grizzly, like a video game monster, like Hell come to Earth.

And then the groaning sounded again, and Erin felt the ground shifting underneath her feet as the monster-thing hovered in the air for an instant and then simply, impossibly, plunged down into the ground, mixer and fire pit and cooler and lawn chairs crashing down, too.

For a second, Erin couldn't understand what she was seeing, and then she recognized the pit in the ground for what it was: a sinkhole.

The sinkhole spread wider, and Howie was wailing, but Erin was free, and she wasn't staying a second longer to find out what happened to him. Her feet launched her toward the door.

As the ground swallowed up the ruined bakery, Erin sprinted from the building in terror. The sounds of the walls collapsing behind her gave her wings. She had never run so fast in her fucking life.

CHAPTER NINETEEN

THE STRANGENESS REGISTERED THAT THERE WERE now two forms of itself, one networked across the flanks of McIntyre Ridge and several large hills, a carefully tended garden of consciousness whose movements happened with little surprise—and one that had emerged from the tunnel behind the Steadmans' house and picked its way through the woods despite every order the Strangeness emitted. Recent developments had rendered the girl's reproductive capacities unimportant, but the changes to the Strangeness's own threads within her body, possibly caused by other fungi that might have managed successful colonization during her unexpected time unalive, had created a new kind of experiment. Such novelty urged the Strangeness to focus upon this new being.

Calling in an opossum and a bat from the forest periphery, the Strangeness watched as the creek girl picked her way back to Bill Steadman's house and snapped the yellow caution tape on the back door. Someone had turned the lock in the door handle, but the Strange threads in her palms found an opening and feasted on the dirt inside, bursting apart the delicate mechanisms. The door swung open. The creek girl and the possum went inside.

The Strangeness urged the girl to stop in the doorway and observe the place for a minute, and she obliged. The possum touched her ankle with the tip of its tail, and threads inside her fed the Strangeness a burst of information. The threads themselves felt different, more highly charged, their genetic expression transformed by stress chemicals from the girl's body. In other experiments, the Strangeness had destroyed subjects experiencing these effects, but the aggressive nature of the changes were worth studying.

Already, the spores from her rampage the night before were settling into the wood of the kitchen cabinets. A loaf of bread on the counter had burst into colorful life, filaments of the new Strange variant crawling across the vinyl and up into the walls. A thicket had found a warm place behind the refrigerator and exploded in mass, penetrating the metal and drinking up the coolant. With almost no fungal competitors indoors, the new Strangeness could expand its territory at a previously unimaginable rate.

The girl from the creek had taken the Strangeness into an entirely new realm of opportunities. It sent a wash of freshly assembled carbohydrates up through the soles of her feet, eager to see what would happen next.

The girl began moving again, her respiration shallower, her heart rate faster. She did not really need air anymore, but such stress responses never left the body, not really. The strong smell of blood sparked memory, emotion—a burning pain and rage that reminded the Strangeness of the distress chemicals the female coyote had made when her mate had been killed. Her distress had mobilized the Strangeness into destroying the poacher's territory, a decision it still hadn't evaluated as a success or failure.

A stream of spores puffed from the dead girl's skin, as if her rage had stirred a new mutation within her body. Her feet scuffed over the wide brown stain in the next doorway and then into the living room. The beige carpet darkened beneath her feet.

A black Lab lay on a dog bed beside the couch. It looked up at her, its eyes bloodshot and dull. The Strangeness had no recollection of it being here when the girl had first explored the house, but perhaps it had come back in through the dog door after the police had scoured the place. Its breathing rasped loud enough the girl could hear it; perhaps it was having an allergic reaction to the spores filling the air. Plenty of creatures could not tolerate them.

She stooped beside the dog and put out her hand. Filaments darted between her fingers and the dog's nose, but the Strangeness felt nothing.

A cold array of biochemicals flooded its deepest, most self-like of hyphae, far from this place and deeply protected from the world. How could it have felt nothing? What kind of creature was this dog?

The creek girl stood and went to the front door. Hesitated. Instinct or memory made her put on the flannel shirt hanging on the coatrack, slide her feet into the driving moccasins. Bill Steadman had been a big man, and his shirt could nearly pass for a dress on such a slight girl. She opened the door and went out to the porch.

"What the hell are you doing here?" someone asked from the driveway.

The dog stepped out onto the porch, angling its body between her and the man. The man looked from her to the dog and back. "What are you doing with Cletus?"

Even through the dense cloud cover, the moonlight made her eyes ache. She brought up a hand to shield them. The Strangeness urged her to go back inside, but instead, her eyes slid dully over the shape of a small red car and stopped on the man's face. A potent blend of hormones jolted through her veins when she registered the blond mustache and beard. She was looking for a bearded man, after all.

The man walked toward her, beginning to smile. The Strange opossum that had followed her onto the porch darted behind a railing, out of sight, but within earshot. "You've got a familiar face, gorgeous. Are you from around here?"

The girl tilted her head, the words slowly moving through her brain. The Strangeness urged her to run, but she didn't move.

The man's smile was complete now, wide and wolfish. "Why don't you help me take Cletus back to my place, and you can tell me all about how you know Bill and the boys." He put out his hand to shake hers. "I'm Craig, by the way."

"I . . ." the girl struggled to find the word that had been stripped from her when she'd taken her last breath. The Strangeness sent flashes of alarm throughout every Strange being nearby. The old dog stiffened. The possum fled beneath the porch.

"I'm Elena," she managed in a hoarse, dry voice, and the Strangeness knew it had lost whatever control it had over her.

CHAPTER TWENTY

ERIN DARTED OUT THE SIDE DOOR OF THE RUINED bakery, bouncing off one of the enormous old rhododendrons and skidding on mud. She had no idea when the sun would set, but with heavy cloud cover, the forest was already nearly twilight dark. She kept moving, stumbling over roots and sticks and clumps of ferns. Was the sinkhole still spreading? She couldn't hear anything over the sound of her own harsh breathing.

Her foot caught something hard and she went flying. She hit the ground with a whimper. She started to push herself up when a hiking boot caught her in the ribs.

The air went out of her in a rush and she collapsed. Rough hands gripped her shoulders, flipping her around.

Howie Steadman stared into her face, his eyes nearly bulging from his head in fear. "What the fuck did you do?"

"Let me go!" she shrieked and tried to kick herself loose, but the laces on her shoe were caught on whatever had tripped her.

"Those strings—that girl had them, too. What are they?" he bellowed, shaking her shoulders harder.

She clawed at his hands. "Fuck you!"

Something crashed in the bushes behind them, and Howie dropped her so hard her head bounced off a tree root. He darted into the brush, running fast.

Jordan came crashing down the path. Erin called out, but he'd seen Howie and rushed after him. Erin fumbled with her shoelaces and realized they'd caught on the old bicycle handlebar she'd tripped on walking with Madison.

Regret flamed up like heartburn. Madison had been so right.

But there was no time for that. Aching everywhere, she began running after the sound of the men's footsteps.

"Jordan!" she called, and when he didn't answer, she ran faster. Even in the deepening twilight, she could see the trail of broken branches and trampled ferns the two had left.

Ducking beneath the branch of an enormous cedar tree, Erin burst out onto a beautifully smooth, well-graded path. Just ahead, she saw Jordan launch himself at Howie in a perfect tackle. Howie hit the ground with an audible oof.

Jordan cranked Howie's arm up behind him. "What the hell is going on here, Steadman? What did you do to the bakery?"

"Jordan!" Erin jumped on Howie's legs to hold him still. "The others are still in there."

Jordan's face went blank. "Dahlia?"

She nodded. "We're going to need ropes to get down in the sinkhole. I don't know how bad they all might be hurt."

Jordan twisted Howie's arm harder. "Where's your truck, you son of a bitch? I know you've got gear in there."

"Fuck you," Howie grunted.

Jordan gave the arm another yank.

Howie howled in pain. "It's by the Vanderpoel place."

"What?" Erin sat back on his feet. "How'd you get up here, then?"

But Jordan was nodding. "The old hotel road." He looked around. "You and Nick must have cleared enough of it to use as a trail."

Steadman bucked under Erin's weight, and she drove her elbow into his side to stop his wiggling. "Any chance you've got duct tape in your pocket?"

Jordan hunkered down beside her, digging in a waist pack. He pulled out a small spool of the gray stuff and, holding it in his teeth, wrenched Howie's other arm back to join the first one. Erin shifted her weight so she could help hold his wrists, her elbow digging into the small of Steadman's back. She didn't mind the thought she was hurting him.

"Okay, get off him." Jordan used the duct-tape bonds to lever Steadman to his feet. He frog-marched him forward. "Take us to your truck."

"My brother's down there, too," Howie said, twisting to look at his captors. "Tell me you'll help him, McCall. You're a good guy."

"Your brother was fucked up," Erin said. "What were those snake-things coming out of his eye?"

"Snake-things?" Jordan asked.

"I don't know," Howie whimpered. Erin could see his shoulders shaking. "I don't understand anything that happened back there."

"We have to hurry," Erin urged the two men. "They could be hurt down there."

Jordan drove Howie to move faster. The Steadmans' path ran in smooth, steep switchbacks down the hill. Big slabs of ancient asphalt made clear patches, and in places the track was even graveled. Erin wanted nothing more than to run, but her body ached and she was barely able to keep up Jordan's pace.

Howie steered them to the right, where the path curved uphill, and in a few minutes, Erin started seeing lights through the gaps in the trees. "We'll come out in back of the Vanderpoel place," he said. "The old lady never notices a thing."

Erin stopped. "How long have you been using this trail?"

"Why should I tell you?"

She gave his arm a fierce pinch.

He shrank away from her. "Since before Scott died. He caught us once when we were building it. He wanted to know how much work we'd done. Gave us his old wheelbarrow. He was crazy about history, you know. I think he wanted his own access to the hotel."

"Maybe Olivia can help us," Erin said.

"I hope so," Jordan said. "You should go to her house after I get Howie's rig. How close are we, Steadman?"

"Almost there, I think," he mumbled. "Come on, just let me go. Nick's the one you want, really. I'll just go home, and—fuck, no, Craig's maybe—"

The gray evening went achingly bright as a pair of white floodlights came on. Erin threw up her arm to cover her eyes.

"What are you doing in my backyard?" a familiar voice shouted, and then came that *slide-chk-chk* sound Erin had heard in a thousand movies, the one that freezes people in their tracks with fear. At the sound of the pump shotgun, Erin, too, turned to ice.

She threw her hands above her head. "Don't shoot, Olivia! It's me, Erin!"

"Erin? Are you in trouble?"

Erin lowered her hands a little, her eyes watering, but the whole yard was a dazzle. "Kind of. Can you keep your shotgun on us as we come up to the house?"

"Fuck that," Howie hissed, ramming Erin's side as he threw himself sideways.

"Shit!" Jordan shouted.

The shotgun roared.

Erin tripped over some kind of yard ornament and fell into

an azalea bush. Jordan shouted some more, but then came back and helped her up. "Damn it, he got away."

Olivia Vanderpoel appeared at Erin's elbow. "What is going on? Who are these young men and why was one tied up?"

"I can't believe I let him go," Jordan complained. "Slippery bastard."

"Olivia, our friends are hurt and trapped in a sinkhole. We've got to get some ropes and climbing gear right away," Erin said.

"I've got everything we'd need in my work truck," Jordan said. "Climbing gear, pulleys—"

"A backboard? Medical equipment?"

He shot an irritated look at Erin. "No, but I can at least go down there and provide basic first aid. Keep people warm if they're going into shock. I don't know how long it will take EMTs to get up to the old hotel."

"The old hotel?" Olivia asked, her voice sharp.

"I know it's trespassing—" Erin began, but Olivia cut her off.

"That place is riddled with mining tunnels." Olivia turned to Jordan. "How long will it take you to get to the truck?"

"It's in Sandy," he said, "at our office. But *my* pickup's back at the trailhead for the hot springs."

"Let me get my keys, and I'll drive you to your pickup. Erin and I will go to the hotel on foot."

"Can you hike that far?" Jordan asked, his cheeks immediately flaming red. "I'm sorry, that was rude."

But Olivia was already striding toward the house, her gray corduroy pants hissing at the speed of her steps. She looked over her shoulder at them. "Well? Come on. Inside, both of you."

"Should we call nine-one-one?" Erin asked, slipping her hand in her pocket for her phone and then remembering Howie had taken her phone when he'd tied her up, tossing it beside the big green cooler. It was now probably at the bottom of that sink-hole. If Deputy Duvall called, it was going to voicemail for sure.

Ditto for Hari, who wouldn't have been able to get a hold of anyone all afternoon. And fuck, how was she going to tell him about Matt? The wet, hollow sound of Matt's head colliding with the mixer replayed in her head, and she felt her stomach squeeze into her throat. She caught herself on the wall, her legs turning to jelly.

"There's no time to fall apart," Olivia said, pocketing a key chain. "Young man—it's McCall, isn't it?—please grab that Tupperware container full of muffins. And Erin, do you have a head lamp?"

Erin's was still in her backpack, now underground. She shook her head.

"Good thing I have two," Olivia said, her lips compressing. "I'll explain everything on the drive—so let's move."

JORDAN HUNG UP HIS PHONE AND SHOOK HIS HEAD. "There's a huge house fire out in Molalla," he said. "Every am-bulance is tied up until they get back. Dispatch is passing along our information to Search and Rescue, but half of those guys are also volunteer firefighters."

"Shit," Erin breathed, letting her head fall forward against the back of Jordan's seat. The smell of cookies wafting from the basket beside her made her feel carsick. She swallowed down the discomfort and looked more closely at the wicker container, neatly packed with what appeared to be a soft red plaid blanket, a first aid kit, and yes, a small box of vanilla candles.

"They're for home showings," Olivia said.

"I thought you ran the chamber of commerce," Erin said at the same time Jordan asked: "Aren't you, like, retired?"

Olivia shot him a sour look. "The minute you retire is the minute you start dying."

"Some people start dying a long time before that," Jordan said, and set his mouth unhappily. Erin thought of her mother, and for a moment she was ten again, struggling to carry the garbage bag out to the curb as the empty liquor bottles clanked and clinked against her leg. She shoved the memory aside.

"Can we talk more about this plan?" Erin asked. "If Dahlia and Kayla's lives are depending on me, I want to know what I'm doing."

Jordan looked over the back of the seat at her. "Matt's still with Hari?"

She could barely shake her head. "No, he's . . . I'm pretty sure Nick killed him."

"Jesus!" he swore. "I can't believe I fucking let Howie go." He made a face at Olivia. "Sorry for swearing."

"No need to apologize," she said. "This sounds extremely dire." Her hand went to the volume knob on the stereo, emitting barely audible classical music. The radio snapped into silence. "This all begins with my father."

"Your father?" Erin asked.

"He was obsessed with the idea of finding treasure on McIntyre Ridge."

"Treasure?" Jordan asked, skeptical. "Even the most successful mines around here weren't that lucrative."

"He wasn't looking for gold," Olivia said. "But he would spend days out in the woods without telling anyone, not even his secretary at the mill."

Jordan opened the muffin container and handed one to Erin. "Mitch had a real reputation as an eccentric."

Olivia gave a dry bark of laughter. "I know the town called him crazy. I think 'tenacious' might be a better word. He was certain the stories about the 1907 meteor strike were more than just tall tales."

Jordan leaned in closer to the older woman. "He was looking for the impact crater, wasn't he? No one's ever discovered it."

"My father had an entire filing drawer full of mineral samples he'd collected around the area. They were all bits of iridium, an extremely dense mineral rarely found on Earth, except at sites of meteor strikes."

"That's the stuff that helped them track down the dinosaur-killing asteroid, right?" Erin vaguely remembered this from a class on the philosophy of science.

"Yes!" Olivia sounded impressed. "I once followed my father on one of his collecting trips—secretly. He went up the old hotel road. After we passed the hotel, he simply vanished. I almost turned around and came home, but then I heard the sound of the pickax against stone." She paused and licked her lip. "It was an abandoned adit," she explained. "Maybe a test bore, I don't know. But I think he found something there."

Erin wrapped her arms around her stomach, more carsick and anxious than ever. "Why weren't there any signs?" she asked. "People party at that hotel all the time. If there are mining tunnels under there, it was only a matter of time before something happened."

"It's private property," Olivia snapped. "Aren't the 'No Trespassing' signs enough?"

"Your father didn't register any kind of mineral claims, did he?" Jordan said. "He didn't want anyone else to know about the iridium."

"No," the woman admitted. "And I have no idea how much excavating my father did there. Scott might have been helping, too, which would have made a difference."

The Volvo's headlights lit up the sign for the trailhead, and Olivia pulled the ubiquitous orange Northwest Forest Pass from her glove box to hang from her rearview mirror. Erin had stopped being surprised by her preparedness. They slid in between Jordan's white pickup and Erin's Toyota. "Erin and I will see if we can get into the tunnels while you get your truck," Olivia said. "Put your cell number in my phone so we can keep in touch."

Jordan took the phone and added his contact info, then hurried to his pickup. He hesitated, looking back at Erin, his hand on the door handle. "You going to be okay? This could be dangerous."

Erin dug the heels of her hands into her eye sockets. They were hot and dry from exhaustion and fear. "Who else is gonna go?" she reminded him. "Just hurry up."

"Erin, can you help me?" Olivia removed a box from the back of her Volvo and dropped it with a thud. "I don't think I can carry all of this."

From the look of the box, Olivia had been gearing up for this trip for a while. Erin even saw a flare gun between the bottles of water and cases of protein bars. She took one of the headlamps and slid it down over her head.

"You are an amazing woman, Olivia."

Olivia shook her head. "If I was amazing, I would have gone up there years ago." She gave a short, sharp sniff. "I've always suspected that's where Scott went."

Erin reached for her hand and gripped it. She had to blink back tears. Here she was, standing with someone who understood just what it was like to have their loved one vanish into this eerie expanse of trees and yet never give up on them.

She pulled her hand away and started loading the backpack lying on top of the gear. Quickly, carefully, as if playing Gear Tetris could keep her from noticing the flutter of hope in her chest.

CHAPTER TWENTY-ONE

THE WOMAN DISENTANGLED HERSELF FROM THE sticky thing beneath her, freeing her arms from the heavy weight of another person's limbs. A rock dug into her leg through the tears in her pants. She recognized these things—other people, pants, bare skin—but only vaguely. She felt too good to be worried about the way words and concepts were flickering out of her head. For the past day, her head and neck had ached, not badly, but enough to concern her and slow her down. Her hand had itched almost maddeningly. But now her body felt good. Beyond good, actually. She practically floated onto her feet. She luxuriated in a long unfolding of limbs and spine, not even minding the dirt beneath her palms as she dropped into downward-facing dog.

The Strangeness allowed her the moment. Its threads had permeated her brain, her spine, and her limbs, and it enjoyed the moment itself. This woman was strong. Powerful. Unlike some of the other humans it had infiltrated, her mind moved quickly and fluidly, her intelligence opening new avenues for it to exploit. There were no chemical weak spots in the brain, no emotional loopholes. It forced its attention to its first female human, that botched acquisition from the creek. Her rage blunted her senses and resisted all control; the presence of other random bacterial and fungal entities that had colonized her body after her death had caused other confusing changes. The spores her body created had held opportunity, but the resulting fruiting bodies had inherited many of the female's problematic behaviors.

This female held so much more immediate promise. She must be brought into the Strangeness's deep heart, her gametes sampled, her mind mapped more deeply. This was what the Strangeness had been seeking since it first began colonizing mammalian bodies.

It sent a quiet pulse through the woman's limbs, urging her toward the tunnel it had long ago mapped with Strange arachnid and moss outcroppings. She stiffened, that fine brain of hers panicking and fighting for a second before the Strangeness regained control.

Behind her, a voice called for help. The woman tried to turn back, but the Strangeness spurred her onward.

It had tasted and known: the other woman in the cavern was useful only as food for its fruiting bodies. After all, now that the tunnel beneath the old hotel was exposed to the outside air, any spores emitted down there could now spread much farther into the forest. Perhaps even all the way to the river and the towns lining its banks . . .

CHAPTER TWENTY-TWO

ON HER OWN, ERIN WOULD HAVE NEVER NOTICED the tunnel bored into the rock wall—maidenhair ferns and monkeyflower hung over the mouth of it, and the aged support posts were so covered in moss and lichen they could have passed for living trees. Up close, their awkward angles warned of imminent collapse. She thought of Deputy Duvall's list of things that could kill you in the Mt. Hood National Forest and felt her whole body seize up with resistance. "This doesn't look remotely safe."

Olivia stooped so her headlamp played on the wall beyond the opening. "You can see some of the beams my father added in the 1980s," she said. "They look okay to me."

Erin took a hesitant step forward. The tunnel exhaled a musty chill that left the skin on her face damp. "I feel a little better knowing there's airflow."

"I should have packed a canary." Olivia stared into the darkness for another moment, and then straightened her shoulders. "Let's get moving." She waved for Erin to lead the way.

Erin was glad for the headlamp Olivia had packed. In its cold white light, she could see the stream running down the center of the tunnel, chunks of old ceiling beams here and there, a hump of fallen rock farther down. She had to force herself to step inside, the signs of decay only increasing the weight of the mountain pressing down upon her.

"It always amazes me that people can enjoy exploring places like this," Olivia said. The echoing splash of her footsteps gave the disconcerting illusion she walked both in front of and behind Erin. Without their headlamps, it would be easy to get turned around in a place like this. The thought was like a drop of water running down the back of Erin's neck and crawling under her shirt collar. She zipped her raincoat higher.

She had to concentrate as she scrambled over a loose heap of rock, the stones shifty beneath her feet. On the other side, the stream widened and deepened, nearly over the top of her trail runners. The water burned with coldness. She tried to distract herself. "Are you claustrophobic?"

"A phobia is an irrational fear of something. Being afraid of this tunnel is perfectly logical."

Erin chuckled. The sound flattened inside the stony walls, the tone turned menacing.

"Stop!" Olivia grabbed her elbow, yanking her backward.

"What?" But then Erin saw the outline on the floor ahead of her, an aged timber square set into the tunnel floor like a mouth of darkness. "Jesus Christ." She squeezed closer to the wall, her heart pounding. "What the hell is that?"

Olivia played a flashlight over the hole. "Must have been the entrance to the main level of the mine. It's full of water."

A wooden ladder led down, down into the depths, lit a phenomenal turquoise for the few feet their lights could penetrate. The structure looked ancient, preserved by the cold of the water and the mine's isolation. Erin had no doubt if she were to touch it, the wood would be as soft as a slice of white bread. Deputy Duvall whispered in her ear: *I've seen people die a thousand different ways out here.*

They turned sideways to get around the mine shaft, and Erin

moved more carefully after that, scanning the ground before every step. But it was her ears that warned her of the cross tunnel, a soft, terrible moan slipping out of a crack in the stone she might not have even noticed.

She hesitated in front of it. Water trickled over the stone, and the air current blew more powerfully against her face. The moan sounded again, faint but definitely human, yanking every strand of sympathy in her body.

But the opening itself was narrow, the stones mere inches from each other.

"No support beams," Olivia whispered. "This is natural."

That did nothing to ease Erin's mind. She thought about calling to the person making that pained and horrible sound, but her tongue had dried to the roof of her mouth.

"I'll go first." Olivia tugged at Erin's shoulder. The old woman's hand felt delicate and fragile.

"No, I can do it." Erin turned sideways, testing the space. For a second the backpack caught, the water bottles crackling and extra flashlight grinding into her spine, and her breath stopped in her throat, her head empty yet full of dark stars, and then she was freed, the space opening up enough she could almost turn front-wise. "It's not so bad." She forced herself to take a deep breath.

"Look." Olivia steered Erin's glance up and behind them, where faint white letters caught in the headlamp's beam. "That's my father's handwriting."

The sight eased Erin's breathing a little. Someone had used this tunnel, even if it was forty years ago. "He must have been tall."

"So tall. I guess Scott took after him."

The tunnel widened a bit more, and Erin could see places where the rock looked chipped by human tools and not merely water-sculpted. This tunnel was like the Steadman brothers' trail—camouflaged at its endpoints and greatly improved in the middle. The floor was nearly dry and mostly smooth. The black beanie on the floor stood out from the rock all the more for it.

Erin picked it up. "Mountain Hardwear," she read. "This is Kayla's." She put it in her pocket.

"Are you sure?"

"It's not even damp. She must have come through here recently."

"We're going the right way, then." Olivia's words were sure but also small. Erin understood completely. What would they find at the end of the tunnel?

The moan sounded again, a sound of utmost suffering. Like a duck's call, it had no echo. Erin had no idea why that felt so important. She touched the beanie in her pocket and kept walking.

CHAPTER TWENTY-THREE

THERE HAD BEEN SCREAMING. BARKING. MORE screams.

The enormous sounds overpowered the Strangeness's messages to itself for a minute or two. Of course, it wasn't just the sounds. The Strangeness's immune system, hijacked by whatever mutation had occurred in her cold, wet body while the girl lay dead and yet not-dead in the creek, was somehow turning on itself. Traces of foreign fungal invaders only worsened the attack. Sometimes the creek girl vanished entirely from the Strangeness's senses, triggering an instinctual drive to cut off the threads it had planted inside her and watch from afar. But it fought down its instincts, retaining a quiet consciousness deep beneath the new, dominant threads. Watching. Listening. Learning.

The creek girl had staggered toward the couch in the middle of the warm, dim room. The man who had picked her up at the—safe place—lay on his belly, staring up at her with eyes the color of wet wood. He had touched her, in the car. His hands had been warm on her leg. Too warm. When he brought her inside his home, he pressed his warmth all over her. He smelled like wet skunks.

I don't smoke pot, a memory—for once not a bad one—whispered deep inside her head. *I can't risk losing this job.*

It's just waiting tables, the memory laughed. *Why do you even care?*

Whatever she had said in reply was gone, but she felt it, someplace between the threads. An anxiety that took the shape of a pair of hands, chapped red around the knuckles, the veins prominent across the ridges of the tendons, the gullies of the flesh. Hands that had worked too hard, been cared for too little. Hands she didn't want for her own future, but whose memory stirred other, better feelings, older and deeper than the reach of the threads colonizing her brain. The girl's heart ached inside her with a childish need to be pulled into the arms that went with those hands. *¡Mamá!,* her heart cried out. *¡Mamá!* She drew herself together to run from this place.

The threads inside her shivered. The Strangeness could no more control them than it could control the stream of memories unraveling in the girl's mind, but it recognized the mechanism of deep connection. The new threads released a flood of chemicals the Strangeness recorded for later analysis, too massive for instant understanding.

The language center of her brain went dark for a moment, the synapses overridden by the threads' messages. The creek girl straightened. Her body creaked as the threads beneath her skin tightened.

She leaned over the dead man on the couch and drove her thumbs deep into his hazel eyes. So warm. So wet, the slickness sucking her deeper into his inner depths. Dopamine exploded throughout her brain; her back arched, her hips bucked. Her lips peeled back from her teeth, saliva spooled from her lower lip: every inch of her skin crawling, twitching, rippling as seeds squeezed out from her pores, rising like blue smoke to fill the room.

She collapsed.

For several long moments, nothing happened. Out of habit, the Strangeness whispered to the threads inside the back of the girl's neck, encouraging them to dissolve and absorb the dead flesh pressing against it, the man's knee or thigh or some similar leg part, but its ability to send messages was now completely blocked. The new Strange inside the girl's body did not seem to recognize a need for nutrients. Dark spots bloomed on the girl's bare legs where threads rebuilt themselves from her own fading reserves. The black dog whimpered and nuzzled her leg, but she didn't move. Parts of her brain turned off and on as new electrical currents rerouted inside its folds.

Light spilled into the room as the door opened.

"Look, I'm telling you Craig doesn't know anything," a man's voice said, a little bit shrill. "You're barking up the wrong—Oh, fuck!"

The girl stood and faced the two men frozen in the doorway, one familiar to the Strange as a hunter of creatures, the other new.

"You poor thing." The new one stretched out his hands to the girl. "It's okay," he said. "Everything's going to be okay."

Okay. The word made a warm place inside the creek girl's head. She stared at the man, his soft brown hair, his gentle face. She liked his voice.

"I'm Hari," he said. "I'm going to help you."

"Cletus? What are you doing here, boy? Are you okay?" The hunter strode toward the dog and then froze. "Oh, fuck! Craig!" He spun around, knocking Hari into the doorframe. Then he bolted down the street, shrieking.

The gentle man rubbed the spot where he'd hit his head and turned his attention back to the girl. "It's going to be okay," he repeated. "Let's get you some help."

He was different from the man who had brought her to this house, the men she had found in the house at the edge of the woods. He seemed . . . safe.

The safe place. She had to get back there. She should bring this safe, kind man—Hari—too.

Echoing his earlier posture, she stretched out her hands to him. "You poor thing," she echoed, her voice the rasp of something insectile, something dead. "Everything's going to be okay."

CHAPTER TWENTY-FOUR

THE CREVICE WAS NOW WIDE ENOUGH FOR ERIN to walk without turning sideways, the walls even smoother. In a few places, she saw small boreholes labeled with chalk notations. One or two were labeled in a different, less tidy hand. The way Olivia's fingers lingered on them told Erin the writing was Scott's. It must have felt a little like looking at those photos of Bryan paddling on the Clackamas.

Erin hesitated, asked anyway. "Are you nervous about finding Scott?"

"I don't know."

"I'm scared to find out what really happened to Bryan," Erin admitted. "When I started thinking about Faraday, it was exciting and even kind of fun imagining there was something weird going on out here. But when I think about Bryan getting caught up in it? I don't want to think about him suffering. I don't want to think of him being scared and hurt and alone. A part of me wants to go home and write my fluff piece about a cute town with good rafting and never think about this place again."

She felt in her pocket for a handkerchief and swiped her nose. Stuffed it back in her pocket.

Her light caught on a speckling of red on the tunnel floor. She paused beside it.

"Is it blood?" Olivia asked.

"I think so."

The older woman put her hand on Erin's shoulder. Erin could feel the shivers running down it. "If you wrote that article, you'd be endangering a lot of people."

"I know." Erin shielded her headlamp and looked up at the older woman. Olivia's teeth were chattering. "Are you okay? Do you want this hat?"

"I didn't plan for the cold."

Erin gave her Kayla's beanie and they walked onward. She realized she hadn't heard the moaning sound since they had first entered the tunnel, and that was worse than the blood.

The drops and spatters continued. It took Erin a few minutes to realize they were getting easier to see.

Then up ahead, the tunnel was nearly blocked by a heap of dirt and rocks and fallen timbers. A ribbon of light shone from the gaps between the debris and roof, a cruel promise of escape.

A naked pink arm stuck out from the rubble.

Erin broke into a run. "Dahlia! Dahlia, oh my god, are you there?" She threw herself at the pile, pawing rocks and dirt. Her fingers touched the arm, and she gasped at its coldness, its rigidity. She was too late. Too goddamn late.

Then her fingers found the seam running down the pale pink surface and she doubled over with relief. "The blow-up doll." Her knees refused to go steady. "Oh, fuck, that was bad."

"What's going on?" Olivia called. "Did you find someone?"

"Nothing," Erin said. "Just some trash that was in the bakery."

The other woman squeezed in beside her. "I think we can widen the gap between the debris and the top of the tunnel."

Erin pulled out a timber from above her head. "Wish we'd brought a shovel." She dug the boot of her toe into the rubble so she could better dig into the uppermost strata.

"Careful," Olivia urged. "Just shift enough to squeeze through. We don't know how stable any of this is."

They went quiet then, using rocks and broken timbers as makeshift shovels, spreading the dirt out behind them. Erin got another foothold and pushed her way over the heap, rocks digging into her ribs hard enough to nearly make her cry. Then in a great sliding whoosh, the rocks and dirt went skidding out beneath her and she half slid, half tumbled on her side down into a chamber about the size of the Vanderpoel dining room. She lay still a moment, rubbing her ribs and getting her breath back. Everything hurt.

A hole in the roof of the cavern cast enough light that she could see the giant mixer standing on end against the far wall. The Steadmans' green cooler lay on its side beside it, spewing ice packs and food across the floor. A Nalgene water bottle sat perfectly upright in a thick, dark puddle.

Erin's memory shot her a vision of the deer kidney lying in the dirt at the riverside picnic area. It had seemed so terrifying, so revolting, and now that bit of dead flesh seemed almost ordinary.

Ordinary compared to the pulped pink thing lying beneath the mixer, the thing that still wore the remains of Matt's puffy coat. She didn't want to look at it, but it compelled her eyes back to it again and again.

"What do you see?" Olivia called.

"Sunlight," Erin answered, not yet ready to describe her friend's remains. She turned off her headlamp. "Do you think you can get over all the rocks?"

Stone pattered on the other side of the mound, as if in reply. "I'm not sure," the older woman admitted. "Maybe after I've had a rest."

"You just stay there, then." Erin hated the thought of walking up to that pink mess by herself, but she wasn't going to let Olivia get hurt just to keep her company. "I'll let you know what I find."

She made herself stand up. The edges of the space lay in deep gloom, but to her right, she could see something draped over a low ridge of dirt and rocks. She turned on her headlamp and took a few steps toward the thing, trying to make sense of what she was seeing.

This cavern was bigger than the opening in its roof, she saw now. The debris from above had made an enormous heap and then spread long low fingers out into the room, pushing all the way into the tunnel where she and Olivia had entered. Debris and junk had been flung loose here and there. Her toe clanked against an empty beer can and sent it ricocheting into the darkness.

"This room must be bigger than the entire bakery," she realized. "No wonder the building collapsed."

Olivia made some kind of reply, but Erin couldn't make out the words. She took another step forward and stopped. The thing caught on the rocks lay flattened and wet, like—her brain struggled to find a comparison. Her mind hit on her father's attempt to duplicate Wiener schnitzel, hammering veal cutlets until they were transformed into something more fabric than meat. She had joined Bryan as a vegetarian very shortly afterward.

This thing could only be described as meat fabric.

In the cool light of the lamp, she watched a chunk of it slide free from the main mass, suspended on some kind of white string. It hung motionless for a second before falling to the ground with a damp plop. That's when the smell struck her hard enough to gag.

She covered her mouth and nose. Spoiled meat, wet leaves, and mixed with it all, that awful bitter stench. She forced herself to go a little closer. Close enough to make out the red flannel shirt, fallen to pieces around damp matter—brown and pink sewn together by the same white threads—draped over the rubble.

"It's Nick Steadman," she shouted. Now it was curiosity that made her bend at the waist, that weirdly human fascination with things like car accidents and pimple popping. "It's like he's been liquefied," she added to herself. She wished she had a stick to poke at the white strings tangled in with the gooey stuff. It looked like they were the only things holding his meat fabric together. She didn't even think there were bones left.

She pulled back, remembering the wriggling threads in the cuts on his face and the strings that had come out of his eyeball. Those white strings had gotten tangled with threads that had also come out of Kayla's hands and hair. How had those things gotten inside them? Was it infectious? She put her own hands in her pockets to make sure she didn't touch anything.

A rattling wheeze sounded behind her. Erin spun around. The sheer gory wonder of Matt's body and Nick's tenderization had distracted Erin from the dim area beside the mixer. Now she saw the small mass pressed up against the huge machine.

Erin rushed to Dahlia's side. "You're alive!"

Dahlia struggled to lift her head. "Erin." Her voice was barely audible.

"Don't try to talk." Erin took a water bottle out of her pack and filled the cap with a few drops of water. "Can you lift your head?"

Dahlia's head rose a few inches. Her beautiful hair hung lank and matted around her head, the red stained darker on one side as if her scalp had bled profusely and then dried. Her eyes had been swallowed up by purple bruising that spread into her temples, which couldn't be a good sign. Both her right arm and leg looked wrong, misshapen maybe. When Erin looked closer, Dahlia's fingers were as purple as the bruises under her eyes.

"Shit, Dahlia, you're hurt bad." She gave Dahlia a little more water. "You should lie back down."

"Thirsty."

"Just a little at a time, okay?" Were people with concussions supposed to eat and drink? Erin couldn't remember. She wished she had taken one of those wilderness first aid classes Bryan was always talking about.

She had to look away from Dahlia then. What if Bryan had fallen into a sinkhole like this? Mitch Vanderpoel could have been digging all over the forest. A small sinkhole would have definitely been overlooked by the helicopters Search and Rescue used, and the forest was so dense, someone could walk past one and never even notice. Bryan could have been lying in a pit like this, too broken and sick to call back when they shouted his name. He could still be lying dead somewhere, his bones lonely and pale among the rocks.

Erin shook her head. It was all coming full circle now, the weirdness of the woods, the tunnels, the missing girls, Bryan. All of it bearing down on her like the mixer that had slammed down on Matt's broken body. Erin's breath hitched in her throat.

"Wish I could see the trees," Dahlia said, her voice barely audible. "Hate to die without getting to see them a last time."

"Don't talk like that."

She lifted her head the tiniest bit. "Water, please?"

Erin supported the back of Dahlia's head and used the other to hold the bottle to her cracked lips. Something gurgled deep inside Dahlia's chest, and Erin had to squeeze her eyes shut on tears. "You're going to be okay."

Dahlia let the weight of her head sit on Erin's palm for a moment. Then she pushed Erin aside. "There's something inside me that's not me."

"What?"

Dahlia laid her head back on the ground, her eyelids sagging. "It wants . . . to take me over. I've been fighting it in my head, but I can still feel it. Wiggling. Tickling."

Erin took off the headlamp and shone it up and down the length of Dahlia's body, but all she could see was dirty clothing and blood. "I don't—"

Dahlia grabbed Erin's wrist hard enough the joint popped. "I'm not crazy."

Erin held her gaze. "I know you aren't."

Dahlia's fingers slid away from Erin's wrist. Erin caught her hand and focused the light on Dahlia's abraded palm. At the edge of one deep cut, something glinted for a second, moist and pale, before vanishing inside the flesh like a startled worm.

"Fuck!" Erin nearly flung Dahlia's hand aside. For a second, she thought she might vomit. She found herself scrubbing her palm and her wrist on her pants like she could wipe off the contagion. How did it get inside somebody? And was it already inside her?

A light played down the cavern wall, and Erin craned her neck to see a dark outline on the edge of the pit.

"Erin? Oh my god, is that Dahlia?"

"Jordan! Don't—"

She wasn't sure what she wanted to tell him, but it was too late. Jordan's shadow swung out from the top of the wall, hanging silhouetted against the twilit sky for an instant before dropping into their underground realm. He landed lightly, smiling a little like a kid on a rope swing. But the smile died as he unclipped from the line.

"Oh, Dee, you look terrible." He rushed toward them and dropped to his knees.

"Thanks a lot," Dahlia whispered.

He grabbed her hand and pressed it to his face. "You're so cold. Jesus. We've got to get you out of here."

Erin gently pushed the hand out of his grip. "I don't know if we should move her."

His eyes flashed toward her. "We can't just leave her down here. She needs a doctor."

"Erin's right," Dahlia said. She had made her voice stronger for him. Put on a brave face. "I'm hurt bad, Scene. I'm not gonna make it out of this pit."

"No." He shook his head. "I'm not going to let you die down here."

He reached for her hand again and Erin blocked him. "You shouldn't touch her."

Jordan shoved her hand away. "Stop that! Dee, come on, I got you. I can rig up a stretcher, haul you out of here. I know what I'm doing."

Dahlia lifted her head a little. "Do you hear that?" Her left eye began filling up with blood.

"What?" Erin managed to whisper, staring at that red-black eye. Jordan's breath hitched in his throat.

"It's Kayla," Dahlia whispered.

"Kayla isn't here," Erin said, but Dahlia only panted and shook her head.

"She says . . . we're in trouble. That we're never getting out of here. Oh god!" She fell backward, jerking and twitching.

"Dee!" Jordan screamed.

He grabbed her by the shoulders, perhaps to stop the seizure, perhaps to comfort her, but it was the wrong move. Dahlia's shoulders peeled off the ground with an audible *rip*, a sudden stench of bitter mushroom and rotting wood. The sound that burst from her mouth was not a scream, but something worse, something cataclysmic. As she slid from Jordan's hands, her mouth widened around that awful sound and the corners of her lips tore, the flesh ripping into two long red seams stitching her lips to her ears. Erin dug the heels of her hands into her ears.

No one could scream like that. The sound couldn't exist in any human body.

And then Erin saw the threads.

They flailed from the rips in Dahlia's cheeks. They writhed from beneath her shoulders, scrabbling and scurrying across the flaking wood. Erin threw herself backward and the headlamp went flying from where she'd dropped it. Its light spun around the cavern, lighting up Dahlia's body, Jordan's pale face, the dark heaps of debris around them. For a second, Erin saw the twisting cords of flesh-colored threads running from Dahlia's body across the cavern floor, connecting her twisted lower half to the pink mass of flesh Erin had dimly recognized as Matt.

It was Matt no longer. She recognized his black clothing, but he was otherwise as reduced as the husk of Nick Steadman, his limbs flattened and seeping from the seams in his clothes. A series of white and pink cords had bound Dahlia to him and to the fallen timbers and miscellaneous crap that had rained down from the ruined bakery. Every bit of organic material near Dahlia's broken body had been stitched to her by the alien fibers, and their surfaces showed the same erosion as Matt's body.

"Erin!" Jordan shouted, and she saw one of the cords scuttling toward her hand.

"Fuck!" She leaped to her feet, stomping on the wriggling thing, but her running shoes were too soft, the rubbery string resisting her attack. Jordan grabbed a rock and brought it down hard on the cord, the sharp edge of the basalt cutting into the fibers. A thin, pale liquid seeped out, and Dahlia screamed one more time, softer and weaker than the ones before.

"Dahlia." Jordan dropped back to his knees. "Dahlia, don't die."

Her broken mouth opened and closed, blood running down her chin. The fleshy cords beneath her twitched and dribbled out more of the pale liquid. Dahlia's eyes widened. Her breath went out of her in a soft gasp, and then she, too, stopped moving.

"Dahlia!" Jordan fell forward, his face pressing to her chest. "Dahlia, please!"

Erin pried him away, squeezing him tight. "You can't touch her, Jordan. Those strings—"

"Dahlia!" he howled, and then he buried his face in Erin's shoulder, sobbing. She had never seen anyone cry like this, never felt the hot damp of heartbreak seep through her clothes and trickle down her neck. She remembered lying on her bed in her dorm room, crying for Bryan. She had cried just like this.

"It's okay," she lied, rubbing the knobs of his spine. "It's okay."

They sat a long time like that, the cavern going quiet around them. The smell of sunblock and bug spray and male sweat made a pleasant counterpoint to the stink of dirt and death and the bitter stench she'd begun to associate with the thread-stuff. Then Jordan shook once, twice, and then pulled away, wiping his eyes.

"Thanks."

"I'm so sorry," she said. "I barely knew her."

He made a little gasp but caught the sob. "She was my best friend. She *knew* me, you know? Even when I was some stupid kid with pink hair, she *knew* me."

Erin rubbed his back. She was crying, too. She didn't have any real right to cry for Dahlia, so maybe she cried for Jordan and his loss, and maybe she cried for Bryan, and maybe for all the lost people who had never been known by anyone the way Dahlia had known Jordan, her best friend in the world. She risked glancing at Dahlia's body, and flinched at the horrible smile split into her face. Deep inside the tissue, she thought she saw something writhe.

The spell broke. "We have to get out of here," she said.

"No." Jordan shook his head. "I can't leave her."

Erin got to her feet. "We have to get back and tell somebody about this. Those thread things are contagious. Kayla had them, and Nick Steadman, too." She led him away from the bodies and toward the tunnel where she'd climbed in. She didn't think she was in any shape to climb out of the hole in the roof.

Jordan followed. "Steadman. Fuck."

"We have to get Olivia and find Kayla," Erin said. "She must have gotten out through the tunnel before it closed up—we found her hat. And we've got to find Hari, too. Get everyone together, talk to the police."

"You think this is all connected? The weird shit down in this sinkhole and the missing girls?"

"Missing people," Olivia corrected from the other side of the rubble barrier. Erin felt a surge of relief at the sound of her voice. "My son is missing. And Erin's brother. It's not just girls."

Erin hesitated. She'd been waiting for the right time to bring it up, and she wasn't sure this was it. But his mother deserved to know the truth. "I've seen Scott," she called. "He's the one who freed me before the collapse."

She could hear Olivia's breath go out of her, and then a stifled sob. "I knew he was alive. I knew it."

"You were right, Olivia," Erin said. "About Scott, your dad's mining, everything."

Something rustled behind them. Erin spun around, expecting the flesh-cords to reach for her or more debris to come loose or something dangerous. She didn't see a thing.

"Let's get out of here," Jordan said.

"Yeah," Erin agreed. She nodded for Jordan to scramble up the heap of debris first, then followed. At the top of the mound, Erin turned to look back into the dimly lit cavern of death.

A thin blue haze hung over the heap that had been Dahlia, motes inside it twinkling like tiny stars. Erin's skin crawled as they roiled in the faint air currents of the room and then settled over the debris. Were those spores? Was this how the threads started?

"Come on," Jordan shouted. Erin launched herself up the rubble, and wished she could hold her breath.

CHAPTER TWENTY-FIVE

ERIN STARED AT DAHLIA'S HOUSE AS OLIVIA SPOKE softly into her phone. Erin supposed it wasn't Dahlia's house any longer. She wondered how long it would take for someone else to move in and take down the orange curtains in the front window, to scrape the "Protect Our Winters" sticker off the frame of the screen door. The back of Erin's nose felt swollen with unshed tears. Improbably, she could still smell the vanilla cookie scent of the trove of candles in the back seat.

Olivia hung up her cell. "I left a message with my friend at the station."

"They wouldn't put you through to Duvall?" Erin wiped her hands with another baby wipe, certain she could still feel the grit of the cavern clinging to her skin. Dirt—and who knew what else.

Her knee was jiggling. She pressed it down with her palms and then wanted to wash her hand again. Every inch of her felt contaminated. What the fuck was that glowing dust down there? She knew it was the same stuff she'd seen in the pool house. Knew it with total certainty. Had she touched it there? Had Dahlia or Kayla? She couldn't remember. All the events of the past three days spun in her head, her brain too tired to keep it all straight. Tired and terrified. Fuck, she wished she knew where Hari was.

Olivia gripped Erin's hands on the package of wipes. "Stop."

The old woman fixed her gaze on Erin's face. "Stop thinking about the cave."

Erin's lips quivered. "I can't." Her breath hitched in her chest. "Oh my god, what if Bryan—"

"*Stop.*" Olivia's voice was fierce. The furrows around her eyes and mouth looked deeper today, the hollows beneath her eyes darker. The trip underground had aged her, Erin realized. But she kept going, kept making phone calls, kept driving them places. She was just a tiny old lady, fragile and tired, and she kept going.

"Okay," Erin whispered.

Olivia pulled a tissue from the packet tucked in the sunglasses holder on the dashboard and offered it to Erin. "What's next? Your friend Kayla is still out there somewhere."

"I don't know. We find Hari, I guess." Erin wiped her nose. "He's not here, so maybe he's chasing a lead."

Jordan flashed his headlights in their rear window, impatient. Olivia ignored him. "Any ideas?"

"He mentioned . . ." Erin thought back to the last time she'd seen him. "A guy. A suspect. Somebody who worked for the Steadmans. Craig something."

"Martin." Olivia turned the key in the ignition.

"You know him?"

"I sold him his house." They pulled out of Dahlia's street, winding uphill toward the elementary school. Jordan followed. He didn't even text to ask where they were going.

"Hari said he was a sex offender."

Olivia tapped her turn signal. Sirens sounded in the distance, headed toward the highway. "I didn't say I *liked* selling him a house."

They parked in front of a good-looking ranch house, but the

older woman pointed across the street to a much smaller unit painted an unfortunate shade of brown. A concrete walkway ran like a berm across the shaggy lawn, beelining to the tiny front stoop. The rain had returned, and the pits and pockets in the cement sparkled with rain. "Looks like he's home," she said. "He's been driving that red Camaro for nearly a decade."

Jordan rapped on the passenger side window. Erin lowered it, and he stuck his head in the window, his ball cap emblazoned with the insignia of the arbor company. He looked official, like he was about to inform someone he needed to take down the neighbor's dying maple. "What are we doing at Craig Martin's house?"

Erin frowned. "Did you go to school with him like the Steadmans?"

"Everybody knows Craig. I'm embarrassed to admit it in front of Olivia, but before pot was legal . . ." He crinkled his nose. "Don't make me finish that sentence."

Erin had to laugh. "Okay, so he probably won't shoot you on sight." She scrubbed her sweaty palms on the leather seats, but only smeared the dampness further. "What do we say to him?"

"Let me do the talking," Olivia said, opening her door. "People are used to nosy old ladies."

Miserable as she was, even Erin had to chuckle at that. Jordan was still smiling as he opened the door for her. "Milady." He waved her onto the sidewalk.

Then he paused, looking up the block at a Dodge Ram parked half on the sidewalk. "I think that's Howie's pickup."

"Shit," Erin whispered. "I don't know if we should be doing this."

"The door's open," Olivia called out.

"What?" Jordan rushed forward, Olivia hot on his heels.

Every instinct warning her not to proceed, Erin took a deep breath and followed the two locals toward the house.

The gap between the door and its frame was a dark seam. Whatever hid on the other side, Erin was certain was nothing good.

"Craig?" Jordan called out, the door swinging open at his touch. He stopped with one foot over the threshold. "Do you smell that?"

Erin took a tentative step forward and the gray smell of unwashed dishes and wet dishcloth slapped her in the face. She covered her nose with her baby-wipe-scented hand.

Craig Martin kept the curtains tightly drawn over the house's small windows, and the light from the open door barely penetrated the entryway. Not that it was much of an entryway—just a two-foot square of linoleum in front of the door, a black rubber welcome mat squeaking under Jordan's foot. Someone must have jacked up the thermostat because it felt nearly tropical inside. Erin pulled her sleeve over her free hand and felt for a light switch beside the door.

A floor lamp stuttered on the far side of the room, the light bulb taking a moment to warm to life. Craig had decorated his home in the style of Affordable Man Cave. A brown microsuede couch had its back to the door, fleece throw blanket emblazoned with the Seahawks logo dripping off one arm. A fifty-two-inch flat-screen TV filled the far wall, speakers angled from the corners on either side. Watching a movie in the small space would have felt immersive or perhaps even claustrophobic.

In the center of the room, a black metal coffee table had been kicked out of square, most of its shape hidden by the bulk of the couch. Erin knew just by looking at it something had gone very wrong. Small as it was, Craig Martin took pride in his home, in his entertainment center, in the movie-theater darkness of the space. He would have never allowed his coffee table to get cockeyed.

Jordan turned left, where an open doorway with a hint of daylight promised a bathroom. "Oh, shit." He pulled his shirt up over his nose. "You guys, check it out."

The bathroom must have been assembled in the late 1980s and never redone. Counters were square peach tiles, the trim and cabinet faces all light gold oak. The mirrored surface of the three-sectioned medicine cabinet was spattered with toothpaste.

And all along the countertop, just at the points where someone's fingers might trail over the tile, ran four lines of blue mildew. Beside the door the lines coalesced into a mass of marbled green-to-brown-to-purple-to-yellow . . . stuff. It reminded Erin of the turkey tail mushrooms she'd seen out hiking, but the thickness and the fabulous crenelations made it like no fungus Erin had ever seen before. Its ruffles ran down the front of the bathroom cabinets all the way to the floor and then crawled up the interior doorframe, where it grew so thickly it prevented the door from closing. Erin craned her neck to follow the fungal explosion into the shadows of the living room ceiling.

"I've got to take a picture." Jordan pulled out his phone and turned sideways to pass through the bathroom doorway, sucking in his belly.

Erin understood. The thought of letting those threads brush against even her shirt . . . she shuddered and took a step back herself. Now she noticed the warped and buckled texture of the living room wall. A tiny shudder ran down the Sheetrock, and then something twitched beneath the beige carpeting, scurrying toward her feet.

"The floor!"

The ground gave a sudden heave, knocking Olivia into the couch. The older woman caught herself and screamed, her whole body vibrating with shock and terror. Erin rushed to steady her, but then she, too, saw over the back of the couch. A man in a red shirt sprawled on his stomach across the cushions, his head spun impossibly backward to stare at them.

Only Craig Martin couldn't stare at them, would never stare again, not with the pink and purple and white tendrils boiling out of the bloody sockets where someone had gouged out his eyes and replaced them with hell.

"Fuck!" Jordan shouted. The floor gave another buck and jolt, smashing him into Erin's side.

The floor lamp toppled. The light bulb popped, plunging them into darkness. The smell of mushroom and mildew thickened, driving the air from Erin's lungs.

"Erin!" Olivia shouted. "Jordan, where are you?"

Erin tried to draw breath to answer her and burst into a coughing fit. They'd only been inches apart a few seconds ago, but in the darkness, Olivia could have been a mile away. Erin felt around, hoping to catch the other woman's arm. Her hand felt only hot, moist air.

The floor roiled beneath Erin's right foot and she hopped backward with a gasp. Something squished beneath her other foot. Blue and green glitter shot up in the air, roiling in the air currents. Flickers of light darted around, lighting up Jordan's pale face, dancing across the surface of the TV, settling in drifts along the back of the couch, billowing up on the currents of heat rising from the exploded light bulb.

Erin's breath stopped in her chest.

Then something tickled the skin above the tops of her socks.

She screamed again, kicking and stomping, but her pants tightened around her calf as if something had seized her leg.

"Jordan!" she shrieked. Her skin burned as if touched by acid.

The front door swung open, the light nearly blinding. "Come on!" Olivia shouted from the doorway.

Erin tried to yank her foot free and nearly fell as the burning grip on her leg tightened. "Help me!"

Jordan grabbed her by the wrist. With a nasty, damp-sounding squelch, the hold on Erin's leg ripped free. She stumbled again, but Jordan shoved her toward the door. She leaped down the stairs, gasping for clean air.

Jordan collapsed on the sidewalk. "What did we just see? The *fuck* did we just see?"

"They looked like mushrooms," Olivia gasped.

Erin yanked up the bottom of her jeans. Her skin looked irritated, but not broken. She rubbed her hand on the wet sidewalk and then scrubbed the rain into her skin. Every inch of her felt contaminated.

"I'm never eating mushrooms again," Jordan said.

Mushrooms. Erin knew nothing about mushrooms. It was time to catch up. And no matter what Scott Vanderpoel had said about the man, Ray Hendrix was probably the closest expert on the subject around.

Erin adjusted her jeans and then stood up, catching their eyes. "We need to talk to the Mushroom Man."

THROUGH THE SMALL WINDOW IN THE TOP HALF OF Ray Hendrix's door, she could see into an entryway. If she leaned to her right, she could see the living room, and if she leaned to her left, a kitchen, both of those rooms wood-paneled and cabin-cozy. Someone had painted the woodwork in the entryway white and installed a bench with open cubbies below. A neat row of Shaker pegs held a pair of binoculars, a fishing creel, a yellow rain slicker, and a collapsible umbrella. The whole array gave off a sense of crowded tidiness.

Her hand on the clean white wood looked wrong. Even after using more of Olivia's wet wipes, her skin felt dirty. Between the ridges of her tendons, she thought something slithered.

She squeezed her eyes shut. They burned with tiredness. When she opened them, the veins on the back of her hand were just veins again, immobile and blue, not creeping white strings.

"Do you hear anything?" Jordan asked.

She shook her head and knocked again, and this time Ray emerged from the kitchen, wiping his hands on a dish towel. He threw it over his shoulder as he opened the door. The smell of spaghetti sauce wafted out, making Erin's stomach howl.

"Hi," she began, and stopped, because even though she'd had the entire drive to his house to come up with a way to explain why she was on his doorstep, she still couldn't imagine explaining this shit to another human being.

Olivia stepped forward. "Sorry to disturb you at dinnertime, Ray, but we have some pressing questions about mushrooms, and as you're the local expert . . ."

"Olivia Vanderpoel! What a delight. Of course, come inside." Beaming, Ray Hendrix beckoned them into the living room. He shifted some books off the leather couch and encouraged them toward it. "Please. Have a seat."

"Thank you," Olivia said in tones so gracious she herself might have been the hostess.

"Coffee?" Ray asked. "I just made a pot."

"No need to trouble yourself," she murmured, even as Jordan said, "Oh, god, yes," and they all had a little laugh at that.

"I'll be right back," Ray said, chuckling.

Erin got the sense he rarely had company. She looked around the living room, noticing the table by the window with the houseplants. Scott's statue had been sitting there when she'd come by yesterday, but now it was gone. The skin of her arms prickled.

Ray appeared with a carafe and a stack of mugs. He put them down on the table and fanned himself with the dish towel. "Awfully warm for April, don't you think? Does anybody take anything in their coffee?"

"Black is great," Jordan said.

"Thank you," Olivia said.

Erin just nodded and accepted the cup when Ray handed it to her. Scott Vanderpoel had warned her to stay away from this man. But he seemed so kind, so friendly. He had been nothing but helpful since the first moment she met him. She clasped her hands tighter around the coffee mug and tried to let its heat comfort her.

"So, what kind of mushrooms are you interested in?" Ray asked, settling into a battered chair that faced the couch. "I can steer you toward a patch, if it's something in season around here."

Jordan leaned forward. "We found a kind of mushroom we're not familiar with. Is there any way to identify it?" He pulled out his phone and brought up the photo he'd taken in Craig Martin's bathroom. "Sorry about the lighting."

Ray leaned in, squinting at the photo. "You can't always ID a mushroom on just its looks," he warned. "There are a lot of look-alikes, and those you'd need a spore print for. These look a little like *Stereum ostrea*, or false turkey tail, but there's no way to tell without studying its physical structure."

Jordan looked pointedly at Erin. She put down her mug. "We found some threadlike . . . stuff, too. We were wondering if it might be mycelium."

"Mycelium?" Ray frowned. "I suppose. Although it was probably a rhizomorph, not mycelium."

"And what is a rhizomorph?" Olivia asked. Erin admired the way she didn't sound irritated by his jargon.

Ray sat back in his seat, smiling now. "Well, a hypha—the technical term for a strand of mycelium—is maybe half a millimeter thick at its thickest. A rhizomorph is like yarn, a bunch of hyphae joined together into one thicker cord. They can grow to tremendous lengths. There's an *Armillaria* in Eastern Oregon that covers almost four square miles of ground, and they've got rhizomorphs that might go all the way across the structure."

"Unbelievable." Jordan gaped.

"Could you identify a mushroom from its rhizomorph?" Erin asked.

Ray shook his head. "Not every fungi produces rhizomorphs, but plenty do. They all pretty much just look like little roots or threads."

"Threads," Erin repeated, seeing once more the strands wriggling out of Nick Steadman's face. "Can those move?"

"Move? I mean, they grow, like roots, but no, they don't move." He was giving her a concerned look.

"She's just asking," Olivia interjected, "because we were reading about how fungi is more closely related to animals than plants. And animals move."

"I'm no mycologist—that's a fungi scientist," he mansplained, "but it seems unlikely. Fungi have perfected the art of life at a standstill."

"You said something about spores?" Erin was nervous about saying something else crazy-sounding, but they needed more information. "I think these glow in the dark. I saw a bunch on some wood where we found the mushrooms."

Ray was making a face. "That's also pretty unlikely. You wouldn't even notice the spores of most fungi, they're so tiny. They can take twenty-four hours to produce enough for a good print, and that's on white, untreated paper."

Erin sagged back in her seat. She had been certain Ray would be able to help them, but she could hear how little information she actually had, how desperately she was flailing for answers.

Ray reached for his coffee mug and stopped. "Although, those questions remind me of something. Something I saw, oh, way back in the seventies."

Olivia clasped her hands over her crossed knee. "Oh, goodness. We were practically kids then."

"Mm-hmm." Ray took a long drink, his eyes unfocused with thought. "I was actually out with your dad, Olivia. It was before I got hired by the sheriff's department; I was eighteen or nineteen maybe, working summers at the old sawmill. Me and Mitch were both interested in mushrooms, so sometimes we'd go out hunting together. He took me to a place where he'd found what he called 'the mother of all shrooms.' An old mine shaft, out past Hillier."

"Hillier?" Jordan repeated. Erin sat up straight.

"Yeah, there're a lot of old test bores out there. Most of them never panned out, but Mitch always thought they should have been better explored. The Hillier mine brought up lots of quicksilver, back in the day. A bit of gold, too. People have always said these mountains had more hidden inside them."

Olivia leaned in. "He was obsessed with mining."

"Yeah, well." Ray crunched up his face, going back into his memories. "It was a weird site," he said. "A short, shallow tunnel with a collapse like something had punched in the roof at some time. He'd managed to dig through the rubble. The tunnel went into—I wouldn't call it a sinkhole, but maybe a landslide or something had cut away part of the mountain. A big gouge in the land. He said it had been full of shrooms just days earlier, big ones, colors like he'd never seen. But it was all gone by the time we got there. I thought maybe he was misremembering the site, but when we cut back the duff, we could see the rhizomorphs. Big, thick cords, nearly as big around as my pinkie."

He shook his head, came out of his reverie. "I'd almost forgotten about that! I never did see any of those mushrooms. But your dad insisted they were out there."

Tears had come up in Olivia's eyes. "It's good to talk about him," she said. "He had a strange dementia, at the end. He couldn't even speak."

Erin got to her feet. The coffee was doing its work, and this seemed like a good time to let Olivia enjoy a moment longer with Ray's memories of her dad. "Could I use your restroom?"

"Sure. Through the mudroom and the kitchen. Can't miss it."

She hurried past the tidy entryway and the spaghetti-scented kitchen. The bathroom continued the motifs of wood paneling and tidiness; a Mason jar full of eucalyptus provided a particularly pleasant touch.

Leaning over to pull her pants back up, she noticed a small red heap under the old claw-foot bathtub. She washed her hands with the bar of oatmeal soap, but then looked back at the red fabric. Ray didn't seem like the kind of man to own a tee shirt, and that's what the knit fabric looked like to her.

She stooped and stretched to reach it. Its folds were stiff, crispy with some kind of white glue reminiscent of papier-mâché; she dropped it and felt an immediate urge to wash her hands again. But she could see the serging on the hems of what looked like cap sleeves, and the curve of what had to be a collar. A polo shirt. A woman's polo shirt. She nudged it with her toe, and it flopped over so she could see the three small white buttons, the embroidery over the heart.

She stared at the words.

Cazadero Brewing.

Ray had been a sheriff's deputy. He'd lived here his whole life, knew every back road and every hiding spot the woods had to offer. If anyone could get away with kidnapping girls and hiding their bodies in secret places, it was probably him.

He seemed so fucking nice.

Erin doubled over, retching but keeping it down. She kicked the shirt back under the bathtub and then forced a few deep breaths, trying to pull herself together. The last thing they needed was for Ray to realize she'd figured him out.

It took everything in her to walk out of the bathroom and calmly smile as she headed back into the living room. Jordan was laughing at something Ray said. Even Olivia looked like she was having a good time.

"Hey, I just heard from Hari," Erin said, her voice so fake and sweet she almost didn't recognize herself. "He'd like to meet up at the brewery, so we should probably get moving." Jordan's eyebrows knit together, and she fixed him with a piercing look. "Seriously, he's really excited about something."

Olivia got to her feet. "Certainly. We wouldn't want to keep him waiting. Thank you so much, Ray."

"Of course." He stood to sweep a bow over her hand. "And don't be a stranger. I can't believe we've never gotten to chat like this."

Olivia beamed at him and motioned Jordan to move along. Erin held the door.

"Thanks, Ray!" she called behind them, and closed the door gently. She wanted to scream and run down the driveway, but she managed to keep herself at a walk.

"What the hell is going on?" Jordan hissed. "How could Hari call if you lost your cell phone?"

"I found something," Erin whispered.

"What?" Olivia asked, bumping into Erin's shoulder. Too interested. They had to look relaxed.

"Just keep walking," Erin said. "Tell me something about one of the houses you're selling."

But Erin couldn't take her own advice. Even as Olivia started describing some house near town, Erin found herself glancing over her shoulder.

Ray Hendrix stood on his front porch, the dish towel back on his shoulder as he watched them leave. And he didn't smile when her eyes accidentally met his.

He held her gaze as he reached for the dish towel and held it in front of him—and gave it a savage twist.

CHAPTER TWENTY-SIX

THE BLOND WOMAN—BARELY BLOND, AS MOST OF her head was now covered in wriggling white threads— worked her way deeper into the tunnel, squeezing between the warm and pungent outcroppings of Strange flesh. Rhizomorphs grew to the thickness of her waist, charged with the electrical communications of a million Strange organisms. Shelves of pink and purple and teal fruits, in shape and texture something between a turkey tail mushroom and a scallop shell, formed the new ceiling and floor of the old mining shaft. Some of these hard extrusions dated back to the landslide that had opened this tunnel and stirred the sleeping spores to life. The shelves had grown now to the size of a child's sled. The woman had to hang on to their crenelated edges to balance on the rough ground, her fingers vibrating with the thrum of the Strangeness's call.

Here in the heart of it, that voice was impossible to ignore. The pupil of the woman's left eye had blown open from the final conflict in her brain, the moment where the Strangeness had forced her to climb into the test bore and she had tried so desperately to reclaim herself. Now she scrabbled forward, her body a machine, her mind a shadow.

Fruiting bodies narrowed the tunnel. The room grew hotter. Once this had been a small cave, sacred to humans who had come here in long-forgotten days, but a cosmic accident had ripped it open, spearing the Strangeness through the lid of the cave and deep into the ground. It had barely stayed alive here in the cold and the dark with nothing to fuel it except the occasional cave spider. And then the landslide had brought the first man, and everything changed.

The Strangeness vibrated with pleasure, recalling that moment. Its rhizomorphs flickered with a peachy inner glow as its chemistry shifted, and the woman let out a soft, happy sigh. She burrowed into the wall beside her, moving her cheeks over the threads lining the tiny, softer growths that flourished here now, peach and yellow and neon pink shades she saw even with her eyes squeezed tight. The past and present merged here, all of it pure chemical experience: she felt, tasted, smelled Mitch Vanderpoel, his blood running metallic from a scrape on his knuckles. She heard, felt, smelled his breathing change as he discovered the silver nodule in the rock at his feet, the carbon in his exhalations seeping into the hard carapace of her tiny, purple body and stirring it from the torpor it had entered a thousand, no, a million, no, a billion years earlier when it was shattered from its place in its world and swept into the void of space.

Warmth and light and carbon were what it craved, and here was something that could provide it with all three.

The woman's fingers brushed other fingers. The threads on her skin sparked against the other's. Memory flickered in the broken depths of her brain, but not her memories. Something shared. A river ran green beside the thinker's bare white feet. A woman with red hair smiled, and she felt her stomach flip—not her actual stomach, but the one belonging to the person doing the remembering. Another one of the Strange.

The moment passed. The Strangeness increased the peach-hued chemicals in its rhizomorphs and directed larger threads into the woman's shoulders, abdomen, uterus. Tasting. Sampling. Storing.

Her lips moved to herself as the chemical cocktail blurred the borders between now and then, herself and the other beings the Strangeness had absorbed into the cave.

The wind stirring every hair on her body in a frisson of speed, her paws barely touching the ground.

The taste of chocolate, the round orb of a cherry pressed to the ridges in her hard palate.

The soft crunch of an insect's carapace between her mandibles.

The mineral tang of water flowing over her body, seeping into her pores as she slowly dissolved the wall beneath her.

Matt's mouth on her neck, the steaming water of the hot spring with its faint tang of sulfur.

The border between what had been the woman and what had been the Strange vanished, and for the first time in her life, the woman felt completely and utterly safe. Perfectly at home. Loved as she had never been loved.

The smile stretched across her face even as the threads and the rhizomorphs slowly pushed her back out of the place she was already calling Haven. Her marching orders appeared in her mind, and she hurried to follow their directions, meeting her assistant at the end of the mining tunnel.

The Strange were in danger, and she was the only one who could save them all.

CHAPTER TWENTY-SEVEN

"RAY HENDRIX? A SERIAL KILLER? I CAN'T BELIEVE IT," Jordan said. "In sixth grade he gave a presentation to our class about how to watch out for kidnappers."

"He's in the perfect position to abduct girls," Olivia said, hunching over the steering wheel, her face grim. "We have to do something about this."

"But first we have to find Hari," Erin said, grabbing the bar above the window as the Volvo skidded around a corner. The windshield wipers pounded a frenzied rhythm. "We don't know where Howie Steadman is, either—he was supposed to go to Craig Martin's, but we only found one body."

"We only looked in two rooms," Jordan reminded her.

"We're going to the police," Olivia announced, glancing into the rearview mirror toward Erin. Her face was drawn, the lines around her mouth gullies. "All of this is too much. We need help."

"Watch out!" Jordan shouted as something, no some*one*, darted into the forest road. A pale face was lit up for a moment in their headlights before the blue-and-brown-clad man leaped for safety.

Olivia stomped on the brakes, throwing Erin into the dash. The man crashed into the bushes, vanishing into the undergrowth.

"That was Scott." Olivia threw open her door. "Scott!"

Erin grabbed at her, but the older woman was already running into the night. The seat belt clip fought against Erin's fingers before she was finally free and out the door. In an instant, the warm rain soaked her hair and her tee shirt. "Olivia!"

"Scott!" Olivia screamed, the force of her voice nearly doubling her over on the edge of the road. The cords in her neck stuck out. "Come back!"

The woman stumbled out of the range of the car's lights, tripping on a branch or rock at the shoulder of the road. Erin barely caught her. The woman trembled in her grip, the rain flattening her silver hair, her trench coat wilting in its force.

"Come on, I've got you." Erin pulled her back toward the Volvo, where Jordan was already moving the real estate supplies onto the floor. He shook out the red plaid blanket and wrapped it around Olivia's shoulders as Erin eased her into the back seat.

"I'll drive," he said.

"That *was* Scott, wasn't it?" Olivia whispered.

"I think so," Erin said, getting back in the passenger seat. She turned around to meet Olivia's eyes. "He was wearing a blue fleece both times I saw him."

"Why would he run away from me?"

Now it was Erin's turn to hand the other woman a tissue. "I don't know."

"Maybe he didn't recognize you," Jordan said. "In the rain. Or maybe he was in a hurry."

Olivia wiped her cheek on the blanket. "He looked like he was headed for town."

"Let's go to your house," Erin said. "Maybe he's going there, too. If he cuts through the woods, he's on the right path."

Jordan gave her a significant glance, and she made a noncommittal face. It didn't matter if Scott was headed home or not; she wanted to get Olivia someplace warm and dry. The old lady had risked enough for one day.

They drove in silence for a few minutes, the Volvo's heater going into overdrive. The vanilla cookie smell thickened, not so much cloying as soporific. Erin pinched her arm to help her eyes stay open. How long had it been since she'd had a decent night's sleep?

She turned her gaze out the window, at the thick darkness of the woods. The occasional white alder stood out in the mass of firs and hemlocks, like a figure dressed in pale clothing trying to catch her attention. Like Bryan, begging her to look for him.

Why didn't you come, Erin? his ghost whispered in her ear. *Why didn't you try to find me?*

She pinched herself again and they turned onto another road. The sight of an actual house with its lights on was so comforting she nearly waved.

They took a back route to the Vanderpoel house. In the middle of the driveway, a Clackamas County sheriff's SUV sat beside Jordan's work truck.

"Oh, shit," he breathed.

The door of the SUV opened, and Deputy Duvall stepped out. Only the lower half of her face showed beneath her plastic-covered trooper's hat, and that half was scowling.

They pulled up beside her because what else could they do? At least she already knew their story.

"Inside," Duvall barked. "Now."

Olivia led them forward, still huddled in her blanket. Duvall waited for them to enter before following them inside and locking the door behind her. They all took seats around her dining room table.

Deputy Duvall dropped her dripping hat on the floor beside her and looked around the table. "You people have been involved with a lot of crazy stuff the last few days," she said, "but what I want to know is: Why did a fugitive from the law have your cell phone when he died, Miss Harper?"

She slapped a plastic bag with Erin's phone down on the table. The screen lit up with about a million notifications.

"Oh my god, Hari," Erin breathed. And then the full weight of Duvall's sentence crashed down on her. "Wait, Howie Steadman is dead?"

Duvall folded her arms across her chest.

"Deputy, I believe—" Olivia began, but Duvall cut her off.

"I'm talking to Miss Harper." Duvall's eyes didn't move from Erin's face.

Erin took a deep breath and began to unspool the events of the past twenty-four hours. Every word of it made her more exhausted. As she spoke, Olivia got up from the table, making noise in the kitchen. A microwave beeped a few times as Erin finished explaining their escape from the sinkhole.

Deputy Duvall sighed. She glanced up at Olivia, now carrying a plate full of what smelled like banana nut muffins. "May I? And do you have any coffee?"

"I'll make a fresh pot."

For a minute, everyone was quiet, focused on normal things like eating. Olivia must have heard Erin's stomach, because she appeared with a hunk of cheese and a box of crackers, as well as a clean coffee mug for the deputy. Erin's hands shook as she shoveled food into her mouth. "What happened to Howie?"

"He ran out into 13th Avenue a little after five o'clock. He was hit by a school bus. Luckily, no kids were on board—the driver had just finished dropping off a group of fourth graders coming home from a field trip," Duvall said with a scowl.

Five o'clock. The dry cracker stuck in Erin's throat. It must have happened just minutes before they arrived at Craig's house.

She managed to swallow down the lump. "Is the bus driver okay?"

Deputy Duvall ripped the top off a muffin. "Two other cars were struck and a woman had to be airlifted into Portland for urgent care. Howie died on the spot."

"13th Avenue?" Jordan shot a look at Erin. "That's two blocks from Craig's house."

Erin looked up as Olivia brought in the coffee, the ramifications of it all spinning in her head. "Were Howie and Craig friends?"

Olivia shrugged. "I mean, they worked together."

"And drank together at the A-Street," Jordan added.

"Do I even want to know?" Deputy Duvall filled her mug. "Since you arrived in town, Harper, I've dealt with more bodies, missing people, and criminals than I have in my entire career."

Erin glanced across at Olivia, unsure how to break the news they had solved at least one of the mysteries on the deputy's list. But the words "missing people" had hit Olivia hard. She was staring into space, her mind obviously on Scott.

"Deputy Duvall," Erin began. "We—"

"I'm not done asking you questions, Harper." Duvall put down her coffee cup. "I need you to explain the connection with Craig Martin."

Jordan shifted in his seat. "You know who he is, right?"

"Of course."

"Okay, so we went to his place, because Erin thought her friend Hari might have gone to interview him for their podcast. And the door was open, so it wasn't exactly trespassing."

Pieces slid together in Erin's head. "It must have been Howie who left the door open!"

"Stop it," Duvall ordered. The tiredness was gone, her posture bristling. "Tell me straight up what happened at Craig's house."

Olivia raised a commanding hand. Despite her damp hair and the circles under her eyes, she had drawn herself back into the severe businesswoman Erin had met beside the visitors' center. "We walked in and found Craig's body on his couch. Someone had broken his neck and dug out his eyes. Is that clear enough for you, Deputy?"

Her tone was pure ice. At that moment, Erin realized there were two Olivia Vanderpoels, one a perfect hostess and loving mother, and one an iron-willed executive who had cannily profited from the crash of the Oregon lumber industry to keep her town in a steely grip just like her father and her grandfather before her. The two overlapped, but only because she could switch them on and off as quickly as she needed.

Erin was glad she was on their side.

Deputy Duvall stood up, her face going cop-blank. "And did you report this?"

A flashing light from the plastic bag on the kitchen table caught Erin's attention, but Duvall and Vanderpoel only had eyes for each other. Erin shifted her weight forward, trying to see what had popped up on her phone's home screen.

"I'm not finished," Olivia said coldly. "I'm reporting to *you* right now we have discovered proof Ray Hendrix is behind the death of Elena Lopez."

Duvall sat up straight in her chair. "What kind of proof?"

"Her work shirt," Erin said. "But if you go there, it'll probably be gone. I think he knows we're onto him." A wave of unhappiness spilled over her. She should have taken the shirt. Hari would have.

"Ray Hendrix," Duvall repeated. She rubbed her eyes, the exhaustion redoubled. "The detective in charge of Elena's case brought Ray on as an advisor."

"What?" Erin shook her head. "Why?"

"It's my fault." Duvall sighed. "I thought the mushrooms on her body might have been significant, and I recommended Ray as our local expert. The only time this asshole from HQ has listened to me yet."

Jordan reached for her hand. "You couldn't have known, Claire."

She pulled her hand away, giving him a sad look. "I don't think the department is going to believe your story, Jordan. Not after all the weird shit you and your new friend have been involved in. I'm gonna need physical proof."

"We don't have any." Erin's stomach felt like someone had dropped something heavy and indigestible into it. Something like despair. "My friend Hari might have some leads, but we don't know where he is."

"You've got through the night." Deputy Duvall got to her feet. "I'm going to need all three of you to come to the sheriff's office first thing tomorrow morning to give your statements." She turned on her heel and strode through the doorway into the kitchen—leaving Erin's phone on the table beside the muffins.

Erin pounced on her phone and the text preview. She got only a second to read it before the floor in the kitchen creaked again, and Erin quickly dropped the baggie and went for the cheese instead.

Duvall gave her a sly look. "Almost forgot my hat." She put the bag with the phone in her pocket. "I'm legally required to take this to evidence. You should probably buy another." She stooped to pick up the damp hat and gave it a shake before putting it on her head. "I'll see you all in the morning."

Olivia followed the deputy to the front door. Jordan waited until he heard the sound of the door latching. "What did it say?"

"It was Hari," Erin said. "And all it said was 'Steadmans' house.'"

EVEN PARKED ACROSS THE STREET, ERIN COULD TELL something was wrong with the Steadman house. A blue-gray film covered all the windows, black goo trickling from the drainage holes in the aluminum frames. Beneath the flickering porch light, the front door hung cockeyed, a broken strand of police tape wavering in the breeze. The leaves of the rhododendrons in the front yard hung limply, patches of gray blooming against the waxy green.

"Jesus," Jordan whispered.

Erin turned off the Volvo, and they sat in silence for a minute. The night was muggy and hot, darkness settling thickly around the blocky ranch house. The porch light's small range left the edges of the yard in shadow. "I'm scared to go in there," Erin admitted.

"Yeah." The word came out muffled. Jordan cleared his throat and tried again. "Yeah. We've already seen a lot of weird shit today."

"I kind of wish I could go back to the Erin who walked into that pool house and warn her it was only just the beginning."

He shot her one of his crooked grins. "You wouldn't believe yourself." He opened the car door, letting in the stink of wet washcloths left to fester on the back of the kitchen sink, the fetor of an open drain choked with black grime, the rancid stench of wood breaking down under a constant Oregon rain.

Erin gagged as she got out of the car. It smelled a hundred times worse than Craig Martin's house.

"What do you think it is?" Jordan mused. "It can't be natural, right? Like, it's a mutant fungus caused by toxic mining waste, or created by climate change, or—"

"Maybe it's both of those things," Erin said. "Maybe it's every bad idea we've ever had, rolled up into one foul package."

They stood in the driveway, bracing themselves. A multicolored ribbon ran around the front door as if a rainbow was trying to squeeze itself out of the house. Erin didn't want to take a step closer to the rotting place, but Hari was in there. She stuck her hand in her pocket, feeling for the canister of mace Olivia had given her—neither Jordan nor Erin feeling confident enough in themselves to take the shotgun—and then forced her feet toward the front door.

When the dog door burst open, she was almost ready for it.

The . . . *thing* hit her in the chest and knocked her backward, the mace flying out of her hand, her head hitting the ground. Hot slaver splattered her cheeks and only her arms kept the snarling creature from sinking its teeth into her face. Black fur sloughed off its flesh, a liquid the pale blue of skim milk dribbling all over her. She thrust her forearm into its throat, and it made a choking sound. She bucked and twisted, pushing harder into its windpipe. Its claws dug into her right arm, pinned beneath its weight.

Jordan leaped onto its back, grabbing its ears, which ripped off in his hands. He fell backward, the air going out of him. It yipped in pain.

A dog. It had been a dog once. A black Lab.

No time to dwell on it. Her arm was free. She drove her fist into the dog-thing's belly, the flesh bursting under the force of the blow, her fist plunging into hot, squirming goo.

The creature screamed in pain and twisted away. Erin tried to pull her hand free, but a mesh of white tendrils held it fast, twining into the gaps between her fingers and forcing her skin into the shattered ruin of the dog's ribs. Shards of broken bone dug into her flesh.

Jordan swung his leg into the back half of the dog, sending it flying. Erin clutched her hand to her stomach, still feeling the slimy threads, the suction, the scraping bones. She didn't want to look. Had to. Her fingers still moved.

"Are you hurt?" Jordan gasped.

If there was blood, it was hidden beneath the dog's, thick and chunky as if it had been coagulating inside its body. Everything stank of rot, flesh and wood and otherwise. She couldn't control her stomach; dry heaves nearly doubled her over.

Snarling, growling, the dog rushed back out of the bushes. From somewhere inside the house, someone screamed, a hoarse, furious sound that matched the dog's snarl note for note. Like they were in sync. The idea was more terrifying than the dog.

In mid-jump, the dog's body changed, its hind legs stretching, the threads in its ruined belly closing into a flat sheet of rippling mycelium. Its jaw opened impossibly wide, green and pink ropes shooting from its jaws. The fungal flesh latched onto the sides of Jordan's face, reeling him toward the creature. For a second, they balanced in midair, man and dog, impossibly tangled, the green threads swarming over the back of Jordan's head. His face pulled closer and closer to the dog's open maw.

It happened in slow motion; Erin's feet glued to the ground. She lunged for Jordan, but now he was falling backward in a glowing cloud, spores exploding from the dog's skin as its whine grew louder and louder.

A woman dressed in black dove out of the trees behind the

creature and grabbed it by the throat. Her hands glowed yellow, and when they touched its flesh the dog's scream nearly pierced Erin's eardrums. For a second, the smell of burning hair overpowered the stench of decay.

The green mesh ripped free, the dog tearing loose from Jordan and flying up over the woman's head. Her long blond hair swirled around her; no, not hair, but white and pink and gold threads moving to pierce the dog's fungal belly.

"Kayla?" Erin gasped.

A hunk of pale flesh like a portobello mushroom ripped away from the dog's side. The dog bucked and twisted in her grip, biting at the air. Jordan began coughing. Erin stumbled to his side, unwilling to look away from the battle. "Are you okay?"

He retched, but nothing came up. Blood dripped down his cheeks from four deep punctures where the dog's teeth had driven into his skin, and raw pink strips showed where the fungal net had ripped away hair and skin on the back of his head.

The voice in the house gave an enormous bellow. Behind Erin, bone crunched impossibly loud. She spun around. The dog made no sound as it fell from Kayla's hands, limp as a worn sock.

Erin could only stare at the woman who had once invited her to housewarming parties and organized hiking events. Kayla wiped her hands on her black pants. The glowing light had subsided from her skin, and she could almost pass for herself again—if you could ignore the pink coral crawling out of her hairline and the way her irises had turned electric blue.

"You're not supposed to be here," Kayla said.

"Help!" Hari's voice screamed from inside the house. "Somebody help me, please!"

"I've got to get him." Erin leaped to her feet, but then stopped, staring at the house. The rainbow of mushroom flesh was a seal, she realized now. The dog had come out through the dog door, but she would never fit.

She looked back at Kayla. Whatever she was now, she had been Hari's friend once.

"Please help me."

CHAPTER TWENTY-EIGHT

I F IT HAD BEEN TOURIST SEASON, EVEN A NOVICE
hiker would have noticed a change in the creatures of the Mt.
Hood National Forest that day. Chipmunks sat in place beneath
the ferns, motionless even when the wind stirred the fronds
beside their heads. Crows perched immobile and silent on the
roosts above the hiking trails. Coyotes stood in broad daylight,
their eyes fixed toward the town of Faraday. The songbirds forgot to sing. Animals crossing into the area kept their distance
from the odd creatures they saw poised and motionless, as if
they could feel the difference permeating their flesh.

The Strangeness had expanded slowly at first, but recent cli-
matic changes had helped it grow exponentially. A space the
size of a bathroom stall had taken the last third of the twentieth
century to double, and then within one extraordinarily warm
summer cubed itself. Six years before it colonized the girl in the
creek, the Strangeness enjoyed its first successful takeover of an
avian lifeform, which had allowed it to spread its spores farther
and in directions it had never predicted.

Now its networks spread throughout the southern foothills of
Mt. Hood and nearly to the Clackamas River. Its ability to trans-
late biomass into connectivity had been fueled by a relentless
electrochemical intelligence only the unimaginative would find
analogous to the human brain. Its thoughts moved throughout

its threads, transcending epistemology to jump through minds so different they could barely recognize each other as living.

It had never felt threatened before.

The Strangeness delved into cellular memories stored in hyphae deep within its most protected center. Ancient enemies flickered to life inside chemical formulas that made raccoons twitch and a pack rat bite its own tail. Knowledge radiated throughout the network, crackling and transforming whatever it touched.

The creek girl felt the threads in her spine twitch and tense, but her own network had separated the Strangeness from her brain. The message entered her body and dispersed; the formulas rewritten into scrambled forms. Clouds of methane boiled up from her skin. Acids dripped from her fingertips. The paint on the walls of Bill Steadman's living room bubbled.

Outside, tendrils crawled from the flattened dog's belly into the soil. Information flickered in and out of its gray flesh. One eyelid lifted. Its head, tilted sideways on a neck whose bones were now gravel, focused on the woman in black.

A million sets of intelligences registered her, spreading her image across the landscape. The girl inside the house bared her teeth as she, too, saw what the dog saw.

If the Strangeness wanted war, she would bring it to them.

CHAPTER TWENTY-NINE

THE WOMAN WHO HAD BEEN KAYLA LIFTED A hand, her lip curling to reveal a mouth full of writhing white threads. Erin took a step backward. The wormy strands in Kayla's hair and mouth—it was too much. Too horrible. She couldn't possibly convince this . . . *being* to help her or Hari.

"Wait."

Scott Vanderpoel simply appeared beside Kayla, his footsteps silent. Wherever he had come from, he wasn't breathing hard or even sweating. Kayla shot him a look, and he put out his arms, palms facing each woman as if he could brace them apart from a distance.

"We're here for the creek girl," he said, and Erin wasn't sure if he was reminding Kayla or explaining things to herself. "We don't need to fight these two." He glanced at Jordan, who raised his own hands above his head.

"She is inside," Kayla said, her voice a dull rasp. "Anything that gets between me and her must be destroyed."

"I just want to help my friend," Erin said. Her heart squeezed. She couldn't imagine what it was like for Hari inside that horrible house.

Kayla narrowed her eyes. Scott cocked his head, listening to something no one else seemed to hear. "He's in one of the bedrooms."

"It's Hari, Kayla," Erin blurted. "*Hari*. You remember him, don't you?"

The pink and yellow threads in Kayla's hair lowered a little. "Hari," she repeated. A muscle beneath her eye twitched.

"I can help this girl and her friend," Scott said, "if you distract the creek girl."

The blue light in Kayla's eyes burned brighter. "She must be stopped."

"She must be stopped," he agreed.

"Go," Kayla said. "Find your Hari. Do what you must. But if you get between me and my target—"

"We won't," Erin said. "You won't even see us."

The pink and yellow threads rose up again, and Kayla turned toward the house. The sound in her throat was not human.

Jordan grabbed Erin's arm. "Are you nuts?"

"You don't have to come. It's okay."

He looked from her to Kayla, now on the front porch. She gave the door a tremendous kick, the wood splintering against the blow. "Fuck," he whispered. "I'll keep watch, all right?"

Scott reached for Erin's hand. "We've got to get moving." His palm prickled against hers, as if covered with tiny hairs. She resisted the urge to yank her hand away as he led her around the side of the house.

"How do you know all this?"

"We're all connected." He glanced back over his shoulder at her, his mouth working as he looked for the right words. "The girl in the house, the creek girl—she started out like the rest of us. But something changed inside her. She's on her own side now."

There's something inside me that's not me, Dahlia had said. This is what she meant. The fungus had gotten to Scott and Kayla and bound them together, somehow. And then the next thing he'd said penetrated her brain.

"Her own side? She's not one of you?"

But they were at the back deck now, turning sideways on the stairs so as not to brush against any of the purple and pink bracket fungus bulging from the railing. Erin rushed to the back door, but white tendrils like Halloween spider webs covered every inch of it, sealing it tight. Scott kicked the brake on the gas grill and took a tentative step up onto its collapsible shelf. The metal groaned, but he was already hopping on top of the lid. "Come on." He held out his hand.

"Where?"

He balled up his fist and slammed it through the window beside his head, clearing the glass from the frame. "Through there."

Erin stared at his fist, now a ball of throbbing white fibers. A shard of glass ejected from their midst. Scott shook out his wrist, and it was a hand again. "We don't have much time."

She stared at the appendage. The prickles were bad enough, but the thing it had become—it would have been like grasping a spider's egg sac or some equally revolting thing, and even though his skin was now skin, his fingers now fingers, just knowing it could change made her stomach squirm.

"Help me!" Hari screamed, and Erin grabbed Scott's hand. She tried to jump onto the grill like he had, but he was already launching her through the air, her body arcing through the open window like a fish through a hoop. His arm stretched improbably, revoltingly, slowing her fall so she only slid down the interior wall.

Fungal bodies sheared off beneath her weight, releasing the potent stink of decay, moisture seeping through her jeans. She'd never been so glad for a rain jacket before. She dropped to the ground and spun around, colliding with something hard and nearly falling over. Her hands identified something like a bench, the kind people installed at the foot of the bed to make taking off their shoes easier. She felt what had to be a stuffed animal and would have smirked to herself if she hadn't been in the dark in a house filled with mutant mushrooms. Something slammed into a distant wall and made the whole house shake.

There were sounds coming from the other room, dull roars and rumbles she couldn't put names to. It reminded her of the time she accompanied her mother to an MRI, the constant alien chords and washing-machine sounds it had emitted. The floor wobbled beneath her feet.

"Hari?" she whispered.

"He's in the closet," Scott said. She hadn't heard him come inside.

"I can't see anything." It was hot in the bedroom, hot as a sauna. Her armpits were already running with sweat.

"This was Kayla's." Something elastic pressed into her palm. She turned it in her hands for a second before feeling the central plastic square of a headlamp. "Don't turn it on yet!"

"Why?"

"The Strangeness is distracted. It won't be for long."

The Strangeness. In the dark, she felt like she understood what he meant. Behind all the missing people, all the scary fungal shit, all the glowing spores and fucked-up spaces, that's what it was: the Strangeness. It was what she had felt when she'd looked at Bryan's postcard and seen the figure with the binoculars studying the child on the lake. It was the missing people and darkness and the faces between the trees. A pure and horrible strangeness.

Now Scott hummed to himself. The bellows and rumbles from the other room melded with the song, nearly obscuring the actual tones, but now Erin found herself humming along with it, years of retail and childhood memory dragging the melody out of the depths of her brain. Across the room, she heard Hari's voice quietly singing along—"Santa Claus is comin' to town"—and for fuck's sake that song was creepy, the scariest thing in the whole damn world, only what Scott meant was worse, because if she understood—and she was pretty fucking sure she understood, because he had said *We're connected*—and when you were connected like they were all connected, the Strangeness didn't really need to make a list and check it twice, because it was watching, and it *knew*. Except for this short moment, it was distracted.

"Why are you helping me?" she whispered, although of course it didn't matter how loudly she said it, because if Scott heard it, the Strangeness heard it, too.

"I was never good at playing with others," Scott said. "My mother said I had a special mind."

"Different kinds of minds," Erin said. She thought of the dog. She thought of the creek girl and Nick Steadman. Each one of them so different, so good at such varied things. "The Strangeness finds different uses for them, doesn't it?"

"Your friend Kayla is so smart, so good with people. A natural leader."

"Erin? Is that you?" Hari whimpered. "Who are you talking to?"

Wood splintered inside the other room, and chunks of Sheetrock fell from the ceiling, blanketing Erin in powdered gypsum and chunks of paperboard. She doubled over coughing.

"Now, Erin! Turn on the headlamp and get to Hari. I'll try to make the window bigger," Scott shouted.

His words didn't make much sense, but she flipped on the light, ready to run. Except she couldn't because in this room there was no place to run that wasn't horror.

The wall had eaten the bed, layers of fungal shells and ropey tissue merging the two. An indentation on top suggested the dog had rested here while the fungus grew up around it. The encrustation continued around the doorframe of the closet, the wooden sliding doors standing together at the wall end to make one large opening, like a mouth in a scabrous face. Wisps of white hyphae waved in a breeze too soft for Erin to feel.

"Erin?" Hari called. "Can you help me?"

His voice came from inside the closet, a cruel joke Hari himself would have hated. She picked her way around the bed, careful not to touch any of its crusted surface. Someone had plugged in a space heater in the gap between the bed and the wall, the heat turned so high she felt the skin on her face tighten.

"Hari?" Her voice shook.

"Help me, Erin!"

She turned sideways to see inside the closet, pushing aside dress shirts and dry cleaner bags to see into the back. The white beam from Kayla's headlamp filled the small space, and Hari whimpered in pain. The sound made Erin's heart ache. She still couldn't see him, just more of those fungus's shell shapes, pink and purple and teal, climbing up the whole back wall of the closet, swallowing the clothes bar. Plastic hangers stuck out of the mass as if they were being eaten.

Then, on the floor, a large, lumpy mass. A suitcase handle jutted out of the top, but the rest was all fungus, purple scallops and greenish-yellow tendrils like sick tree roots, a greasy, glistening substance running over their surface. The smell of mold everywhere, choking the breath in Erin's throat. She flung aside men's slacks, a flannel shirt, but they only flopped over the crusty bulk of the fungus thing, their sleeves and hems already absorbed into this alien growth.

"Hari!" she shrieked, and then her fingers felt warm flesh, the dampness of a blinking eye. "Oh my god, Hari. You're okay." She remembered the headlamp and twisted it sideways so she wouldn't blind him.

"Oh, fuck, Erin, I am not okay."

His voice sounded so muffled. She dropped to her knees, carefully pulling back the fallen pieces of Bill Steadman's wardrobe until she could see Hari's eyes, dark and gleaming and no longer neatly aligned in his face, but stretched, skewed, diagonal, blues and pinks and yellows stretching out his face and tilting the bones the wrong way.

"What the fuck!" The words climbed in her throat to pierce her ears.

"I thought I could help her," Hari managed to say, except his voice seemed to come from all around her. A Nike shoe wiggled beneath her knee, its tongue flapping in a grotesque parody of a mouth. "You've got to get out of here."

"Hari." There were no words for this. No words for seeing your best friend absorbed into a closet and redistributed across its walls and contents.

The thrumming, roaring, snarling on the other side of the closet wall seemed to speak the real meaning of Hari's situation, guttural and violent and surreal. What the Strangeness meant was something beyond connection—beyond the meaning of individuality itself. Erin lost control of her legs and fell sideways in the cramped closet space.

She hit the wood and just kept falling. The light of her headlamp wrote a white line down the middle of a space that had

probably once been a kitchen and living room, but those defini-
tions had been destroyed by some kind of battle.

Erin remembered the way Kayla had broken down the front
door looking for the creek girl, and it appeared that had only been
the beginning of the violence. A refrigerator sat in a melted pool
of linoleum, its plastic parts bursting from its sides and turning
to fungal threads. Some piece of furniture had exploded, spewing tufts of foam rubber across every surface. A soft crackle of
static sounded, and Erin wriggled to see the source of the sound.

It came from Kayla as she stepped out of the depths of the
living room—or perhaps from the vintage television set that
had sprouted arms like an octopus and scuttled behind her, its
matter unspooling from its top half though the yellow tendrils
dangling from the back of her scalp. *They eat plastic,* Erin's brain
whispered, words babbling up from her stricken mind.

The being in the center of the kitchen turned to stare at her.

For a second, Erin thought of a xenomorph with its long bug-
like legs and awkwardly canted body, but that alien queen had
been beautiful, intentional, and this thing looked like an acci-
dental hybrid between a woman and a coatrack. Which is what
it was, of course: a coatrack and a vacuum cleaner and half of a
coffee table all melting into the hyper-attenuated body of a dead
girl. Her flesh had turned gray, and black liquid wept from her
pores, but despite the changes, Erin could still recognize the
face of the girl on the missing posters.

"Elena," she whispered.

The tears in her eyes were for the girl, and for Hari and Kayla,
and Scott, and Bryan, all of them, all the people lost to this
hideous Strangeness. How unfair it all was.

The cord of the vacuum cleaner shot out, its metal prongs
driving into Erin's arm. She screamed in pain.

Kayla lashed out, sending Elena flying across the room, smashing into the wall above Erin and sliding down just inches from Erin's head. The cord in her arm drilled deeper and she grabbed onto it, her fingers slick in her own torn flesh.

"You don't have to do this, Elena," Erin said between gritted teeth. "You don't have to hurt me!"

Elena snapped her head around to snarl at Erin. Green light blazed deep within her pupils. "Hurt?"

Her voice sounded as if it had been scoured out of the bottom of a pit, a well of pain far worse than the agony of Erin's arm.

Erin realized Elena could feel Erin's own pain through the prongs now scraping through Erin's flesh. She closed her eyes and focused on that feeling. *I'm sorry*, she added. *I'm sorry you hurt.*

Hurt. The voice came from everywhere. The pain of it transcended sides, transcended individuals. Elena Lopez's pain surged up Erin's arm and resounded through each strand of fungi in the room. Even Kayla stopped, her hands going to her belly as if someone had struck her in the gut.

Hurt.

An image of Ray Hendrix exploded in Erin's head. Kayla let out a shriek so piercing the last of the glasses in the kitchen exploded. Hari and Scott wailed in agony.

Ray Hendrix opened the passenger door of his pickup. *Would you like a ride, pretty girl?*

"Never again," Kayla growled. It was her own voice, but damaged. Erin remembered Kayla gripping Nick Steadman's shoulder back at the Cazadero Brewery and heard herself sob. This was Kayla, the real Kayla. Somewhere inside this grotesque monster, she was still in there.

Kayla's eyes rolled back in her head, going entirely blue.

Elena's head snapped backward, a strange hum burning in her throat. Kayla's voice echoed it.

And then a new image of Ray Hendrix appeared. The view came from high above, as if a crow or an owl watched him: Ray standing outside his house, his head turned as if he'd heard something out of the ordinary. He took a cautious step down the stairs.

"Never again," Kayla repeated, her voice twining with Elena's, and the words echoed through Erin's head, the whole house, the whole of the Strangeness.

The image shifted, blurring with motion as the bird swooped. Ray flailed and screamed and toppled down the stairs, but the view expanded as a rat shot out from under the porch, burying its teeth in Ray's ankle. The owl ripped into Ray's ear, blood hot across its beak and tongue.

Erin's hand went to her face, feeling the heat as if it poured over her own mouth. Elena and Kayla echoed the motion. The rat was still chewing, the owl still tearing. The man screaming, screaming . . . then silent.

"*¿Está muerto?*" Elena's voice cracked, as if something had broken deep inside of her.

"Yes," Kayla said.

"It's done," Elena whispered. She said something else in Spanish that Erin didn't catch. She was crying now, her tears black like melted plastic. "Please. Please. I don't want to live like this."

And Kayla's fist shot out so fast, so hard it pulped Elena's head through the wall.

CHAPTER THIRTY

KAYLA'S FIST DIDN'T JUST TRANSIT THROUGH SKIN and bone and wood; her Strangeness-imbued tissues slid past layers of Elena's mutated mycelium and then crashed into the fruiting bodies that had unraveled Hari's body.

Information flickered across chemical receptors faster than the speed of sound, jolts of near understanding that pushed the deep networks of the Strangeness into computational overdrive. The temperature inside the space Kayla had dubbed Haven rose by five degrees as the fruiting bodies and rhizomorphs dissolved organic matter and shuttled chemicals between each other. A colony of bats disappeared into fuel in the instant of processing power. A deer, crusted over for nearly six months, let out a soft sigh as its heart finally stopped.

Hari had changed everything. When the Strangeness had spied on the creek girl inside Craig Martin's house, her mycelium didn't even know how to feed upon the nearest carbon deposits to support itself. The girl's body had been dangerously weakened, running on its last reservoirs of strength. But somehow between leaving Martin's house and giving Hari threads, she had learned to reach out to the world around her, her mycelium warping in new and amazing ways during the transition.

The Strangeness did not feel emotions like jealousy or covetousness, but it recognized the utility of the changes within Elena's cells. The mycelium that had once been Strange had transformed into something nearly as alien to the Strangeness as the Strangeness was to Elena. As the threads in Kayla's skin brushed the threads in Elena's brain, the Strangeness tasted hybrid mycelium, a blend of its own genes with some resilient terrestrial fungus that must have colonized the creek girl during her transit to the mill wheel. Something stealthy, something the Strangeness hadn't deigned to notice before. Its presence, combined with the unique chemistries of a decaying body hyperstimulated by a locked emotional state, had created an entity capable of things the Strangeness had never achieved. Distributed networking—not only of thoughts and information, but chemical and biological patterns. A mind could be portioned across substances as different as a suitcase and a running shoe but kept in working order by hyphae capable of growing at speeds previously unattainable.

Unfortunately, the power of Kayla's fist had destroyed far too much of Elena's brain for the creek girl to be of use, and the rotting closet had collapsed on the substance that had once been Hari. The scraps remaining would have to be carried to Haven for deeper genetic sampling before they finished dissolving into their chemical components.

Armed with the new flavor of the shifted mycelium, the Strangeness sent out a profile to all its Strange components. Just in case there were others Elena had touched. Others infected with her wonderful threads. Given the speed at which the threads had colonized Hari, the Strangeness felt optimistic they would find someone soon.

CHAPTER THIRTY-ONE

ERIN DRAGGED HERSELF UPRIGHT.

Her wrist burned where the prongs of the vacuum cleaner cord had dug into it, but the wound was already sealed over with a thin white membrane more like rubber than skin. Looking at it made her stomach heave. She tugged her jacket's sleeve down over it. With a low rumble, the kitchen ceiling slumped nearly a foot closer to Kayla's head.

Scott appeared beside her, covered in the white silt of broken Sheetrock. "We've got to get out of here."

"What about Hari?" Erin whispered.

Scott glanced at the wall behind Erin's back. A chunk of Sheetrock broke free and smashed on the ground. "I don't think he made it."

Kayla grabbed Erin's arm and hauled her to her feet. "Come on." She pushed open the back door, a rainbow of fungal ropes breaking like rotten string. How much of their strength had come from Elena's will? Would they just break down like mushrooms in the rain? Part of Erin wanted to study the mess that had been Bill Steadman's house, but the greater part of her wanted to run.

Her feet sided with running, although her legs only managed a sort of stumble. Kayla didn't let go of her arm. Erin's rain jacket hissed as its surface slowly dissolved beneath the other woman's grip. Every second outside the house, Kayla stood taller, her shoulders more squared. Whatever the battle had taken out of her, the fungus inside was feeding back into her. With the fungus spurring them on, someone like Kayla was nearly unstoppable.

The thought made Erin try to yank her arm away, but Kayla only dug her fingers in tighter. That's when Erin realized the world had been lucky for a long time, with the fungus—what had Scott called it? the Strangeness?—only finding animals and a misfit like Scott Vanderpoel. Creatures it could barely use except to spy on the world. But in Kayla it had found the perfect tool, a mind it could mesh with, a body already incredibly powerful. With her help, it could grow exponentially.

They skidded around the corner of the house. Erin's headlamp lit up Jordan's face, pale and scared as he hoisted a broken tree limb. She had forgotten about him entirely.

"Erin? Are you okay? What happened in there?"

She looked back at Scott and saw the blue flicker in the back of his eyes, the soft pink tracing of threads beneath his skin. Then Erin's raincoat gave up its last layer of plastic, the threads in Kayla's fingers drilling into Erin's arm.

Electric blue.

The flash exploded inside Erin's head as thread and membrane connected. The two strands of fungus had started the same, but they weren't now, and the difference yawned inside Erin like an uncrossable chasm. The power of the Strangeness, the hunger at its heart. The hunger for her.

A vision of Haven flashed through her head, and fear exploded through her veins like an icy geyser.

"Get her!" Erin screamed, and threw herself backward,

and Jordan, not knowing what else to do, whipped the branch around so it smashed into the side of Kayla's head. She collapsed in a heap.

"Erin, stop!" Scott shouted, but he tripped on Kayla's legs and went down.

Erin only had a second.

She sprinted toward the car with a speed she'd never felt at any trail race. "Get the dog!" she shouted, and Jordan scooped it up without asking questions.

Scott screamed in rage or pain or some feeling beyond the scope of human imagination, and she threw open the Volvo's door and slammed the key into the ignition, Jordan a step behind. The tires screamed out in the night, and they drove. They just drove.

CHAPTER THIRTY-TWO

THEY SHOULD HAVE KEPT DRIVING FOR HOURS, TAK-
ing themselves as far from the Mt. Hood National Forest
and the Strangeness's territory as possible. Maybe all the way
into the desert of eastern Oregon, where the heat and drought
kept fungus to a minimum. But Erin had no idea if the threads
inside her would die without Elena like the threads around the
Steadmans' back door, or if being inside a living body would
allow the fungus to start again. She wasn't going to risk infect-
ing every person at every rest area along the way if the threads
could spread to anyone else. Bad enough to be sitting here with
Jordan.

"Where are we going?" he asked, twisting around to see
through the back window. "And what am I doing with this dead
dog on my lap?"

"It isn't dead." She had a thought. "Is there anything to eat
in that basket?"

He shifted awkwardly, trying to reach the basket behind Erin's
seat. "No, just these stupid candles."

"Put one in the dog's mouth." She steered them around a corner, trying to remember where they were.

"What?"

"Just do it. And remind me how to get to Olivia's house." Her
head felt funny, very light and hollow, hungry for food and sleep
both. Her brain barely managed the directions or staying in her

own lane. If there had been any traffic, they would have been in a world of hurt.

The dog was breathing again by the time they pulled into Olivia's driveway. Erin's hands shook as she pulled the key from the ignition. Scott would follow them, but where else could she go? She needed time to plan, and Olivia was much smarter than Erin was. She would have an idea. And food. And a bed.

The light on the front porch snapped on. Neither Erin nor Jordan said a word as they got out of the car and trudged up the front stairs, Jordan still carrying the dog. Gray goo smeared the front of his jacket, and Erin had to imagine she looked a thousand times worse. But Olivia let them in without even asking them to take off their shoes. The smell of macaroni and cheese made Erin's mouth run and the dog wriggle.

Jordan dropped the dog beside the table as Olivia delivered plates filled with molten cheesy noodles. Erin finished her first serving before she remembered all the horrible things she'd touched and felt sick she hadn't even washed her hands. Excusing herself, she went and scrubbed her hands in the bathroom sink, the soap burning her palms and making her skin itch. The white membrane on her wrist looked unchanged.

She went back to the table. "The thread-things got me," she announced. And burst into tears.

If Hari had been there, he would have immediately put his arms around her, but Jordan and Olivia just sat there gripping their forks like they might need to stab her. Which she understood. It wasn't like they actually knew her. She had arrived in their lives only a few days earlier and proceeded to drop an ocean of bad news in their laps. Why should they reach out to her and risk contaminating their own human flesh?

She cried harder.

Olivia stood up and pressed a tissue into Erin's hand, patting her on the shoulder. "There, there."

"What are you going to do?" Jordan asked.

"I don't know!" Erin squeegeed her eyes. Another mound of mac and cheese had appeared on her plate while she was in the bathroom, and she speared a bite. Gulped it down. "I mean, I do know, I just don't like it."

Olivia sat down again. "Tell us. Because if this is contagious, I'm worried about all of us. And my town."

Erin dug for the words to explain the knowledge that had burst into her brain while Elena had been plugged into her arm. "There are two kinds of fungus-things," Erin said. "One that's been here for a long time, the one that took over Kayla and Scott."

"Wait—took over? What does that mean? And Scott's a part of this?"

"Yeah," Jordan said. "He and Kayla kind of helped Erin back at the Steadmans' house."

"The fungus, the Strangeness—that's what Scott called it— it's what made those threads we saw at Craig's house. And the threads link them together. The Strangeness sees what they see. Hears what they hear."

"And it's been here a long time?" Olivia's voice quavered.

"Yeah. But now there's something new. Somehow when the Strangeness tried to colonize Elena Lopez, the fungus mutated. Maybe because she died in the process? Or maybe because her brain was changed by the trauma of being raped and murdered by Ray Hendrix?" She remembered the owl and the rat and put down her fork. "Shit, he's dead now. Kayla used some Strange animals to rip him to pieces. She let Elena and I watch."

"What?" Olivia pushed her chair back an inch. "What?"

"The fungus takes over people's minds, not just their bodies. It can take over animals. But the fungus in Elena's body can do even more than the first one. And the Strangeness wants to learn from it. But the only way to do that is to take a living host to the Strangeness's center. The place where it first started. Haven."

"It has to be the place where the 1907 meteor hit," Jordan said.

Erin stared at him. "The meteor?"

He got up and began to pace. "Where have we run into all this creepy fungus shit? Places Mitch Vanderpoel explored as mining sites. What was he looking for? The mineral from the meteor. Remember that place Ray Hendrix described with all the mushrooms? Sounded like a meteor crater to me." He stopped in place, too excited to keep moving. "And let's face it, this fungus is pretty fucking alien."

"Aliens." The macaroni turned to cold grease on Erin's tongue. "I can't believe we're talking about aliens." Or that there was now an extraterrestrial fungus growing inside her body. She twisted her wrist to look at the white patch. It wasn't any bigger, she was pretty sure.

"Again," Olivia said, her voice fierce, "what about Faraday? Whatever this Strangeness has been doing, up until now, it's been happening in the woods. Craig's house is four blocks from the elementary school."

Jordan stopped his pacing, his face going pale. "My mom's house is just three blocks from his."

"I don't know." Erin sank a little lower in her chair. "When Elena died, the fungus in the Steadmans' house got weaker. I think she was like its brain, and without her, it's starting to die. And the patch on my wrist hasn't grown any. That's got to mean something."

"Kill the brain, kill the body," Jordan said.

"That makes sense," Olivia agreed. "But how do we find the brain for the Strangeness?"

Erin hugged her arms around her stomach. "I think Scott will come to take me to it."

A light flared in Jordan's eyes. "Then we'll follow him and burn the fucking thing to the ground." The venom in his voice made the others stare at him. He tightened his lips. "For Matt and Dahlia."

"For your friends," Olivia agreed. "And for stealing my son."

Erin caught herself falling sideways. "I think I have to take a nap," she whispered.

THE BORROWED ALARM CLOCK SCREAMED, AND ERIN'S eyes crawled open. Her arm moved a millimeter at a time toward the nightstand, finally fumbling the thing into silence. The darkness of the guesthouse encouraged Erin to close her eyes again and go back to sleep, but some sound or thought prodded her to sit up. The long day returned to her, all the violence and rot and nastiness, the colors and smells and pain. She pulled her knees to her chest and let herself cry for a second or two. She wanted her mom.

The thought cut off the tears. When was the last time she'd let herself think that? Unbidden, a memory of some beach festival, the family holding hands, eating ice cream cones, laughing at the dunk tank as a guy wearing fake antlers fell into the tub. Somehow she'd dropped Bryan's hand and gotten separated from everyone. A clown had offered her a balloon and she'd run away from its skewed smile, then hidden behind a stand where the owner was on a break. She'd curled up on her side, crying, wishing for her mom.

But it had been Bryan who'd found her and led her back to their parents. He was the one who had known where she would hide. The one who had offered a stack of napkins to dry her eyes and who had bought her a cotton candy to put a smile back on her face.

Bryan.

Something flickered in the back of her head, a dull pink flash of emotion that wasn't hers. Slowly, she got out of bed, fixing her mind on the sensation. She held it tight as she went into the bathroom and turned on the shower. The warm water beating on her head and shoulders helped drive the sleep out of her brain and focus on the pink. It was faint, and somehow enclosed, the feeling tinny.

"Bryan," she said aloud, squeezing shut her eyes to block out anything but the sensation. The pink flashed brighter. It tasted like cotton candy.

She rested her forehead on the shower wall and let the sweetness fill her.

"You didn't turn the light on," a voice said from the doorway. "You should at least pretend you're still human."

Erin didn't jump. She'd been expecting Scott to show up.

She opened her eyes, registering the gray on gray of all the manufactured and artificial surfaces of the room. Tiny speckles of mildew were a soft blue, not a Strange color, but merely the color of life. Sadness settled into the pit of her stomach, heavy and inert. "I'm one of you now, aren't I?"

He didn't answer, only waited patiently on the other side of the dead plastic curtain.

Erin reached for the travel shampoo and gave her hair a quick scrub, then rinsed it, wondering at the simple pleasure of hot water and soap bubbles. Would she ever feel them again? She could sense a tingling inside her chest and abdomen beginning to dissolve the ache for her lost humanity, the Strangeness stealing the sadness to file away in its stockpile of chemical knowledge. She cleared her throat. "Did you know my brother was Strange?"

With a jangle of rings, the shower curtain slid open, and Scott turned off the water. "Yes." He held out a towel. There was no window in the bathroom, but she could see him clearly enough, the soft purple glow beneath his skin, the blue in his eyes. She could see the tiny motes of mildew already growing on the bath towel, one of the ordinary fungus varieties ready to grow on a damp surface at any time. No matter how often you washed things, there were always spores waiting to grow, somewhere. Everywhere.

She buried her face in the towel anyway. It still smelled lightly of lavender and freshly cleaned. No one would have known the spores were even there, unless they were Strange. The pink sense of Bryan was trickling away, almost as if someone had pulled the plug. Or as if someone was sucking it up, his aura a pink milkshake for someone to sip.

"That's why I followed you in the first place," Scott admitted. "You were so nice, just like him."

"You broke into the room," she said, and wrapped the towel around herself. "You moved the statue."

"He would have wanted me to warn you."

"He's in Haven, isn't he?"

He sighed and followed her out to the bedroom. "There are a lot of them. Animals and people who aren't quite the right fit for the Strangeness to control, but can still be useful."

"It's like virtual reality in there, isn't it?" The pink flash had been so hard to understand until she'd locked on the metaphor.

"Their minds are playing while their bodies are . . . what? Dissolved for food?"

"The Strangeness does not eat living things. It has other needs, however."

Other needs. She thought of the way her sadness had been dismantled, the Strangeness intrigued by its function; thought, too, of the pink energy's sudden shrinkage. The Strangeness had drained it away, not like water from a tub, but like energy from a battery. She didn't need to speak the thought out loud, but she wanted to. "They're being used like batteries."

"Batteries and microchips," he agreed. "The more neural connections, the better."

She dropped down onto the edge of the bed and squeezed the ducts at the corners of her eyes. "Why him?"

"He was easy to talk to." Scott sat down on the bed beside her. "But he was so unhappy, Erin. He wanted something better than humanity."

"So you took him to the Strangeness?" Her voice climbed a register. "What the fuck, Scott?"

"People have been studying the effects of fungi for decades," he said, getting excited. "They can use certain kinds to clean toxic minerals out of the soil. Filter water. Stop erosion. Make trees grow faster. The future of this planet is fungal."

"This Strangeness isn't even from this planet! Why the fuck are you defending it?" She slammed her fist on his knee and was glad to feel him wince.

"It cares!" He nearly shouted it, his eyes sparkling not with fungal light but tears. "Whatever it touches, it cares about. Can you say that about humanity?"

The air caught in Erin's chest. He sounded so much like Bryan, she couldn't keep looking at him. Eyes burning, she got up and put on a sports bra, underwear, her least filthy pair of jeans. He was right, as much as she didn't want to admit it. Humans were killing the planet. That knowledge had sent her brother to a shrink and a bottle of antidepressants. Had made everyone from the Clackamas County sheriff's department to his own parents believe he had killed himself.

But he was alive.

"I wish you'd listened to my warning," Scott said. He grabbed her wrist, and the membrane sparked an irritable green against the threads in his fingers. "I'm sorry I have to take you like this."

"Me, too," she said, but her heart was speeding with excitement, not fear.

She hadn't dared to hope she would find Bryan alive after all these years, but why else had she come to this stupid little town? And now Scott was going to take her right to him. But if they were going to escape from Haven, she was going to need backup.

She reached for the bag of Hershey's Kisses Olivia had given her and stuffed it into the pocket of her raincoat—hoping like hell Jordan was ready to follow her trail of wrappers.

CHAPTER THIRTY-THREE

ERIN FOLLOWED SCOTT OUTSIDE, WHERE A THICK bank of clouds blotted out the stars. The summer-warm wind carried the promise of a Pineapple Express as it stirred the tree branches and made Erin unzip her raincoat. The pre-dawn forest should have been dark, but instead it was lit up with life. Scott was six feet of iridescence leading the way into the forest.

He moved fast, much faster than she would have expected. It should have been a struggle to keep up with him, but her legs felt strong and her lungs clear. Even a few feet apart, Erin could feel an inhuman heat radiating off his body. Water vapor rose in spirals from the top of his head. She brushed her hand across her own forehead and registered what felt like a low-grade fever.

"What made you join the Strangeness, Scott? You had a life. You had your art and your students."

"It wasn't enough," he said. "Do you know what it's like, living in a small town where everyone has always thought you were a freak? Where every woman crossed the street to avoid talking to me?"

"You couldn't get a date, so you signed up to serve an alien fungus?"

"Shut up," he hissed.

Erin fell silent. She risked a glance at him and saw threads glowing beneath the skin around his eyes like the strands he'd worked into the bronze statue in her room. She felt a pressure around her own eyes that increased as they sped past the ruins of the old hotel and up the flanks of the next ridge. She was dropping silver wrappers behind her as often as she dared, which wasn't as often as she would have liked. Sometimes she felt other eyes, tiny flashes of blue following behind her. Watching. Listening. As if the spy inside of her head wasn't enough.

Christmas is a-coming, the goose is getting fat. She kept the song running through her brain as she took another Hershey's Kiss out of her pocket and hoped the watchers didn't notice her drop the wrapper behind her on the trail.

"*Please to put a penny—*" Scott broke off, narrowing his eyes at her. "You've been using that stupid song to cover your thoughts, haven't you? What are you trying to hide?"

He had stopped in front of a rock face covered with bushes. It took Erin a minute to realize the hanging vines and ferns obscured the mouth of a tunnel.

"We have to go in there?" The quaver in her voice wasn't acting.

"We're almost there." He pushed open an entry hole. "Come on. And no singing."

Erin dug her fingers in the greenery as she passed through, hoping it was enough to mark the route for Jordan. Scott had checked her pockets before they left Olivia's property, flinging aside her multitool and headlamp. He'd only let her bring the Kisses when she complained she was starving. If this had been a movie, she would have walked into this tunnel with a pair of assault rifles and a crate of dynamite, but instead, she was facing the enemy with only a handful of sugar and the faintest chance her friend was following with a gas can.

Then the ferns closed behind them. Even with her fungal-boosted vision, the tunnel was too dark to see anything. Scott waited for her to move. Her toe caught on stone, and he barely caught her before she hit the ground. The air smelled sour, hints of sulfur and vinegar, but the scent changed as they went deeper into the mountain, growing first more mineral, then thick with the smells of patchouli and rot and the familiar Strange bitterness. Every foot forward, the air became warmer, the walls brighter, faint tracings of pink appearing and then growing thicker, more distinct. Purple growths began appearing where the pink networks met up and twined together.

Blue and yellow lights left tracers in the air. Sounds that weren't sounds echoed in the hollow places of Erin's skull. When she waved her free hand in front of her face, it glowed like a neon green flower at the end of her wrist, tiny white smiley faces beaming from the tips of her fingers. Scott glanced back at her, his face a skull with beams of blue light for eyes.

"Is this real?"

"Define 'real.'" His voice sounded in her ears, but she wasn't sure if either of them spoke. The walls of the tunnel had begun to pulse, the floor propelling her forward. At some point, the stone had changed to scallop shells and flesh. When her shoulders brushed them, they sparked like static electricity.

All of this is a dream, and I'm going to wake up in the guesthouse, still plastered after that hike into the hot springs.

She laughed out loud at the thought. The walls closed behind her and pushed her forward in an obscene parody of childbirth.

Hello, someone said. *Do you know if it's baseball season yet?*

Tell me what a latte tastes like, someone else begged. *I haven't had a coffee in so fucking long.*

A kitten mewed in the back of her head. A bull elk blew out a hot breath, remembering the sensation of plunging down a ravine at top speed, racing after a cow under the open sky. Her

head swiveled as she tried to see the animal beneath the layers
of shelf fungus and twisting rhizomorphs.

A hand reached for her, the rest of the arm swallowed by a
mass of purple turkey tails. A face peered out from a gap between yellow hyphae.

Erin!

The floor shoved her onward, but she grabbed onto the nearest shelf fungus and spun around, searching for the source of the
voice. "Bryan?"

Bright pink: *I'm in here.*

She dropped to her knees beside a hummock of hard purple
flesh, a few tiny mushrooms coming out of the top. A cleft in
the wall revealed the side of a shoulder, a hint of lower jaw,
like someone had lain down on a cushion of fungus and been
grown over in their sleep. She pushed her fingers into the fold
and felt skin, the firmness of a cheekbone, the crinkle of an ear.
No beard. Whatever had been done to her brother must have
stopped his facial hair from growing. The feathered thing that
had lived in her chest for five years stopped flying and settled,
not to roost, but to be imprisoned for good.

"Bryan." Tears ran down her face, soaked her tee shirt. "I've
been looking for you."

I know you have.

His face didn't move as he spoke. Maybe movement was beyond him. Through the threads in her fingers, she felt the buzz-
ing hum of the Strangeness, its current here so strong it made
his skin throb.

The question "are you okay" rose up in her mind and immediately died. Of course he wasn't okay. There was no way
for anyone in his situation to be anything like okay. This was a
prison, a torture chamber, a stomach digesting life-forms while

their minds were alive to feel it. She was kneeling in an actual hell, and her brother was trapped within it.

It's not so bad. He laughed.

It's worse! she thought at him, and he laughed again.

Listen, see, he thought, and her fingertips lit up with him: his thoughts, his feelings.

Comfort filled the center of Bryan's body, the portion still accessible to him. His consciousness swirled in a sensation of warmth and well-being, like soaking in a hot tub while smoking really good weed. Instead of boredom, his mind sent out streamers of joy and curiosity, moving through tree roots and into the dawn sky, becoming both branch and talon as a Strange hawk landed on an enormous Douglas fir. When the hawk launched itself, his mind followed it, feeling its body move through the roller coaster of thermals and air currents rushing over the mountain. In the distance, the sunrise lit the top of Mt. Hood so its peak glowed a vibrant peach.

They hung in that space for a moment before Erin's mind snapped back into her body, her fingers going dull. She had never felt so alone, so empty, so . . . void. What it meant to be human, she realized: living empty, disconnected from the world and all the other beings sharing it.

"It's good, isn't it?" Scott whispered. He was crying, too, as he knelt beside her. "I keep begging the Strangeness to let me stay in Haven, but it always sends me back into the world. I can feel it when I close my eyes, but it's never the same as being plugged in."

Bryan pulsed joy through Erin's fingers. She tried to remember the last time she had heard him laugh and couldn't.

Scott helped her to her feet. "Just a little farther," he said. "The Strangeness needs you at its heart."

He twined his fingers between hers as if they were lovers, but she knew they were connected more deeply than any lovers had ever been. The floor sent waves of pleasure up her legs and when they met the vibrations traveling through Scott's body, she felt herself tremble on the brink of orgasm. The threads in their palms danced and churned. She wanted to collapse into the sensation. She wanted them to melt into the walls and each other and never untangle. She wanted—

But they stepped out of the tunnel and into the space that had once been an open meteor crater and was now a room almost entirely closed in by walls of fungus. The steamy heat glued Erin's shirt and jacket to her shoulder blades. The air hung so thick and richly scented she had to pant, mouth open, as she made sense of the cramped space.

Kayla lay on an extrusion of pink flesh like a sacrifice upon an altar, her hands crossed on her stomach, a mass of threads writhing around her head. Her blond hair was gone entirely. Erin stumbled toward her and heard her feet scuff on rock.

The sensation of bliss instantly turned off.

Erin stared at her feet. Rock, not fungus. Somehow this one tiny outcropping of stone had been left uncovered, and her feet had found it. Her mind, sluggish, tried to make sense of it.

"Come on," Scott urged, beckoning her toward Kayla's side. He patted the table. "You're almost there."

Rock, not fungus.

Rapture, then nothing.

"Come on," he repeated.

If she touched the table, she'd feel it again, the bliss, the wonder, the connection. The connection might be real, but the joy and the pleasure were entirely chemical, the manipulation of an alien being that had mastered the chemistry of its new planet.

Scott grabbed her arm and tugged her toward the altar. Her feet skidded off the rocky surface and warmth rushed up her legs again.

Kayla sat up. The side of her head where Jordan had smashed it was bare and naked, a purple membrane replacing the skin. It pulsed to the beat of the Strangeness.

"Your brother used chemicals to survive living in this world." Kayla's voice issued from Scott's mouth, from the walls of the cave, from Erin's own skin. "What difference is there between that and what We do? At least he is whole here."

Words had fallen to the very back of Erin's brain. "He's a prisoner," she managed.

Kayla smiled, and a silver light escaped from between her lips. Every inch of her looked burnished, touched by a mineral glitter a raver would have envied. Erin remembered Jordan's story of his adventures as a Scene kid when he and Dahlia were young. They could have had all the color and sparkle they wanted if they'd only found the Strangeness as teens.

She remembered the way Dahlia died, her mouth unraveling, her spine dripping goo, and turned her eyes away from Kayla's face. But Scott had begun to glow, too, blue and gold and pulsing rainbows. The walls vibrated and trembled. There was no safe place to look, not in this entire cave, so Erin lifted her face to the ceiling and looked for the one gap she could feel in the roof, a dark and tiny opening onto the sky.

Someone help me, she pleaded. She didn't believe in God, but if there was some kind of terrestrial superpower anywhere to be had, she wished they would look down at this second and strike her dead before the Strangeness could swallow her whole.

"Dead?" Kayla snarled. Her hand shot out and grabbed Erin's

jaw. "How dare you beg to die when We are offering you the chance to join Us?"

"You only want me for Elena's fungus," Erin slurred around Kayla's fingers. "Otherwise, I'm just another cell in your battery cave."

Battery cave, Batcave. Somewhere behind her, her brother chuckled at her play on words. She felt it, and she felt its realness. It steadied her legs and lifted her chin. She closed her eyes to look inside herself.

Elena's fungus was so quiet and weak Erin had nearly forgotten it, but it was still there in her wrist. Its tendrils listened to the Strangeness like a tiny spy in enemy territory, and now it sent Erin the message she'd been hoping for, the travelers Kayla and Scott had been too distracted to notice.

She didn't need God when she had friends who could follow a trail of candy wrappers. How Jordan had found the hole in the cavern ceiling, she didn't know, but he was up there, all right. Scott's eyes widened as an owl caught a glimpse of the man in his climbing gear.

"What the hell?" Kayla snarled, and then a stream of gasoline splashed down onto her head. When the flaming torch soared through the open cavern roof, it blazed as bright as the meteor must have burned a hundred and eighteen years earlier. The pink altar in the center of the cave went up instantly.

Fear and terror exploded through the Strangeness's network, feeding back on itself in a loop of screams. Kayla's eyes went blank, her body frozen.

Even with one foot on the disconnected stone, the Strangeness's pain almost overpowered Erin's mind. Her body vibrated with the enormous resonance of its screams. She wasn't sure how she managed to reach out and shove Kayla into the fire.

The screaming drove through Erin's brain like an ice pick. Something broke free in her nose and blood poured hot down her top lip. She could barely stand, but she knew she couldn't stop yet. She launched herself at Scott.

He didn't struggle, his mind too flayed by the howling Strangeness. She hit him center mass and he stumbled back into the flames. Some of the gasoline must have splattered his arm, because it caught in seconds. Erin felt the melting polyester of her rain jacket's sleeve sear into her arm.

With an awful sound neither human nor Strange, Scott staggered out of the fire. He was a flailing star of flame and smoke so bright that Erin had to shut her eyes against the brightness.

The pain in her head was too much. She felt her legs go out from under her as the smoke and the agony overrode everything. It didn't matter. She was ready to die if it meant freeing her brother and saving the goddamn world. As her raincoat caught fire, she thought at least Bryan would be proud of her.

CHAPTER THIRTY-FOUR

ON THE BANKS OF PLAZA LAKE, A FEMALE COYOTE in mid-pounce went rigid and collapsed. The Douglas squirrel she'd been chasing streaked into a clump of sword ferns and then up a tree, shrieking in terror. A few feet away, her pups yipped in their den.

The coyote's body began to convulse, her legs kicking, her paws scrabbling the dirt. Her abdomen heaved.

A few miles away, a hawk fell out of the sky, striking the ground just inches from a trail runner starting out on the Salmon River trail. The trail runner spun around, sprinting to her car and racing to the Zigzag Ranger Station. There, screaming and crying, she told rangers about the worms that boiled out of the hawk's mouth and eyes before burrowing into the ground. When rangers returned to the site, they found only a mass of blood stained feathers.

In communities all along the edges of the Mt. Hood National Forest, people reported animals behaving strangely: a squirrel that collapsed and stayed frozen even when approached by dogs; a crow that toppled over onto its side, vomiting blue liquid; a buck that rammed its head into a tree trunk. Rangers reported entire meadows turning gray and stinking of rot. Trees collapsed on several forest roads, and a falling Doug fir damaged the Oak Grove powerhouse.

At Plaza Lake, the mother coyote went still. Her tiny pups crept out of their den and managed to crawl to her side, licking her mouth with frantic glowing tongues. Their whimpers were the only sound in a forest that had gone terribly silent.

CHAPTER THIRTY-FIVE

EVERYTHING HURT AND ERIN DIDN'T WANT TO OPEN her eyes, but the voice was emphatic. She tried to swallow and started coughing instead. Her throat burned. Her lungs burned. Something warm and foul smelling slid over her face.

"Get a hold of that dog," a voice snapped, and it took Erin a minute to recognize it as Deputy Duvall's. "Burn victims die from infections."

The dog barked, and Erin opened her eyes. The black Lab from the Steadmans' house stared down at her, panting and making a doggish kind of smile. It lunged free and licked Erin's face again. It felt kind of good.

"Erin, are you conscious?" Jordan said. Black soot darkened his face, except for two circles around his eyes. He must have been wearing goggles when he'd set fire to the cave.

"Don't move," Duvall added.

"How—" Erin started, but broke off, coughing.

"I followed the candy wrappers, like you planned," Jordan said, "but Olivia also got Deputy Duvall to use one of the county's drones to fly over some spots on her dad's map. It captured the opening to the cave."

"Jordan's the one who saved you," Deputy Duvall said. "He rappelled into the cave and smothered the flames with his own body." Erin couldn't see Duvall's face, but she thought the deputy

sounded proud. "I told him he should come work for Search and
Rescue."

The dog leaned into Erin's side, its flanks warm and soft
against her skin. She could see pink strips of her raincoat melted
into her arm, which ought to be horrifying, but somehow, she
didn't mind. Her head felt wrong, heavy and light at the same
time.

"I gave you some emergency painkillers," Duvall said. "Because it's a long way back to civilization, and it's going to hurt
like hell."

"'S not bad," Erin mumbled. The dog nosed at her arm, dain-
tily freeing the end of a pink strip with its front teeth. It gave the
strip a tug. No one noticed.

Olivia leaned in, filling Erin's vision. "Did you see Scott?
What happened to him?"

Erin tried to shake her head, but the skin on her neck
screamed in agony. "I don't know," she lied. She didn't want to
think about Scott or how he had lured her brother into Haven.
She wasn't ready to think about any of it: the linked minds, the
battery cave, the Strangeness's plans for the world.

The dog finished pulling a pink plastic strip free from her
arm. It should have hurt, but the skin beneath looked pale and
smooth and healthy. Erin smiled groggily at the dog. Before
the painkillers took her back under again, she thought it smiled
back.

"YOU GOT LUCKY," DUVALL SAID.

Erin's parents had offered to bring her home, but she had
wanted to stay with Olivia, who put her up inside the main
house in a room still smelling of Ikea. The doctors were amazed

by Erin's progress. Even her lungs were in good shape, better than Jordan's even, because he'd inhaled a lot of smoke dragging her out through the burning tunnel.

The whole Strangeness had gone up in flames, the colorful shelf fungus and ropes of rhizomorphs alike. Firefighters had come to protect the forest, and they'd uncovered the bodies of several missing hikers, including Bryan's. Official statements implicated Ray Hendrix, who had vanished the same night. A suspicious pool of blood had been discovered on his porch, but his body was not to be found. A preliminary search of his property had revealed trophies from three different young female victims.

Emissaries from several cable networks were sniffing around for film rights. Erin hoped Elena's family made a bundle.

"I got lucky," Erin agreed. The black Lab lay on the foot of her bed, its tongue lolling contentedly. She had never thought of herself as a dog person, but the dog's warm presence made it easier to close her eyes at night.

Not that they stayed closed. The night before, with the help of five milligrams of melatonin, she had fallen asleep, hoping for only darkness. Before long, she was in the woods again, the glowing trees clawing at her and the forest creatures hissing at her from the bushes. She kept trying to run, but the roots wriggled out of the ground, long multicolored threads that grabbed her ankles and pulled her to the ground.

Sprawled on her belly, she could hear the footsteps behind her, the screaming. She had to get up. Had to get away. But she knew if she sat up, she'd see them: Hari, and Dahlia, and Matt, their bodies twisted and broken, bits connected only by strings.

Then a hand had hoisted her up, up, up, until she was hanging over Kayla's burning face, the flames becoming spores, the spores filling Erin's mouth and nose . . .

If it hadn't been for Cletus and his gentle licks pulling her awake, Erin might have suffocated in her sleep. She shuddered, remembering it.

Thank goodness for Cletus, whose friendly concern could push the past back into the past. Sometimes she heard Olivia crying in the night, and then she took the dog to the old woman and they all drank hot milk in the kitchen. It helped, having someone who understood. It helped to look at the dog, whose one ear had never grown back, and to know she wasn't insane, but that she had survived. They were both broken, but at least they were whole.

Duvall ran her fingers through her hair. She'd cut it since the night in the cavern, a shaggy cut setting off her cheekbones and the sharp angle of her jaw. If she'd been gay, Erin would have asked her out in a minute. But Madison had been texting Erin. It was weird, lying to her about Kayla. Sometimes Erin struggled to keep the fictions straight in her head. She hoped repeating it made it feel more true: Kayla had been a hero to very end, she had tried to help her friends, she had been human. Better to remember her that way than the monster Erin had killed.

"I have to know," Duvall said. "Is it really gone? Did the fire kill it? Can something like that really die?"

The dog sat up, staring at Duvall. Erin tucked her legs underneath her, looking inside for clues. "I think so," she said, listening to her heartbeat, her own ordinary inner sounds. "I haven't felt anything strange since that night. If the Strangeness isn't dead, at least the stuff that infected me and Elena Lopez is. Which seems like a good sign."

Duvall got up, pushed aside the blinds on the window, stared out into the forest. It was late May now, and the woods had just passed the peak of green. There'd been no green in the cavern, Erin realized. Pinks and blues and purples and yellows and tiny red mushrooms like Disney cartoons—but no green. Green had belonged to Elena's fungus, not Scott's. That made the Strangeness feel more alien somehow.

"They wanted to transfer me to Oregon City," Duvall said, stooping a little to follow the movement of some kind of bird. "But I don't think I can leave yet. I've got to keep watching. Making sure it's really gone. Olivia says she'll help."

The bird fluttered up, revealing the pale belly and orange tail of a northern flicker. Bryan's favorite bird. The thought still hurt, but maybe not as much as it had a month ago. Erin nodded. "I think that's good."

Duvall turned to face her. "Will you stay and help us?"

Erin put her arm around the dog. "I don't think so." She hesitated, looking for the right way to explain it. She gave up, because Duvall already knew about Bryan and climate change, and all the other things that needed saving. "I've got to live my life, you know?"

Duvall's face tightened. It took Erin a second to realize the woman was fighting tears. It seemed strange for someone as strong as Duvall to have such soft feelings. But maybe that was what made her strong in the first place.

"I'll visit all the time," Erin added, and Deputy Duvall smiled.

"We'd like that," she said, and Olivia came in with a plate of cookies, and the world was warm and all right for a moment.

* * *

MADISON PUSHED OPEN THE CAFE DOOR AND STOOD awkwardly on the front mat, her eyes roving the room. She wore a pair of high-waisted jeans and a gold sleeveless top that made her look like a fashion model. Grinning, Erin stood up from the table and waved to her.

"There you are!" Madison hurried between the other tables, smiling at the other eaters as she made her way. She was as friendly and bright as Erin had remembered her, even smudged with grief at the loss of her sister.

It was unfair someone as kind and good as Madison should live in a world of such suffering. That anyone should.

Erin pushed such thoughts out of her head and made herself hum the cheerful song that had been playing in the car on the drive to the restaurant to put her smile back in place. She rose to give Madison a half hug. "You look amazing."

"You, too!" Madison beamed. She took her seat, putting her purse over the chairback and settling into the chair with such neatness and ease, Erin felt a touch jealous. She herself had nearly knocked over the vase of carnations when she'd arrived. They certainly made the odd couple. "I'm so glad you picked someplace with air conditioning," she added. "This heat wave is awful."

"Climate change. What are ya gonna do?"

At that moment, the waitress arrived, offering them coffee, which they both accepted, along with menus. Erin pointed out the specials board, where cornmeal pancakes looked especially promising, and Madison grew excited over house-cured lox. When the silence came, it was short and awkward, and Erin finally broke it by reaching for Madison's hand. She snaked her fingers between Madison's and stared into her eyes.

"Thank you so much for meeting me here." She could smell that soft coconut smell wafting off Madison's skin, a warm, cozy perfume she would always associate with the night at the hot springs. "It's been really nice, talking to you on the phone."

"You get it, you know?" Madison blinked a few times, clearing her eyes. "Most people just say they're sorry about Kayla and Matt, but you really understand."

"And you do, too," Erin agreed. "I miss Hari so much."

Madison squeezed her hands tightly. The waitress reappeared, and they ordered, but even as they talked to the waitress their eyes kept flashing back to each other, their faces turning back into smiles. Erin had never felt this kind of chemistry with anyone else. She was so excited it was hard to breathe.

"You look different," Madison blurted.

Erin pulled her hand back to touch the shiny scar on her cheek. "Oh, god. I'm sorry. This was—"

"No!" Madison covered her mouth with her hand. "No, I'm sorry. You look good. Healthier. Happier." She took Erin's hand again. Her thumb traced over the constellation of smooth spots on Erin's wrist, the fire scars, the electrical-cord gash. "Even your eyes look different. I thought they were brown."

Erin remembered that night in the hot springs, the way Madison stared into her eyes for what felt like an hour. "They're hazel," she reminded her. "The color changes with my mood."

Madison leaned in, so close Erin could feel her breath on her skin. "What does it mean when they're very, very green?"

Erin thought for a second. In the back of her head, she felt the black Lab sit up, its one ear lifting as if to hear her response. A trio of young coyotes stopped wrestling. A raven drifted across the sun, its vision traveling from mouse to squirrel to coyote and all the way back to the cafe table. All of them waited for her to take the next step.

Erin leaned in a little closer. "It means I'm very, very happy."

The threads in her palm found the cut on the back of Madison's finger, and Erin's smile grew into a kiss.

ACKNOWLEDGMENTS

THIS BOOK WOULD HAVE NEVER HAPPENED IF MY husband, John Kaczanowski, hadn't taken me out for a drive along the Clackamas River during pandemic lockdown. All my gratitude begins with him and the river and comes around full circle to both wonderful entities.

For details about mining and underground exploration in the Pacific Northwest, check out Jacob Arciniega's YouTube channel, Pines and Mines. Another great resource I've returned to time and again is local historian Brian McCamish's "In Search of History" page. I'm also grateful to the members of several writers' groups who helped in the writing process: Dale Smith, Rebecca Stefoff, and Jen Willis (go, Masked Hucksters!), and the unofficial Codex Writers horror group (especially Christi Nogle and L.S. Johnson, whose feedback radically reshaped the story).

The wonderful team at Tor Nightfire really brought this book to life. Massive thanks to Kelly Lonesome (editor extraordinaire!), Shawna Hampton (angel copyeditor), Kristin Temple, Hannah Smoot, Jordan Hanley, Khadija Lokhandwala, Saraciea Fennell, Michael Dudding, and Valeria Castorena. I will forever owe a debt of gratitude to Lesley Worrell for her amazing cover design, and Greg Ruth for his stunning cover illustration.

The real hero in this book's journey is my agent, Lane

Heymont. Without him, this story would almost certainly be sitting unread in a folder on my desktop.

And thank you, dear reader. A book remains inert until you bring it to life. Thanks for making mine come alive!

ABOUT THE AUTHOR

John Kaczanowski

WENDY N. WAGNER is a hiker, trail runner, and nature lover. She's the author of the critically acclaimed works *The Deer Kings*, *The Secret Skin*, and the *Locus* bestselling *An Oath of Dogs*. Her short fiction has been nominated for the Theodore Sturgeon and Shirley Jackson Awards, and her short stories, poetry, and essays have appeared in more than seventy venues. She serves as the editor in chief of *Nightmare* magazine (for which she was nominated for the Locus Award), and is part of the Hugo award–winning editorial team behind *Lightspeed*. She lives in Oregon with her very understanding family, a giant cat, and a Muppet disguised as a dog.

Bluesky: @wnwagner.bsky.social
Instagram: @wendy.n.wagner